Who Paid The Price

By

Stuart Jones

Hope you enjoy

S Jones

'on the road to anywhere'

Copyright © 2021 Stuart Jones

All rights reserved, including the right to reproduce this book, or portions thereof in any form. No part of this text may be reproduced, transmitted, downloaded, decompiled, reverse engineered, or stored, in any form or introduced into any information storage and retrieval system, in any form or by any means, whether electronic or mechanical without the express written permission of the author.

This is a work of fiction. Names and characters are the product of the author's imagination and any resemblance to actual persons, living or dead, is entirely coincidental.

The views expressed in this work are solely those of the author and do not necessarily reflect the views of the publisher, and the publisher hereby disclaims any responsibility for them.

ISBN: 9798594849242

www.publishnation.co.uk

Prologue

Hi Daddio

A quick email, honest! I know what you are thinking but I'm up early and wanted to email you. No crime in that. ☺
   Anyway, thank you, thank you for the car... what are you like? I dread to think how long you spent getting her restored and how much you must have spent on her. I'm sure one day you will tell me, no doubt when I have done something to annoy you.... again! I really do love the colour, baby blue, you always said that I was never a pink sort of girl. *So* looking forward to driving in this morning. Good job I have only got birds for neighbours! I am sure they loved waking up to the sound of my MGBGT. I like the sound of that - *my* MGBGT.
   Also sorry for talking shop again last night ... but thanks for listening, again ... and giving me the courage not to back out, again ... I needed to know that I was doing the right thing. Deciding to blow the lid on industrial espionage and dropping someone into a whole heap of pain was never going to be the easiest decision. I can't believe that I am saying those words. Like you say, short term pain - long term gain! ☺ Seriously though, I've got to do what's right ... I think! Scary. I will be glad when I have it off my chest and it's someone else's worry! It's good that Richard has given me space to make the right decision. I meet with him at Gray Grand Prix at 10.00 a.m. We make the call to the FIA and then fly out with the team for the Barcelona official F1 tests so I will catch up with you when I am back. It sure feels a bit awkward.
   Again, thank you, thank you, thank you, thank you or have I already said that? I love her to bits! My MGBGT! You are the best Dad ever!
   I'd better get on with having my breakfast and trying to create something that looks like a human being!
   I'm buying lunch when I am back! (Providing it's McDonalds ... and I've not overspent on 'polishes' for my NEW car☺. Oh

... and we need a name for her .... I am thinking Sally? As in RoseSALLY.

I really need to go as just caught sight of my hair! It seems to be mocking me, tame me if you can! By the way, still not found my phone, very strange! Had everyone looking for it yesterday and no joy, soooo not me! Will text you when I have sorted another, thank goodness for insurance!

I'm going ... Speak soon.

Love you xxxxxx

Rosalie

Chapter 1

His Scottish accent was heavy but deliberate, ensuring clear instruction and a good measure of displayed respect.
"Please ride up in the front with me, sir. I make no apology for boasting about the view of the breathtaking scenery you can soak up as we take a ride out to see the master."
The kilt-wearing gamekeeper, estate manager, security man? It was hard to know exactly what this man's role was, as he stood shielded by the open front door of the immaculate gleaming black Land Rover Defender.
Peter Smith placed his simple, unbranded, green wellington boot onto the black step of the Land Rover and used his left hand to grab onto the handle-like dash and hauled himself up and in. The aluminium door was closed behind him, the main noise being generated by the clunk of the heavy door latch.
"Hold on sir, the run out gets a little uneven."
With a rattle of the long gear stick Peter Smith's 4x4 chauffeur reached forward, turned the ignition on, then hesitated, waiting for the little orange glow plug indication light to extinguish, upon which the ignition key continued its journey engaging the starter motor and causing the 300 TDI engine to rattle into life. A long squeeze of the slightly out of proportion clutch pedal ensured a clean first gear selection and after a reach forward to release the purposeful looking handbrake the trustworthy loyal Land Rover eased off down the rough country track quickly asking for second gear at what seemed like a little over walking pace.
"You keep the Landy in nice condition."
"Thank you, sir. Yes, we do, Land Rovers have been a firm favourite with the family for many a year, especially when they are up this way visiting. The estate is that large that they rarely go off it."
"They? You have a few?"
"Yes, we do, sir. We have three 300 TDIs, two TD5s and two more modern TDIs, which are really Ford Transit engines, but we won't hold that against them, sir."

Peter Smith had quickly got in a little over his head and did wonder how he was going to keep up his side of the conversation but was saved by his chauffeur's Land Rover enthusiasm.

"Prefer the older three hundreds myself, as the saying goes 'old Land Rovers never die'- they just leak, rattle and break down occasionally, but they always seem to come back to fight another day. Just hold tight sir."

The Defender was brought down to walking pace again and dramatically nosed steeply downward and headed towards a small, but racing, brook. Resisting the temptation to dip the clutch, the expert chauffeur allowed the gear box to transfer the engine braking effect to the four slightly skipping wheels, as the front of the Land Rover dipped into the fast-flowing stream. As the vehicle levelled out, the driver squeezed the throttle ensuring a sedate but definite acceleration. This surge of forward motion created a bow wave in front of the bull-nosed Land Rover. The front driving wheels soon grabbed hold of the opposite bank and set about hauling the not so light-weight vehicle out of the cold busy water assisted by the pushing of the rear wheels. In no time, without fuss, the dripping Land Rover seemed to stand proud on the opposite bank having just shown off what it could do.

Peter Smith sat back and made no further effort to make conversation, preferring to just enjoy the rough but fun roller coaster ride. Ten minutes had passed when the verbal silence was broken above the now less rattling, warmed engine.

"Only a few minutes now, sir. We will just follow this bank next to the river and the master should be just around the next corner."

Peter Smith drank in the breathtaking scenery. The surrounding grass seemed harsh in colour and coarse in texture, no doubt hardened against the battlesome weather of the Scottish Highlands. The broad and bubbling river that dominated Peter Smith's view seemed to breathe up and down as the water flowed over hidden boulders and then dipped towards the shale-covered bottom - doubtless catching its breath from the ferocious winter torment that it had recently endured. A thicket of trees stood in front of the slowing Land Rover, hiding the exit of the rightward bend of the restless river. The Defender turned right just before the trees and tracked around the perimeter of them before forming a trio of Defenders as it parked up next to a brace of black matching ones, one of which had its back door open, revealing a makeshift camping stove upon which was sitting a totally out of place solid silver, cooling, coffee pot, a well weathered closed food hamper laying by its side.

"Sir, if you follow the trodden path through the trees there, it will open out on the river front. The team are aware that you will be arriving."

'The team', Peter Smith thought, the highly trained, highly alert security personnel that had also been highly trained in how to be as discreet as possible.

Upon exiting the small gathering of trees, the river, as promised, dominated Peter's field of vision. The master stood alone, knee deep in the river, protected from the circling water by a pair of watertight green waders. His perfectly tailored country jacket allowed the free movement of his arms, as the weighted fly-line formed flowing loops in rhythm with the whipping of his fishing rod. Then, after several false casts, the brightly-coloured lure would expertly land on the river tension imitating a tasty insect morsel ready for an unsuspecting, hungry running salmon to strike.

Peter Smith halted his progress in the shallows - knowing not to intrude on the moment and to wait until acknowledged and spoken to. After what seemed like a lengthy few minutes that gave a chance for the cold water to exert its power, the master's head suddenly jerked around.

"Ah! Peter, I am so sorry! I did not see you there! Either your chameleon skills are developing, or I am too engrossed in trying to be a fly! A warming coffee is in order, I think. Do follow me, Peter, to my Land Rover where I have a coffee pot. I think it can be persuaded to warm up again."

Two wooden fold-out chairs held together with strong, tartan fabric had appeared behind the open rear door of the Land Rover and two steaming coffee cups awaited Peter Smith and his boss.

"Peter, thank you for travelling up to the meeting, it must have been a dreadful inconvenience. Let me get straight to the point. I have looked at the file you prepared for me regarding our next target and I clearly see injustice. A person appears to have gone to jail for another man - and profited quite handsomely for their sacrifice. The crime? Industrial espionage, and although there *are* suspects, I admit that it is likely that a guilty individual is still at large. You referred to a girl that tragically, and according to the police reports, accidentally, lost her life about the same time, but you question this verdict. Clearly, Peter, there is injustice and somewhere within this scenario someone is operating above the law."

"If I may, sir..."

Peter realised he had jumped in too soon as he spoke the words.

A consoling but firm smile was his rebuff.

"Peter, sadly we live in a world of injustice - as you are only too well aware. I have to choose carefully the injustices that we try to put right. When I set this organisation up it was to take on the 'big game', the individuals that had risen above the reach of the law. In this file I see some injustice, yes, and really what appears to be just a hunch that all is not well with the tragic death of the girl. These things, Peter, I do see, but what I fail to see is the 'big game'."

Peter knew this to be the case. Sadly, he knew that the tragic death of a 21-year-old girl excited about her job, her future, even the car that her father had just restored for her, was now five year old news.

"You are, of course, correct, sir. Please accept my apologies. I will remove the file."

"If I may continue Peter..."

Another slightly softer smile filled the gap this time.

"Even though I get the feeling you are not telling me the full story I am confident in your judgment and believe you have your reasons for looking into this injustice."

Peter Smith felt the eyes of his meeting companion attempt to peer inside him.

"What have you seen, Peter, in this case? Why should I leave the other 'big game' sitting in files awaiting action whilst I let you off the leash to chase this one down?"

Peter Smith looked across at his questioner.

"Trust me, sir."

"I see you are using Stirling Speed as your main operative. I can see why. I presume he is fully recharged after the Troutman affair?"

"Yes, I believe he is - although I do need to find him. He went exploring the wilds of the Australian outback six months ago and still appears to be enjoying being lost somewhere over there."

"He is a good choice, Peter, and I see we will have on board the French girl Sian, also from the Troutman case."

"Yes, Sian was keen to get involved with our organisation. She has a unique personality and works well with Stirling. I contacted her in Paris and invited her to join us."

"So, if I remember correctly, Peter, Sian is Stirling's cousin?"

"Yes, sir, something like that."

"You know Peter, when fly fishing, one needs patience and skill to loop the fly line with sufficient expertise so that you can place your lure in the right position so as to have a hope of catching a running salmon. Try to cut corners and the bait falls short and the salmon swim on by. Don't let your salmon escape because you did not maintain your skills, patience and professionalism!"

Peter Smith took hold of the offered closed file.

"Point taken. Thank you, sir."

"Thank *you*, Peter Smith. You are a driven man and I sometimes wonder where that comes from."

Chapter 2

The art of driving a race car is being able to slow speed down in your mind. To be able to see things in slow motion when you are being hurtled down the racetrack at a hundred and seventy miles per hour enables you to assimilate information, process that information, then act on it correctly. You can predict rather than react.

Driving a Kenworth truck with a big cam 625 BHP Cummins engine through an 18 speed Eaton gearbox with a 45-foot tanker trailer hooked on ensured that you did not have to slow things down in your mind; you live in that slow motion world.

Stirling prepared early for the left-hand corner, easing the speed down and pressing the clutch down to manoeuvre the large gear stick into a neutral position. A slight squeeze on the throttle induced a guttural growl from the big Cummins and allowed for the gears deep within the huge gear box to seamlessly mesh when Stirling dipped the clutch again and eased the gear stick forward to collect a lower gear. Checking his chromed, offside mirrors Stirling eased the Kenworth out towards the middle of the road whilst keeping his left-hand indicator on to warn chancers not to think about squeezing up the inside of the turning big rig. A good squeeze on the air brakes and a few more downward changes brought the lumbering animal to a speed that meant it would be happy to consider the sharp left corner approaching.

Stirling checked his near-side mirror this time to ensure no one had chosen to fill the exposed near side lane, then, allowing the nose of the rig to go past the actual start of the corner, Stirling spun the large, wood-rimmed, chrome-spoked steering wheel to the left. The long outstretched bonnet responded accordingly and swung into the awaiting road. Carefully watching his near side mirrors the highly-polished triaxle trailer now came into view as it cut into the corner, carefully skirting the kerb stones. Stirling only had a moment to grab two higher gears before easing the speed back down as he peeled the Kenworth off the hot tarmac and onto a large dusty car park of a trusty truck-stop. He pulled on the handbrake to the accompaniment of a short but sudden hiss of escaping air. As he climbed down the stainless steel steps of the truck and set off towards the cafeteria he knew that he was probably at the end of his Australian adventure.

Chapter 3

Stirling knew who he was meeting, but at first had to peer around the brightly decorated American diner looking for his lunch date. His eyes finally rested on a figure who was partially hidden behind a large upright menu, sitting in the corner looking out of the window. Stirling approached within earshot range. Without looking around the figure spoke.

"Stirling Speed, what on earth have you just pulled up in?"

Stirling replied as he pulled back a chair.

"Well, if it's not man of mystery - Peter Smith."

Peter eased himself back round to face Stirling with an easy smile.

"Stirling, how are you? Are you aware that you are rubbish at answering phones?"

"Most probably out of range Peter, satellite phones are the must have kit when you are deep into the outback."

"And your messages when you come back into civilisation?"

"OK Peter, maybe a little out of range, with a little 'out of sight out of mind' mixed in. Anyway I must have answered at least one, otherwise we would not be sitting here, so stop whinging!"

"Seriously, what have you hauled onto the car park? Our last conversation was that you were buying a camper and looking to become 'at one' with Australian nature. Have you even got a licence for that?"

"Really Peter, how very dare you say such a thing, I have a licence for everything and if you must know, I think your research will show that I passed my HGV, as it was known back then, when I was 18 via a young driver's scheme. What else are winter months between race seasons for if not to get more licences? I came out here to buy a camper, was overtaken by a couple of Kenworths and thought, I *so* need one of those. So, I took an apartment in Mandurah, South of Perth, and focused on getting a drive."

Peter raised his eyebrows in mock derision.

"And the money is good?"

"Certainly is."

"So how does one of the most recognised three-time Formula One World Champion pull off such a stunt without the world's press camping on his bonnet?"

"I used a couple of contacts that I have to get me in at a small trucking operation that delivers fuel to remote villages. I offered the owner a deal he could not refuse."

"You offered to sign a poster for him?"

"I offered to do some private racetrack coaching with him at Barbagallo raceway, then, to complete the illusion, I grew a beard, bought a peaked hat, and 'Chuck the long-distance truck driver' was born! People see what they want to see. With me they saw another trucker. You Peter, of all people, know how to blend into the scenery. Well, I thought, I'll have a go at that, and you know what? It worked! Trust me, I've had a blast!"

A young cheery waitress slid up to the table dressed in a bright red bib and braces over a simple white tee shirt.

"OK Guys, what can I do you for?"

Stirling looked across at Peter Smith who returned the look with a half sweep of his right hand over his stained empty plate and partly drunk pale looking tea.

"Just me then, erm, can you rustle me up a simple salad, a small bottle of water and just a filter coffee please, nothing fishy on my salad!"

The waitress lost her smile for a second as she tapped away on her little mobile device that was no doubt transmitting live to the kitchen.

"Thank you…"

The waitress hesitated as she looked up and lost her smile again.

"…Sir... have you been in here before? You look familiar."

Peter Smith smiled as he looked up and caught sight of an out-of-date advertisement behind the counter. It advertised Goodyear tyres and displayed a younger Stirling Speed with one of his racing boot clad feet resting on top of a fat rear tyre on the back of a dramatic looking Formula One race car, a tyre technician listening intently to Stirling's wise words. The rather corny caption read, 'Stirling Speed never tires of tyres!'

Stirling caught Peter Smith's look and responded with a stroke of his beard.

"I do rock on through this neck of the woods every now and then."

This seemed to satisfy the quizzical waitress.

"Don't say it, Peter."

"Oh, you so owe me Stirling! All I needed to do was to point to the poster, I wouldn't even have needed to say anything."

"So, I take it Peter that you have not flown to the other side of the world just to wind me up?"

Peter Smith took a moment to recalibrate and fixed Stirling with a serious stare.

"Stirling, I need to ask for your help on another case. I know the Troutman case was hard, and I know I pushed you into uncomfortable areas, but I knew you would come through at the end. You have many qualities that my organisation can use out in the field. It takes a special person to become a three-time Formula One World Champion but...,"

Peter hesitated as he anticipated Stirling's interruption.

"Peter, I chose to dedicate my life to motorsport. I knew that in a split second of a poor decision, or in the moment that it takes for a component to fail, I could be asked to pay with pain, or worse, but that was OK because no one had made me do what I did. The Troutman case made me grow as person and also at the end of it I was left with a choice. I could indeed go back to my retirement or I could choose to get involved in your organisation to help bring at least *some* of the injustices that surround us in this world into line."

It was now Stirling's turn to hesitate, although he was not quite sure why he did. Maybe to build suspense? Maybe to just give himself a final opportunity to back away from the decision that he had made..."

"Peter, I have made the decision that maybe retirement is not quite where I am at. Maybe there is a fight in me that still needs an outlet. Maybe your organisation is that outlet. So, Peter Smith, what I am trying to say, in a slightly long-winded way, is that I have chosen to work for you and so the consequences of what may happen rest firmly on my shoulders!"

Peter Smith smiled in a relieved but sincere sort of way.

"It's good to have you on board Stirling, you are just what we need."

The smiling girl came back with the ordered food and beverages and carefully unloaded her tray onto the table. Her smile broadened.

"We know who you are, me and the girls - we have sussed you…"

Two other beaming waitresses looked across with a knowing look.

"It appears your cover has been blown Chuck!"

Stirling flashed Peter a false smile and then proceeded to carefully position his salad in front of him.

"So young Miss…,"

Stirling looked at his excited waitress's name tag;

"So young Miss Suzy, who do you and your inquisitive mates think I am?"

"You're the man that owns the printed t-shirt shop down on the waterfront. The one that sells the t-shirts with bikes, cars and trucks on them and the one that sells the t-shirts with the cheeky messages on the front of them. I have one, it says…"

Peter looked out of the window, shoulders shaking, whilst Stirling quickly jumped in.

"Nope, sorry Suzy, mistaken identity there I am afraid, I am just Chuck the trucker - originally from the UK but presently residing just outside Perth when my rig is parked up!"

"Really?"

"Yep. Really."

Suzy retreated, clearly unconvinced.

"So how much did Goodyear pay you for that poster Stirling?"

"OK, OK, less about me, can we get 'down to business' as they say?"

Peter leaned forward, placed his two elbows on the table and then brought his outstretched forearms and hands together to form a sort of sideways church steeple.

Chapter 4

Ross Keane walked away from Richard Gray's transparent office, past all the other transparent offices, to his own transparent office. To prevent the glass walled offices all looking like oblong fish tanks that housed a variety of busy, slightly eccentric, species of humans, the glass walls had been shaped and curved at, no doubt, great expense to create offices that ebbed and flowed as you walked past them. Clever lighting design ensured that each undulating office glass wall that faced the connecting corridor had its own distinct colour. A brave designer decided the idea would be soothing, break down barriers and create creative thought, and not just look like a psychedelic troubled dream. Ross Keane, chief designer for Gray Grand Prix had accepted that it did work, and visitors were always blown away by the offices - in fact, they were blown away by the whole design of the Gray speed technology centre.

The custom-built centre had been open five years. It cleverly housed all of the Gray Grand Prix activities, looking like it had been designed in the future and then brought it back into real time and yet still somehow managed to retain a 1970's theme that remembered that colourful, but tragic, period of Formula One racing. Richard Gray, after a few years of learning his craft in Formula Three and then Formula Two had finally, in 1973, at the age of only 24, managed to convince a young Spanish aristocrat to fund the purchase of his first Formula One car, a March race car of simple but effective design. History remembers Jackie Stewart storming to the third and last of his Formula One world titles only to be rewarded by the tragic and devastating blow of having his handsome, talented, and hungry teammate, Francois Cevert, fatally crash whilst pushing hard at Watkins Glen. Stewart walked away from the sport that had given him so much but asked such a heavy price. A concerted look through the results journals, though, would turn up the poor performance of Gray Grand Prix. Six non-finishes were only improved on by a number of non-point places and one spectacular crash at Monte Carlo. But Richard Gray was a fast learner. He built on every mistake, every misjudgement, and perfected his art of getting money to go racing. It would take four years for Gray Grand Prix to win its first Formula One race and a further two to win its first Championship. After that, Gray never finished outside the top three of the constructors championship and broke into the stratosphere realms of generating income, hence the available budget to take the gamble and invest heavily in The Gray Speed Technology Centre.

Cleverly integrated cast backs to yesteryear could be seen sprinkled around the centre. The current F1 race cars having gone to final assembly lived down in an area known as The Arches. Each chassis actually had its own arch way, this design feature being a nod towards the place where some of the early Formula One teams began their life, in rustic garages under the railway arches that could be found dotted around most urban sprawls. The large modern staff cafeteria known as 'The Garigista Café' derived its name from a slightly derogatory phrase coined by the great Enzo Ferrari when he spoke of the early British F1 teams. Then there was the relaxation area where all the employers could play pool, table football and talk, this area was known as the Rosalie Lounge, named after a member of staff who had lost her life in tragic circumstances in years gone by. Staff could often be heard making arrangements to meet at Rosie's.

Ross slumped down at his desk and then spun round on his chair to peer out of his window that overlooked the man-made lake that nestled in the middle of the technology centre. Ducks floated across it, totally unaware of the high profile, high technology business that busied itself around them. Ross Keane was a troubled man. He hated having his hand forced. The meeting he had just had with Richard Gray had gone the way he expected, but not the way he wanted. Richard had pulled rank on him, which, as team owner he had every right to do, but Ross hated not being listened to. As Design Director for Gray Grand Prix it was his responsibility to make sure that their race car got results. Putting in a driver with questionable ability, and to add to it, an all-round bad attitude, was not the way to get results. In Ross Keane's eyes Sergio Petrov was not ready for Formula One. His junior race career to date was littered with crashes, licence endorsements and controversy. Ross had compromised and suggested that Sergio be brought into the team as reserve driver, or, at worst, number two driver, but Richard Gray had made it clear that this year, Sergio would be their number one driver. Sergio brought with him 11 million pounds worth of sponsorship from his father, plus a raft of Russian sponsors that all contributed to the 300-million-pound budget required to keep Gray Grand Prix on the Formula One race circuits of the world. Their present number two driver would be retained on a one-year contract. A driver who was clearly past his best and was in it for one last pay year. His only saving grace was his experience testing cars, but his recent announcement that he was having an operation to right an old grumbling race injury had stunted that ray of light. There was more than Sergio's below parr ability as a driver that worried Ross though. Six years ago, Sergio's father turned up at the old offices of Gray Grand Prix. Anatoly Petrov, or, Mr Petrov, as he affectionately liked to be called, turned up in force with an entourage of bodyguards. In the meetings that Ross was privy to, Mr Petrov made it clear that he viewed money like air, it was always available in whatever quantities that were required. Mr Petrov also made it clear that he had a 12-year-old son who wanted to be a Formula One race driver and so would buy whatever was required to ensure that his son realised his dream.

 Gray Grand Prix had just lost a title sponsor unexpectedly. The worldwide chemical producing company had been exposed faking its results to get through stringent tests and suddenly, this billion-pound money making machine had suddenly become a hungry, money eating animal that no one wanted to be associated with. A successful cashed up team like Gray's could normally take a hit like that in its stride, but unfortunately the timing of this sponsor collapse was the worst it could be. Richard Gray had just invested heavily in the technology centre and was too far down the road to reverse out. The temptation of a limitless supply of Rubles proved too great for Richard, and he grabbed the life line with both hands without really calculating the real price that had to be paid for this form of finance. Ever since, Richard had become a puppet controlled by the master puppeteer.

 Ross contemplated his position, as he had so many times before. He had had good offers to jump ship to other teams but just as Mr Petrov controlled Richard Gray, he also controlled Ross Keane.

Richard Gray's final words on the matter were,

"I don't really care whether you like it or not, Sergio is our driver this season, so you need to find a way of making it work."

Ross spun back round to his desk and began doodling on his blank note pad. Doodling on Ross Keane's pad was always a sure sign that he was groping around for an idea.

"Doodling? That's never a good sign."

Ross instantly knew who the French accent belonged to. He looked up to see Sian, smiling, holding a cup of tea, officially Richard Gray's PA but in reality, Ross shared her as well.

"Oh, nicely timed Sian."

"You seemed to have lost a pound and found ten pence Mr Keane."

Ross smiled at Sian's way of putting things over.

"Well Sian, somehow I have to make a third-rate driver into a world champion driver in about three months, so all ideas are welcome."

Ross leaned back in his chair and took a good swig of his tea.

Sian delayed her response, to give the impression that she was contemplating an idea.

"Well actually Mr Keane, I do have an idea."

"OK, let's hope it's not a Baldrick idea!"

Sian tilted her head slightly to one side, causing her silky shoulder length black hair to appear longer on one side than the other.

"A Baldrick Idea? What's that mean?"

"Sorry Sian, it's a reference to a long running British comedy called Black Adder. It would be easier for you to watch it sometime rather than me try to explain my failed little joke."

Sian flashed a smile back.

"Black Adder, I'll have a look tonight."

Ross smiled back and put his hand up in apology.

"Really Sian, it's not that important. Your idea?"

Sian continued with her idea.

"Get a driver coach in. Someone to work with Sergio. See if they can drag some 'speed' out of the boy."

"OK, but who could we use with enough F1 experience, who has not got much else to do, is willing to spend time with a spoilt brat, and associate with his very dodgy father? Please throw me a name!"

"Well, I did throw you a clue in my last statement Mr Keane, Speed...." Sian teased.

"I am afraid my brain is a little too fried today for quizzes, just make it easy for me Sian."

Sian delayed her reply yet a little longer, she was enjoying playing her part.

"Well Mr Keane, why don't we see if we can employ the services of three-time World Champion and retired race driver Stirling Speed!"

Chapter 5

Stirling sat forward in the black leather back seat of the taxi as the dark grey gates started to swing away from each other to reveal the gravel driveway up to home, Drayton House.

"Just give the gates a moment to open fully. I am not sure why you have to do that but the guys who fitted the gates told me that is what I should do."

"No problem Mr Speed, bet you are glad to be home."

The executive taxi service employed good drivers who seemed to be able to make just the right amount of conversation without being too intrusive and Stirling had quite enjoyed telling someone about his undercover Australian truck driving adventures.

Stirling's gardener had clearly tipped off his housekeeper, as the large, solid wood front door swung open before Stirling could extract his keys from his well-worn leather hold all. The discreet taxi driver eased past the open arms of Stirling's housekeeper with Stirling's equally well-worn leather suitcase. Stirling gave his welcoming housekeeper a big smile in reply.

"Stirling, you look really well. Everything is in order, the Jaguar has been serviced as requested and the garage have made a note of a couple of observations for you to look at. I have left that and your private post on your desk in your study. Now are you ready to eat, sleep...?"

"Thank you, it is good to be home and actually, I am ready to go for a run."

Stirling's over caring housekeeper frowned.

"Oh Stirling, surely after such a long flight back you need to take it easy?"

Stirling walked past her and into the parquet floored hallway.

"Taking it easy is just what I have been doing for the last 20 hours. First Class on British Airways will not allow you to do anything else but take it easy. Trust me, it is time for a run."

"Why, Stirling, do I get the feeling that the run is to help you plan another adventure?"

The taxi driver spoke next.

"I'll be leaving you sir. Your pickup will go on your account."

The driver turned to leave as Stirling reached into the inside pocket of his sports jackets to fish out his brown, slightly scuffed, oblong leather wallet. His searching thumb and index finger, by using a rubbing together motion, managed to extract a single £10 note that he passed to the departing driver with a....

"Thanks, great service."

"Sir, you know that we are not supposed to accept tips. We are paid well enough."

"I know that but, hey, live dangerously."

"Thank you sir. You have a good day sir."

The housekeeper swung the big door shut and closed out the cold but bright, crisp, winter's day.

Stirling grabbed his suitcase to take upstairs and continued his conversation with his housekeeper as he climbed.

"I don't know about another adventure, but I have been asked to help out on another little project."

Chapter 6

Stirling soon settled into his running rhythm. It was time to awaken his body from the long flight and to give some serious thought to the information that Peter Smith had given him, back in Australia.

Peter had leaned forward on the table at the American diner and brought his outstretched forearms together to form a point with his hands almost as though this was going to help direct what he was about to tell Stirling.

"Stirling, what do you know about Gray Grand Prix?"

Stirling knew the team well.

"Very successful team, still owned by a nice guy, Richard Gray, seems to be linked with some Russian oligarch who by all accounts is not a man to cross, whose son, if I remember rightly, seems to have made it his personal mission to hit every barrier, try every gravel trap, and bounce off as many competitors as possible in the junior championships."

Peter Smith went to speak but was halted by Stirling's interruption.

"Oh, and they had a load of trouble a few years ago - not sure how long ago now. They were involved with some sort of industrial espionage, ended up with a huge multi-million pound fine, and had to pay massive damages because it was proven that they stole a load of data from the Stragatti team - of all people! I remember it all got very messy. There was a whistle blower whose identity was vague. At first it was thought to be their designer, Ross Keane, who had been the mastermind behind it, but, in the end, I think it was a member of his family that had actually done it. Sorry I can't remember all the details, that was during a period of my life when I was quite blinkered, or maybe that should be, focused."

Peter Smith hesitated as Stirling still seemed to be in recall mode.

"You are…"

Stirling continued, now oblivious to Peter Smith's attempt to continue.

"Correct me if I am wrong, but around the same time I think that a young girl who worked for the team was found dead at home. I think she was called Rosie? I only know that because their technology building has a lounge in it that all the staff call Rosie's lounge in memory of her and...,"

Stirling rolled his head slightly to one side. Peter Smith decided this time to make sure that Stirling had finished.

"Have you finished? You've trawled through your memory banks?"

"Yep, that's me done. You can now fill in all the blanks."

"Well, actually Stirling, that is the problem - we can't fill in the missing blanks. We are pretty certain that the family member you mentioned was paid to take the rap for the espionage."

"What's the evidence for that?"

"The original whistle blower...,"

Stirling interjected.

"The original? There was more than one?"

There seemed to be a thoughtful pause before Peter Smith replied.

"That gets a bit complicated Stirling, and it's information that will only cloud even more the murky waters. The evidence we have is..."

Peter Smith held up his right hand and stuck up his thumb.

"One. The original whistle blower named someone else as the mastermind behind it all, but we can't prove that.

Two. The case built around the family member was too complete, too perfect. There were no missing pieces in the jigsaw. The jury had no option but to convict. It was a watertight case. Whenever I have come across watertight cases in the past, I have found that they are always set-ups.

And three.."

Peter Smith raised his middle finger to match his outstretched thumb and index finger.

"The individual went into prison, a race engineer on a race engineer's wage, and after good behaviour in prison came out three years later as a multi-millionaire GT race team owner."

"So, who is this individual? Have I come across them?"

"I doubt it, probably well down the pecking order for you in motor racing terms."

"But you have a name?"

"Yes, Sam Keane."

"OK, I think I have heard the name somewhere. So where do I come into this Peter? What are we trying to achieve?"

"Someone out there, Stirling, did not go to prison when they should have done. We need to find who that individual is. Although the team lost all its points for the season, the team avoided a life ban because Richard Gray proved without doubt that he had no knowledge of the trading of team data that was going on. Stragatti had clearly found a performance gain and the case was that Sam Keane, who worked for Stragatti, was offering the secret performance data to the highest bidder, and had approached Ross Keane. Ross apparently then sat on the information because, I suppose, it was tempting to know what Stragatti were up to, but also, he was being offered this illegal, jail baiting, information by a member of his very own family. We need to find out who was really behind it all. Someone paid Sam Keane to take the drop. I also need you to check this Russian character, who we know is certainly familiar with organised crime although, how familiar, we are not sure."

Stirling was surprised to feel a slight sense of excitement at the thought of getting stuck into this next project.

"OK, so am I in cold, or have you already been preparing the field for me?"

"We have set some things in place for you Stirling, but before I get to that, I want you to look into something else. I know that there are unanswered questions about the death of Rosalie and I feel strongly that there is a connection."

Peter Smith had a moment to regroup, almost like he was starting a new paragraph of the discussion.

"I have it on good authority that Rosalie had knowledge of the spying that Gray Grand Prix was involved with. This has always been vehemently denied by the team. They insist that she would never have had the access required to discover any of the undercover dealings."

Stirling had taken another swig of his coffee, then polished off the last mouthful of his slightly dry salad. He had caught sight of the trio of staring, smiling waitresses and responded with an upward squeeze of his cheeks that did not really pass as a smile, but more a forced facial expression.

Stirling had then turned his attention back to Peter Smith.

"So, do you know how this girl was popped off, and do you know where the police got to with the case?"

Peter Smith was clearly rattled by Stirling's last comment.

"Stirling, never lose sight of the gravity of what we are dealing with here. 'This girl' did not 'pop off', she tragically lost her life, and 'this girl' was called Rosalie. This is the ugly world we have to deal with, and we should never try to minimise the gravity of what has gone on here, otherwise we are taking the first steps to normalising it."

Stirling took a moment to show that Peter's point had been digested.

"Thanks Peter, I take your point. Please go on. Where did the Police get to with Rosalie's death?"

Peter Smith had gestured and silently mouthed a glass of water request to one of the passing waitresses.

"Rosalie was poisoned."

Peter Smith took a moment to look out into the car park as another double trailered truck pulled onto the truck stop in swirl of dust.

"She was found by her father, who had received a call from her workplace of two years, which was Gray Grand Prix, to say that she had, very unusually, not turned up for work. She had lain there for four days. The office thought she was at a race test, the test team thought she was at the office. The police could find nothing. Their suggestion was that it was an accident. I am certain, Stirling, that more was involved, and that if murder had been proven then it would have been a sophisticated and well thought out murder."

Stirling digested the information.

"So, what lead the police to the conclusion of accidental death?"

"Because of the type of poison. It could... have been ingested by mistake!"

"OK. So, I am presuming this was not a nice death. Is it instantaneous or drawn out?"

"Rosalie was next to the open door of her car. She had dragged herself, vomiting and convulsing, out of the house and was trying to get help. She would have been in agony and known that she was in dire trouble. She fought for her survival to her very last breath."

"Wow, horrible."

"Rosalie lived in a quiet and secluded cottage that had actually been left to her by her grandmother. It was, and still is, actually, a designated nature reserve. Her grandmother was a highly respected academic and researched flora and wanted to keep this area available for the study of nature. Because of its remoteness, Rosalie had no chance."

"By mistake? She took the poison by mistake?"

"The police could find no evidence of it in Rosalie's house. They could not find any evidence as to how Rosalie could consume the amount that the autopsy found she had ingested. There was no conclusion of how she had taken it."

"Anything else suspicious, and why try to make it to the car? Why not call for help with her phone?"

"My next point. She could not call for help because she had lost her phone the day before at work. It was found a few days later in the bottom drawer of her work desk."

"And that is suspicious?"

Peter Smith had sat back in his chair.

"Stirling, you once said to me that when you had a bad handling race car in a race, all the theory and all the rules went out of the window. Sometimes you had to rely on instinct, you had to just chuck it at the corner, sort it out and hope you came out the other side. Stirling just trust me; I am chucking this case into that corner and I know that you are the one that can actually make sense of it all, so that we can come out on the other side. Rosalie lived in a remote cottage; her phone was important to her. She was known for being well organised, hence becoming PA to Richard Gray at only 22. She would not have randomly lost her phone in the bottom drawer of her desk, and more importantly, I have it on very good authority, despite what Gray Grand Prix say, that she did indeed have knowledge of who was behind the industrial espionage."

Peter Smith had sat forward in his chair.

"Stirling, I believe that she was murdered. In fact Stirling, I *know* that she was murdered!"

The word 'murdered' hung in the air long enough for Stirling to know that it was time for action.

The slight incline which was made more difficult by the slippery wet mud brought Stirling back to the here and now. Inclining slightly forward, Stirling shifted his weight onto his toes and dug in for the steady climb, his legs starting to feel the burn.

Stirling had been surprised by Peter Smith when he had announced that Sian, whom he thought he had lost whilst working on a previous case together, the Lawrence Troutman case, was now working for the organisation. Stirling allowed his mind to wander slightly. Wow, what a story that was, Lawrence Troutman, the reason that now Stirling Speed, retired three-time Formula One world champion had ended up working for a secret organisation that brought about justice. Crazy...

Although Stirling had not seen much of Sian over the last few months due to his Australian adventure, he had made time to keep in touch with her via email and was looking forward to spending more time with her again when he was back in circulation. Typical of Sian, she had neglected to mention that she would be working for Peter Smith and that they would be again working on the same case!

Sian had apparently been positioned in Gray Grand Prix working as PA for Richard Gray and Ross Keane. It was her job to be an inside ear and to try to position Stirling closer to the team somehow. It had been a gamble that Sian would legitimately get the PA's job which had become available. Peter Smith had seen the opportunity, coached her well as to what they would be looking for, and Sian had played her part perfectly and managed to get her feet under the table there. When she had picked up that they would be promoting the young Sergio to the team, she took the initiative to offer Stirling's services as a driver coach. Peter Smith was pleased that young Sian had used her initiative and was also pleased that, in this case, the cards had all fallen well for a change.

As Stirling needed to get close to Sam Keane as well, it was Peter Smith's suggestion that they encourage the young, inexperienced, and somewhat struggling Sergio to spend some time driving one of the GT race cars that Sam Keane ran so that Stirling could evaluate and start to coach him. Mr Petrov was not happy with the situation, but Ross Keane saw it as a way forward and pushed hard for it, insisting that it had been a stipulation of Stirling Speed and that this was the only way he would get involved. Even Mr Petrov found it hard to turn down the offer of coaching from a three-time F1 world champion.

Upon hearing the case he was due to work on, Stirling was keen to get up to speed on all aspects of the case, hence his last request to Peter Smith;

"Peter can you get me the actual police files for both the industrial espionage and the death of the Rosalie girl?"

Peter Smith was pleased at the way Stirling was responding and engaging. Ex racing driver Stirling Speed was morphing into Private Investigator for The Special Investigations Bureau quite naturally.

"Really no problem Stirling. I will make sure that all the files are made available for you when you are back in the UK."

Stirling's path levelled out now as he ran the last mile which ended at the start of the meadow that belonged to his property.

At least the first test that Stirling was scheduled to do with the young Russian was only a few minutes drive from Stirling's home, Drayton House. Stirling eased his jog back to a steady walk for the last hundred metres. After a good hot shower, snack, and a quick check through his race kit bag it would be an early night, ready for the test day tomorrow at Oulton Park race circuit. Although Stirling had no idea what was in store for him yet, maybe naively, he had a quiet confidence, just as he always did when he was starting a race in the past - confidence that he knew he had a good chance of getting the result he wanted.

Chapter 7

Sian had been quite - excited? No, perhaps that wasn't the right word. Proud? No. Satisfied? Yes – satisfied. That was it. She was satisfied with herself, satisfied that she had handled herself in such a way that Peter Smith felt that she warranted an assignment with his Special Investigations organisation.

'Well, he must think there is something about me and I suppose he must think that I am someone who can be trusted' Sian had thought to herself when Peter Smith had taken her by surprise and broached the subject with her.

In the past, sometimes her French accented English, combined with her cheeky sense of humour and her tomboy approach had, maybe, caused some to write her off as just a silly young girl.

Sian had decided that it was time to visit Paris. One reason for the visit was, considering that she had spent her whole life in France, she had never actually set foot in the capital. Another reason was that Sian was starting to ask herself that inevitable but still uncomfortable question -what am I going to do with my life?

One week into her Paris adventure she had been sitting across the rue from Notre Dame in a typical Parisian corner café, the autumn sunlight turning the leaves in the trees even more golden. The busy and, judging by the regular usage of the horn, frustrated traffic, jostled for position as mopeds, motorbikes and cyclists eased through the traffic cracks, like rainwater disappearing between paving stones. Lost in watching the people, traffic and life pass by, Sian had jumped when a familiar voice had suddenly broken the moment.

"Hi Sian, fascinating isn't it, just watching the world? How have you been keeping?"

Peter Smith was apparently looking into a new case and needed an inside person. He had gone to great lengths to explain the case and he stated that Sian should thoroughly understand that she did not have to get involved. He had also made it clear that he felt strongly a murder was connected with the case and that whilst he took extensive precautions to protect his operatives, he could never one hundred percent guarantee their safety.

"Sian, we are dealing with a despicable group of people that attempt to operate above the law and just underneath the veneer that is our day-to-day life. They will stop at nothing to achieve their selfish wants. If you choose to become involved with my organisation Sian, you will rub shoulders with these people. I must make that clear. Sian, you of all people know about injustice. I would like to give you the chance to help right some of the wrongs in the world. The decision is yours though."

Sian knew this was her moment, her very own crossroads, and she knew exactly the direction she was going to take. That had been six months ago. Peter Smith had wasted no time, integrating Sian into the organisation, sending her on field training and then preparing her for her first undercover role at Gray Grand Prix. A month had passed since she had got over the first hurdle and been offered the PA's job for Richard Gray and Ross Keane.

Sian eased her 1968 off-white Alfa Romeo to a standstill at the security gates of Gray Grand Prix next to the security guard, who was waiting with his hand outstretched. She rolled her window down and smiled at the slightly grumpy looking man.

"Bonjour, ça va?"

Sian's cheekiness seemed to make the security man slightly grumpier.

"Your pass, please Miss."

Sian froze for a moment whilst she wondered where she had secreted her pass this time, then suddenly flicked an index finger up in an, 'ah just remembered' moment, turned away from her unconversational security man and began rummaging about in her far too large, chaotic bag.

"Miss, you do know you have a queue behind you, a queue that includes Mr Gray?"

Sian looked back up at the man, bit the right side of her lip and mouthed a sorry to him whilst attempting her best smile at the same time.

"Miss if you don't mind me saying, we do have this every morning that you come in. Can we not organise a set place for your pass?"

The security man lowered himself down to Alfa window height.

"Try down the side of the seat Miss, that is where we found it last week wasn't it?"

Sian fished down between the hand brake and the red leather seat and felt the sharp plastic corner of her pass holder. With a triumphant smile she presented the now positively angry security man her pass.

After noting the pass number on his clipboard he pressed the little fob attached to it which remotely lifted the barrier.

"Thank you, Miss."

Sian flashed another smile, squeezed the clutch, and brought the little Alfa engine on to cam. Then after a quick,

"Au revoir,"

through the open window, Sian stepped off the clutch. Instantly the overloaded near side rear tyre squealed with delight and the Alfa barked abuse at the shaking head of the security man as it scurried across the Gray Grand Prix car park to parking bay number 26.

Chapter 8

"Sian."

"Mr Gray."

"You seem to be settling in well?"

Sian turned away from her open laptop and turned to face her questioner.

"All good, sir. I hope I am living up to expectations?"

"Well, I don't think our gate security man is your biggest fan, but I have to say I have been impressed with your whole approach and Ross thinks you are doing a brilliant job. In fact, he tells me it was your suggestion to get Mr Speed to coach Sergio."

"He prefers Stirling, but yes I did. In fact, they are at Oulton Park up in Cheshire testing a Porka today with Sam Keane's team."

"A Porka? I presume you mean a Porsche. Oh dear, I have to say that sounds expensive. I'll wait for the damage bill to arrive shortly then! Did I hear that you are related to Stirling or am I making that up? I have always rated him as a driver and an all-round good guy."

"I am actually, I am sort of his cousin or half cousin or something. It's complicated."

"Let's hope Stirling gives us mates rates then, I seem to remember that he has the record for one of the highest paid F1 drivers ever, in fact, maybe we should get Stirling to run a test for us in the F1 car. That would certainly get the press in a lather and maybe even get Ross off my back.

"Oh, I am sure that it's not about the money anymore."

Richard drew up a chair and sat at Sian's effective but somehow slightly chaotic desk.

"Sorry Mr Gray, but should I not be coming to your office?"

"Honestly, really don't worry about all that sort of thing. There are just a couple of things that I do need to check."

Sian picked up a pen in preparation for any notes.

"You have organised a restaurant for tonight?"

"Yes, I will email the details to you."

"Thank you. Mr Petrov will be flying here via helicopter from Oulton and then we will be heading out for dinner together. Please Sian, ensure everything is right, even if it means double checking everything. I am afraid that Mr Petrov has a rather short fuse. Then we are all flying to Switzerland tomorrow in the Lear. Can you just check that transfers to the airfield for Mr Petrov and Sergio have been arranged for tomorrow? Looking at the itinerary, that detail appears to have been missed off so if you could just check that with our travel office. Also, whilst I am away, I do have a specialist calling in to run some soil checks in the glasshouse. He will come to the main reception and ask for you. If you could afford him full courtesy and assistance, Sian, that would be great."

"No problem Mr Gray."

"So, Sian, is there anything you want to ask me about before I do my factory tour? Anything? I really want you to settle here. I do not like change around me."

Sian did not know if the timing was quite right but decided to go for a quick prod.

"There was one thing Mr Gray, Rosie's Lounge - what's the story behind that? It's in memory of an employee?"

Richard's reply was not instant and there was a moment of hesitation which demonstrated that he had clearly not been expecting that particular question.

"Well Sian, you got me there for a moment. I was thinking more along the lines of holiday pay, etc. Erm…"

Richard took a moment to reset.

"I live in a world where death can be hiding around the next corner and I lost two drivers in the early days to this, at times, cruellest of sports, but the death of Rosalie hit me so hard that even today I find it difficult to talk about."

Sian genuinely felt a stab of guilt.

"Oh, I am sorry, Mr Gray, I was inquisitive that is all, but really it's not that important."

"But it is important Sian. We should never forget Rosalie. A race driver rightly or wrongly goes out in a blaze. Yes, all around suffer, but a driver knows what can be asked of him. Rosalie was my PA, and Ross's, just as you are. She was so efficient and really brightened your day up when you spoke to her. Nothing was missed and nothing was too much trouble. Then one day, she didn't turn up for work which was really out of character. In the two years she had worked for us she'd never had a sick day. It was a little chaotic as we were flying out for winter testing that morning. She was due to fly out with the senior members of the team in my plane so that we could get some work done on the way out. No one could get hold of her, so we had to leave without her as we were on a tight schedule. We were taking some prototype parts out to test and the team who were already at the circuit were waiting to fit the parts. Test days are expensive enough, without having the cars sitting doing nothing whilst they wait for parts."

Richard turned away from Sian to look out of the window as he continued.

"She was not found for four days. The office thought she was with us, and we thought she was with the office. It was four days before anyone contacted her father to see where she was. He found her."

"I am sorry Mr Gray."

Sian agonised about whether she should dig further, but she knew that she was there to do a job and, if possible, right this wrong.

"May I ask how she had died?"

Richard turned back to Sian.

"By accident. She had somehow ingested a poisonous root, would you believe, and died before she could get help. A stupid, cruel death. Working so close to her I just was not prepared for it. The police did a thorough job. It was just a stupid, stupid accident."

Richard then fell silent but continued to stare at Sian. Not so much looking through her, but more a case of seeing someone else in her place. Then without a word he smiled, got up, and walked to Sian's office door.

"I think I am going to delay my workshop floor walk for 50 minutes or so Sian. If anyone wants me, I will be in the glass house."

"Mr Gray."

Richard delayed his exit. He turned and produced a smile that said, 'don't worry, ask.'

"What happened to her father?"

For a second time Richard Gray was not expecting this curve ball and was expecting another question about Rosalie.

"Her father? I really don't know to be honest. We went into a very difficult time for the team. It was when all the industrial espionage stuff was kicking off, so I ended up with my hands full of that."

Sian drew a line under the questioning.

"Thanks, Mr Gray, for taking the time to tell me all that. I'll get onto the travel department straight away to check out the travel plans."

Richard flashed another smile back and silently left Sian's glass office that not only exposed what was in it but had also just exposed a still-hurting Richard Gray.

Sian made a mental note to do some research on Rosalie's father and also to ask Peter Smith if he had any further information on him.

She decided to at least look busy for now and picked up her phone.

"Hi. Is that the travel department?"

"Can you book me a holiday please?"

"Sorry, I do know you are really busy, it was just a joke. It's Mr Gray's PA here, Sian,"

"Sian, spelt, s,i,a,n you pronounce it She-arn,"

"That's it. Could I just run through his travel plans for the next few days please?"

"Yes, I will hold but hold what? OK, OK, it was just another joke, I'm holding!"

Chapter 9

Stirling held the grumbling Jaguar in second gear as he guided the bulging nose of his battleship grey E type along the tight little lane towards the scenic Oulton Park Race circuit buried in the Cheshire countryside. Second gear at this low speed ensured the Jaguar did not suffer a bout of congestion thanks to its mildly modified camshafts. Stirling loved having to drive around his Jaguar's eccentricities rather than sitting back to allow some computer to enjoy the drive instead. A surprisingly glittering pond passed to the left, surprising because Stirling had expected a damp day at best, based on the time of year and the weather forecast. Instead, Stirling looked out at the snaking road in front through his driving sunglasses, the clear blue sky and bright early spring sun bouncing around on the E Type's curved, sculptured windscreen. Stirling eased the big Jag to a halt, right hand indicator on, his right string back leather driving glove-covered hand resting on top of the Jaguar's wooden steering wheel, his left, similarly clothed hand resting on the first gear selected chrome gear stick, whilst he waited for a tractor to chug past in the opposite direction. Then with a slight growl from the twin exhaust, Stirling steered the Jag right into the Oulton Park entrance. A sign read, No Admittance, Exclusive Test in Progress.

'Well, someone is throwing their cash around to exclusively hire the circuit!' Stirling had been half expecting an open test day or a semi exclusive at least.

The sleek lines of Stirling's Jag were a familiar sight around the Cheshire lanes so the keen-eyed security man recognised the Stirling Speed driven Jaguar straight away and gestured for Stirling not to stop, but to drive straight through to the paddock. Stirling chose to stop though, everyone else would have been made to, and Stirling hated taking things for granted.

"Go straight through Mr Speed, the team are all set up inside."

"Stirling please, thanks. Great morning for it."

"Absolutely sir, still not warm enough for the old thermals to be left off yet though, sir."

"Good point."

Stirling gave a thumbs up and eased the Jag away from stand still but then gave the throttle a cheeky squeeze as the Jaguar nosed up over the Bailies bridge entrance, the exhaust notes gloriously bouncing back off the walls of the bridge. Stirling left the throttle alone down the other side of the bridge, the tuned engine coughing back through the exhaust, then when on the flat he decided to announce to the team that he was here. A quick first gear, a careful selection of second gear, then a big slice of throttle ensured the engine got the fuel it craved and all in the paddock would look up to see an inflight Jaguar devouring the long straight road that ran alongside the paddock area.

Sergio looked up as well and spoke through his heavy Russian accent to whoever wanted to listen to him.

"Ah, so the man who thinks he can show me how to drive has arrived. Tell him he can find me in my motor home."

Stirling halted his Jaguar opposite the immaculate race transporter of the strangely named Catch Me Race Car Team. The transporter, predominantly white with blue and red stripes swirling along its side caught the sunlight well. All the very black tyre walls had clearly been dressed and accentuated the highly polished alloy wheels. Stirling could not help noticing that the Goodyear lettering on the shiny rubber tyres that adorned the tractor unit had all been positioned at the top of the wheel.

"Wow"

Stirling thought to himself,

'When the transporter parked up, they must have jacked each wheel and rotated them to ensure the Goodyear name was positioned at the top! That is attention to detail!'

Stirling switched the rumbling but silky, straight-six engine off and reached across to retrieve his favourite blue cashmere scarf from the dark ruby red, slightly cracked leather passenger seat. He had bought a light sky-blue cashmere scarf at the same time as his dark blue one, convinced that he would wear it. Indeed, each time he reached into his accessory drawer he always reached for his sky-blue one first, and would even take it downstairs to put with the gear he was leaving the house with. Yet, as always, he would change it at the last minute for his dark blue one, promising himself that he would wear it next time! He now folded his dark blue scarf in half, wrapped it in half around his neck, then pulled the two ends of the scarf through the loop formed by the other side, and pushed it up tight to his neck to seal out the bright but still cold day. He swung open the rear boot door of his Jaguar and reached inside for his large dark brown leather race kit bag. It was at this point that he realised he had not done as he had promised himself and done a little research into Sam Keane, or the Catch Me Race Car Team!

"I don't even know what this Sam Keane looks like. Come on Stirling, poor prep!"

He made a mental note to himself,

"Must try harder!"

He smiled to himself as he allowed the large rear door of his E type to swing and then clunk shut.

Even after all the years that had passed, Stirling still remembered those words being scrawled all over his school workbooks. The teachers did not seem to understand that he was busy planning how he could get himself into a race car and conquer the world, not about the mundane matters of day-to-day schooling. Stirling even allowed himself a little private chuckle.

"How life turned out!"

Choosing to ignore the large motor home to his right and the door into the race transporter to his left, he strode over to the only open garage door that contained racks of tyres, both slicks and wets. He negotiated them to find himself on an empty pit lane and so followed the sound of music coming out of a garage where all the activity seemed to be.

Inside it he found a wheel-less plain white Porsche 991 911 GT spec race car with a huddle of race engineers looking at a laptop precariously perched on the car's expensive back wing. The laughing engineers did not notice the presence of a three-time world champion of their chosen sport at first, but then, like a group of mere cats, they seemed to look up all at once. The centre of the bunch carefully closed the laptop.

"Hi guys, Stirling's the name and speed's the game."

No reply came back.

"It was a joke, guys! I am here to do some coaching, all arranged with Sam, Sam Keane."

Stirling stood at the entrance of the garage and stared at his clearly uncomfortable race engineers for the day. The centre of the group composed himself, handed the laptop to the nearest hand and walked forward, hand outstretched in preparation for a greeting handshake.

"Mr Speed, sorry mate, you caught us on the hop. One, we thought it was Sergio walking in, we were all just looking at his latest testing crash. My word, that guy's got nine lives - and two, of course we knew you were coming, but it's not every day we get to work with drivers like you, so I for one am a little awestruck if you don't mind me saying, and I make no apologies stating that I will be getting a photo with you at some point today to put on my Instagram to prove to all that I am now officially a mate of Stirling Speed. Oh, I'm Trevor, this is Pete, Mario, Charlie and Sam, not *the* Sam, I might add."

Stirling laughed.

"Well, that's a relief, I'd been told that all GT race car engineers were weirdo's, but it turns out that actually they are all just freaks!"

The comment broke the ice well and all joined in pointing at each other to highlight who was the biggest freak.

"So, a few things that we need to get on top of today."

Trevor grasped his clip board from the top of one of the Beta toolboxes, ready and willing to take down Stirling's requirements.

"First point. It really must be Stirling, not Mr Speed. Anyone else calling me Mr Speed will have an airline inserted where the sun don't shine, the airline will be switched on while we all take bets on how long it will take before they explode. Second, I will need a good supply of tea all day long, so please show me where the tea urn is, I hope, already boiling, and third, where can I find Sam Keane?"

The guys all laughed, it was going to be a good day despite having to deal with Sergio.

Trevor piped up.

"Sam is up in the race transporter and you will pass the tea urn on your way inside, Stirling."

"Cool. Do we know when we go live?"

Mario confidently chipped in.

"The track has just gone green Stirling, but apparently Mr Petrov has had a delay flying up and for some reason we can't start running until he arrives."

Stirling picked up his kit bag and headed out to the transporter, walked up the aluminium railed steps to the door, clicked it open, walked past the steaming tea urn to a polished wooden door that looked like it belonged on a super yacht. Stirling opened the door and was presented with a narrow flight of steps. He turned slightly sideways as he started up the steps so as to keep hold of his kit bag whilst calling out,

"Ahoy! Is there anyone on board?"

He crested the short staircase to be confronted with a smiling and quite stunning lady. Maybe late thirties? It was hard to say, clearly someone who looked after herself. Her shoulder length blonde hair settled a moment later than her head, which had settled its change of direction to look directly at Stirling. A correct, refined and very English voice conveyed the words,

"Hello Mr Speed, who prefers to be called Stirling."

Stirling smiled back, conscious that time was ticking by.

"Hi, sorry to disturb you."

The heavily English accented voice came back.

"No problem."

"Do you know where Sam Keane is? He seems to be a little elusive."

By the time Stirling realised his mistake his words were already on their journey out of his mouth.

The smiling lady said nothing but lifted up the folded over zipped edge of her open team jacket to reveal clear but unmistakable embroidered letters that clearly spelled out, Sam Keane.

Chapter 10

A blade that sweeps through the air gives the impression of motion created by a powerful controlling arm. The victim of that blade can see it arching in slow motion towards them but is powerless to react to it, paralysed in the moment. A blade that whips through the air creates an altogether different impression. It strikes like a venomous snake that has slithered through the undergrowth to ambush you.

The man had no choice but to stand and watch the demonstration as the thin, glinting, un-tipped fencing sword whipped through the irritated air. Like the lunge of a rattle snake the blade suddenly whipped in the direction of the man's chest, piecing the white cotton shirt, the absolute tip of it coming to rest on the man's moist skin.

"Fencing is a discipline of respect, speed, technique and, fortunately for you, precision. I give you a chance to change your life, to play with the big boys, yet you repay me with failure. I give you time because you are young, and you make mistakes. Yet still I think you laugh at my generosity. Now I ask you to come to my house and again you disrespect me by turning up five minutes late. When you drive up my drive, tell me, what do you see on my front garden? What?"

The man swayed slightly causing the blade to flex more and so causing an indentation in the stretching skin that was now at breaking point.

"Yo... your helicopter Mr Petrov?"

"Yes, my helicopter, that costs me one million pound to keep in the air. I have that helicopter to save me time. Even to save me five minutes it is worth it for me, yet you turn up five minutes late. Those five minutes have now been the most expensive five minutes of your life. I will take back my money from your house and your cars and your boat. As you stand here, already you have nothing."

The blade is retrieved. The master of it turns his attention to the man at the door.

"See to it that my helicopter is ready for departure in fifteen minutes. As for this sweating failure, remove him from my life and take his Rolex and his rings from him and make sure they are given to my son."

Chapter 11

"Well, Mr Stirling Speedy, I really didn't think you would fall into that trap. Bet you didn't think Sam Keane had a pair of these."

Sam folded her arms and pretended to hitch up her well layered up, cold protected, boobs!

"Sam, sorry, sorry,"

Stirling put his head down in mock submission and his hand up to emphasise his apology.

"I have to say, Miss Keane, not the sort of mistake I usually make. If I can start again. I believe I am here to drive one of your cars today."

"You are, providing I am not picking up the bill for your services."

Sam stood, continued her smile, and held out her hand. Sadly it was something she was used to, it was a common mistake.

Stirling met her hand with his own outstretched one.

Sam then clasped her hands behind her back, rotated slightly away from Stirling and tilted her head a little to one side in a sort of pseudo coy stance.

"So, poster boy, Sam Keane has turned out to be 'bad girl' ex-convict Sam Keane."

"Poster boy eh? May I?"

Stirling gestured at the sofa to sit down.

"Please do. Don't feel too bad Stirling, everyone makes the same mistake and I'll get my own back on you at some point. It's good to have you on board and yes, I suppose I had better confess that I may have had a poster of you at some point."

"No doubt a poster of me advertising some obscure thing. The things the teams got me involved with."

"For a man that holds the record for receiving one of the most expensive pay cheques in F1 I bet you didn't complain too much."

"By all accounts I don't believe that you have done too bad for yourself, Miss Keane."

"Well, that is a long story, maybe for an evening in an expensive restaurant, paid for by you, if you really want to hear about bad girl Sam Keane."

Sam put her hands on her hips and shook her head.

"Did I just think that in my head, or did I actually just say that out loud?"

Stirling sat down on one of the leather sofas and placed his kit bag at his side.

"I am afraid it was out loud, and you know I might just take you up on that. At the very least you can tell me where the ridiculous name of your team came from?"

Sam pushed her laptop away and sat on the opposite sofa.

"So, you're the man responsible for us having to run this little runt in one of our cars. Have you met the lovable young man yet?"

"No, I haven't had the pleasure, although his reputation does precede him."

"Oh yes, you will have your hands full with this little soul. How do you want to run it today, Stirling?"

"Let's get him out on the track first and then I'll have a run out. Then we can compare the data."

The dramatic noise of a low hovering helicopter filled the transporter and drowned out any further conversation.

Stirling turned to look out of the window.

"Is he allowed to land that thing in the paddock?"

Sam stood up, zipped up her jacket and pulled on a team branded bob hat.

"Oh, you'll find, Stirling, that Mr Petrov does not play by the rules that us mortals have to."

After putting on more protection against the Cheshire cold in the way of a pair of gloves, Sam picked up her closed clipboard and gave Stirling a mock grin.

"Let the fun begin, oh and you will find his dad, Mr Petrov, more lovable than his son!"

Sam turned to leave, then fired back a cheeky,

"You can get your kit off in here if you want!"

Stirling returned the fire -

"Well, that's the best offer I've had for a while. I'll get my kit off, then get my race kit on and then perhaps we can all convene in the garage and say our hellos to the Petrov family and maybe, just maybe, we can get this show on the road."

Chapter 12

Stirling was sitting on a flimsy looking blue deckchair lacing up his race boots, whilst the race engineers busied themselves with the final checks on the slick shod Porsche and set the tyre pressures, when a large, very large, bald headed man with no significant neck entered the garage from the pit lane. Stirling expected the man to approach him, but instead the bulky man positioned himself next to the far wall, out of the way of any activity, and then just stood there, his arms dangling by his admittedly bulky waist, although not bulky when compared with his even more bulky shoulders.

'So, I presume that is not Mr Petrov then?' Stirling thought.

Sam Keane was the next visitor to the garage. She entered hugging her clipboard.

"We good to go Trevor?"

"All good Sam. Stirling has run through with us how he wants to run the car. We are running the car quite soft as Stirling wants to evaluate Sergio's feel for the car and his feedback."

Sam looked through the settings that Trevor had just handed over.

"OK, can we crank on a couple degrees more rear wing please. We are not going for a time today and I really want the car nailed going through Island bend and Druids, especially as Sergio is used to running a lot higher, down force cars. I'd also bring the cold tyre pressure up a tad as well, with it being so cold. Just keep a good eye on the hot tyre pressures when the car comes in so we can see where we are at. I see we have not gone too aggressive with the front camber settings. OK, that's cool for what we are doing today.

Sam looked up at the car and went through a mental checklist.

"And we are OK with the seat fittings for the two drivers?"

"Yeah, they are both about the same size. Stirling has said he would have the pedal box set up slightly differently, but he said to leave it for today."

Sam turned to Stirling who was busying himself putting on a team jacket that he had just been handed and the obligatory winter testing bob hat.

"You cool with everything Stirling?"
Stirling replied with a simple thumbs up.
"OK."

Sam lingered with a stare at some tools that were now not in use yet had been left out on top of one of the toolboxes.

The offending race engineer followed the stare and realised his mistake.

"I do hope that I do not have to insert those tools up someone's left nostril when I come back into the garage. I seem to remember that I personally made sure that there is a place for everything when it's not being used."

Trevor glared at the offending engineer who responded with a,

"Sorry guys."

Sam turned to exit the garage but was met by a man wearing a black overcoat. A fine example of a sharp crease in his black trousers could be clearly seen with the quarter of his legs that were exposed under the long coat. His shining black shoes were angled into a flat toe and seemed to emphasise the crease in his trousers. A large grey woollen scarf wrapped around his neck partially hid the lower part of the man's defined jaw line and chin that sat below the not large, but sharp, nose. The man's cool blue eyes were not sunken as such, but the pale surrounding skin ensured that the dim light within the garage made his eyes look darker than they actually were. His longer, rather than shorter, black hair was swept back and clearly held in place by some, no doubt, expensive hair product and one could deduce that for the age of the man, maybe 50, his hair had been expertly coloured, as no grey hairs dared to make an appearance.

Stirling made his move to the front of the garage and decided not to hold his hand out for the obligatory handshake in fear that it would be left dangling by this man who clearly worked hard to make his presence felt.

"Mr Petrov, I presume?"

"Yes. Sergio tells me you have kept him waiting in his motor home."

Sam, who by this time was standing behind Mr Petrov, looked over his shoulder to Stirling and rather cheekily gesticulated and silently mouthed,

"*My* motorhome actually!"

Stirling ignored Sam's correction.

"Well Mr Petrov, you could do with getting your door man over there to pop over and tell young Sergio that the action is in here in the garage and out there on the race circuit and certainly *not* in the motorhome playing Super Mario!"

Mr Petrov eyed Stirling, unsure how far he could push his attitude.

Stirling eyed back with a look that said, 'I will eat you alive if you even think of pushing me!'

Petrov decided to play the safe middle ground.

He nodded towards his bodyguard.

"Go get him."

Then he turned back to Stirling who had not removed his stare.

"Remember who is paying your extortionate wages today, Mr Speed."

Stirling maintained his stare.

"That's just my expenses. Wait until you get the bill for my time, my man."

Stirling turned to the very silent Trevor.

"Change of plan Trevor. I'll take the car out first. I don't like being kept waiting."

Sam could not hide a slight smile.

"OK lads, let's get her warmed up and can we get Stirling's seat set up. On track in ten please."

Chapter 13

Stirling gave his safety harness one last tug out and down and waited for Trevor's voice through his radio ear plugs.

"OK Stirling, you're good to go. Three good warm up laps please and remember the new front pads. The tyre temperatures will be sub-zero!"

Stirling squeezed the right-hand paddle shift behind the steering wheel and it clicked rather than clunked into first gear. As he eased onto the throttle pedal and the car rolled out of the garage he couldn't help but smile at the perfect, though by chance, timing. Sergio had finally walked around the corner into the garage at the same time, helmeted and gloved up ready for his run. Stirling could see that he was not impressed that 'his' race car was just going out on circuit. Young Sergio turned to his father with outstretched arms.

"Oops, I think I might have just upset the boy. I'm sure Sam will handle it."

Five laps in and temperatures were starting to get within the vicinity of their operating zones and Stirling was really starting to get used to the 911's unique handling properties. A rear-engined 911 Porsche could never be confused for a mid-engined sports car. In years gone by, the 911 had a reputation for being a tail happy diva, but years of racing development had seen Porsche hone the 911 into a beast of a car both on the road and on the track. Stirling soon sussed that it was best to play to the car's strength, its traction out of the corners. Heavy, sudden braking unsettled the thoroughbred and caused the rear weight of the engine to become something that suddenly had to be managed. Squeezing the brakes still firmly but long into the corner ensured the whole car settled into the corners and meant that the lighter front end weight of the car could be persuaded, without too much effort, into the corner. The 911 derivative likes to be busy and does not welcome neutral periods of time where it is waiting for the driver to decide on what to do next. As the brakes are unloaded and the steering starts to roll off at the corner apex, a very definite squeeze on the throttle shifts the weight onto the rear wheels and, when combined with the weight of the rear engine, the massive rear tyres can dial up plenty of grip that sees the car sling shot out of the corner to the accompaniment of the howling flat-six engine.

Stirling loved Oulton park, the venue of his first race win in a Formula Ford 1600, so many years ago. His delayed turn into Lodge Corner ensured a straighter exit as the track dramatically drops away into Deer's Leap, enabling him to get onto the throttle earlier to ensure a good terminal speed on the start / finish straight. Stirling reached for the right paddle and short shifted from second to third at the bottom of the dip so that the big Porsche was settled as it came up over the rise where the circuit kinks to the left slightly.

Keeping the steering as straight as possible over the brow gave the growling car one less thing to do and resulted in it following the slight camber towards the pit lane wall. Even though Stirling knew that he was the only car on the circuit, he instinctively looked in his left mirror, just after checking his lap board that had been hung out early for him to see the only information on it, the lap countdown. Easing the Porsche to the left-hand side for the approach to the right hand 'Old Hall' corner, Stirling chose to brake a little early. The time loss would be marginal, but the safety margin would be increased, the cold day resulting in a cold tarmac and the bumps in the braking zone for Old Hall all added up to a chance that was not worth taking. Stirling peered through the corner, straining to see the exit, almost imagining it so that he could squeeze back on the power. The Porsche pushed slightly at the front through the first part of the corner, but the slight understeer was negated by the arrival of the power and the slightly more favourable camber on the exit of the corner. Stirling judged it perfectly as the Porsche's outside wheels just about irritated the exit kerb. That flat-six, now at flat-chat, sang as Stirling kept the car to the outside of the track down the avenue, pulling for fourth gear ready for the flat right kink. A breeze of right-hand lock and the car swaps sides of the track in a blink of an eye to the right side, ready for the critical left hand Cascades Corner. Over a soft 'yump' and again an earlier brake than feels necessary is applied as Stirling's left hand instinctively reaches for the left paddle shift and asks for third.

The electronics blip the engine accordingly and third gear is ready to do its job. Turning in just before the service road on the right, Stirling turns his head to search out the apex and the awaiting exit kerb. The Porsche howls as the accelerator pedal runs out of any more movement and the tyres skip across the track, desperately trying to win the battle over the lateral forces that are trying to fling the car off the track. Now, the twin clutch system really justifies its presence on the car as Stirling flicks for fourth gear, the glorious Porsche cacophony not noticing the gear change and only acknowledging the higher ratio with a slightly deeper noise. The process is repeated as fifth gear is asked for. The fast and committed Island bend now fills Stirling's concentration as he leans on the left-hand side of the steering wheel and coaxes the galloping thoroughbred into the bend. Relaxing his commitment, Stirling blends off the throttle then climbs back on it as the now happier Porsche commits to the long left-hander, the rear wing working hard to show the rear of the car who is boss. The race car is now looking as though it is heading for certain oblivion as it heads flat out in fifth gear for the second gear, right hand, banked hairpin. At the point where it seems that its driver has forgotten about braking, Stirling loads the brake pedal for an instant, the car responds by compressing its exotic suspension, then Stirling heaves onto the brake pedal - the heavily braking car skipping under protest, but Stirling is ready to correct any protests that get out of hand. As the steering is turned into the tight hairpin, there is still braking work to do, but the hugely scrubbed off speed and the selection of second gear now gives Stirling confidence to bleed off the brake pressure as he applies more steering lock. The outside tyres dig into the tarmac and the Porsche sweeps round the corner faster than seems possible. Stirling is well back on the throttle before the corner is finished and allows the car to run to the absolute outside edge of the tarmac on the exit. Short change to third and allow the car revs to hit the big numbers, then another determined brake to bring the race car tight into the left, right, left, Britain's chicane. After demanding some of the entry kerb, Stirling is careful not to ask too much from the first and second aggressive apex kerbs but then asks for all of the available exit tarmac as the Porsche flies over hilltop and starts its head long flight down to

Hislop's chicane - introduced to the circuit after the tragic death of up and coming, promising race driver and all-round nice guy, Paul Warwick. The hundred-meter marker board on the left is used as a visual reference for the critical braking point where the tricky chicane is. Being careful not to get into a situation where the big rear-situated engine arrives at the corner first, Stirling realises that he has carried a little too much speed in and so decides to put the Porsche design engineers to the test and releases the brakes, committing to the start of the chicane. The Porsche responds gamely and only expresses its slight displeasure with a little understeer, then a kick of oversteer as the front tyres grip up. The protest scrubs off the remaining excessive speed. Patiently, the Porsche is kept under careful control so that maximum concentration can be given to the all-important run out of Knickerbrook corner. Stirling switches the power on carefully, but straight away the Porsche complains about the adverse camber on the exit. A quick lift of the throttle shifts the weight forward and engages the front wheels again so that they can do the job that they are supposed to do. Stirling realises that he has lost his exit line slightly, but commits to holding onto the throttle. A lift at this point would be a death blow to the quick lap time that he is carrying, according to the digital delta display on Stirling's dash top. The reluctance to release the throttle from its duties means that the committed Porsche is heading out well onto the aggressive kerb and the whole car vibrates, almost blurring Stirling's vision as the Porsche grabs what purchase it can to help it in its quest for the mind-blowing acceleration away from the corner. Accelerating hard up the hill, under the bridge, and over the hump at Water Tower, Stirling aims the almost leaping Porsche in the direction of a big treetop on the exit that has grown higher than the rest. Another service road flashes past on the right and Stirling steers his high-speed projectile to the left side of the track in preparation for the notorious double apex right hand Druids bend. Stirling decides to hold it in fifth in an effort to give the 'on the limit' Porsche one less gear change to worry about, the torquey engine growling at the extra work. Stirling's dancing tyres do not worry the first apex too much, but make sure that the second one is on their bucket list. The fifth gear entry, even after a brake squeeze, has set up a slight push from the front tyres, maybe caused by an over efficient rear wing. Stirling has no choice but to manage the situation and modulate the throttle a little, being careful to roll all the steering off at the exit to allow for the awkward bump taken at full power on the exit of Druids. Throttle nailed; Sterling still has time to glance at his digital delta readout as he flashes under Baillie's Bridge. The red numbers preceded with a minus sign on the digital delta confirms that this is his fastest lap. A quick visit to sixth gear then sees Stirling calling for the lower gears as he controls the lively Porsche, under-braking on the undulating approach to the last corner, Lodge Corner. Being careful not to overdrive, Stirling commits to it with surgical precision, the game race car rotating towards the apex. The exit of it is un-spectacular, neat and controlled, perfect. The Porsche is howling again, happy to be off its leash as Stirling pulls for more gears and the hyperactive race car careers onto the sweeping start/ finish straight. In the time it takes for an eye to blink, Stirling flashes past his wide-eyed team as they look at their busy lap timers and wonder how Stirling Speed has just equalled the lap record on a day like today!

Chapter 14

Reaching through the steering wheel, Stirling squeezed the collar located behind it and released the steering wheel from the column to assist his cockpit exit. Trevor leaned in, took the wheel from Stirling and placed it on the dash.

"You certainly had her singing Stirling. Any changes?"

Stirling swung his legs over the high side impact bars and clambered out whilst tilting his head to one side to gain better access to the buckle holding his helmet chinstrap tight.

"Thanks. No changes, great job guys. Nice set up for what we are doing today."

In other circumstances he would have asked for some rear wing to be trimmed out and would have looked at improving the turn in abilities of the car, but all was good for the Sergio onslaught.

Sam wandered over.

"You pedal well for an old guy!"

Stirling pulled off his fireproof under helmet and attempted to straighten his hair.

"Ah it's a cold day, I think the engine was quite enjoying ingesting the cold air charge. Where's our young Sergio? I take it he was not happy with me jumping in the car first?"

"Oh no, we had a proper, 'toys out of the pram' moment. I think you are definitely off his Christmas list before you even got on it. He's retired for a sulk in my motor home. Come on, I'll walk with you. This should be fun."

Stirling set off towards the motor home.

"I'll find a way to get him to work with me, but I just need to get him to learn a bit of respect if I am going to get him to listen to anything that I am going to say."

"Good luck with that one."

Sam turned to her waiting crew.

"Let's have some more scrubbed tyres on please. Can we get the fuel topped up? Trevor, I am happy with the tyre temps. Can you just balance them all round?"

Sam pointed to the temperature she wanted all the tyres balancing to.

"We are just going to get our little diva, so let's be ready to rock and roll in...,"

Sam looked at her square, original 1970's Tag Monte Carlo watch.

"Let's rock in 15, so, say 10:30. Let's use the dry track as much as we can. Knowing the UK at this time of year it could be snowing by lunch."

Stirling had not hidden his long stare at Sam's watch well and as they commenced walking Sam pulled her sleeve back for Stirling to have another look, who replied to the gesture with,

"Sorry, I have a bit of a thing for watches, especially original ones. Nice."

"A present from my big brother."

"Nice big brother!"

Sam turned to look at Stirling.

"We don't talk, well we do, or should I say, we have just started talking. We have not talked since all the trouble. I am afraid I did not turn out to be the nice little sis that he thought he had. I turned out to be a conniving, fraudulent little cow actually."

"He bought you a watch though."

"That was before I tried to blackmail him and ended up nearly nailing a prison sentence on him for a crime that he didn't commit! Now if that has not whetted your appetite for an evening in discussion with Sam Keane then nothing will. You driven Porsche's before? Are they an acquired taste?"

Stirling found Sam's directness quite captivating.

"I have, but not for a while. But I do have a guilty secret when it comes to Porsche's, just don't let my Jag hear. Maybe if you come round to my place tonight, I can let you into my guilty secret and you can tell me how you ended up blackmailing your brother. Now we are probably equal on the whetting of appetites front."

"No, I think I trump you on that one, but still, I would like to take you up on the offer. I have come up in my motor home though and need to be back at the workshop tomorrow. We do actually have real customers that we run cars for."

"OK, without sounding too much like I am trying to lure you to my lair, I can have my housekeeper rustle up erm, well something. She will put a nice white wine in to chill and freshen one of the rooms for your stay and, to seal the deal, I will personally drop you off at your workshop tomorrow on my way down to Gray Grand Prix, and that's my final offer."

"You are sounding a little desperate Mr Speed, but I will take you up on your offer."

Sam looked across at Stirling's E Type sitting resting in the paddock, minding its own business.

"And that is not going to break down on us on the way down?"

"Quiet, quiet she gets jealous over other women."

"OK, deal. I'll get one of the lads to take the motor home back. That will get the tongues wagging!"

Stirling had just got hold of the motor home door when it was taken from his clutch.

"Sergio, just the driver we were looking for. How about we have a brew together? We can have a quick run through some data and then get you out on track."

Sergio pushed past Stirling, then turned to look him in the eyes which prevented his father from making progress down the motor home steps.

"No. How about you learn your place? Don't ever make me look stupid again. My father decides who runs and when they run, he pa.."

Sam now stepped forward and cut off Sergio's rant.

"With all due respect young Mr Petrov, I run this team, and no one farts around here unless I say so. OK?"

Sergio turned to his father, who responded,

"Sergio, don't get yourself riled before you get in the car. Let your driving do the talking. Go show them, my boy, what you can do. Then we all talk!"

Stirling made no sound but swept his left arm down as if to say, "after you". Sam and Stirling then followed the mini entourage headed by a striding Sergio with his bald headed Teletubby on one shoulder and his upright, trying to not appear to be over-striding, father on the other.

"Well Sam, just as you said earlier, this is fun."

The Porsche was not happy as, yet again, the brakes were hit hard and far too late for turn one, Old Hall corner, the young driver wrestling to keep the rear of the car behind him. The hot and bothered race car was hauled to an acceptable but slow entry speed and responded poorly to the heavy steering input by flinging its rear tyres into a time consuming oversteer that needed urgently controlling before the point of no return.

Mr Petrov unnecessarily shouted along the pit wall to one of the stopwatch holding guys.

"That looked fast, what time did he do?"

The un-impressed engineer replied silently by turning the stopwatch for Mr Petrov to see.

"That is fast, No?"

Stirling spoke up.

"He's close on four seconds off the pace. He is trying to hustle the time. I think we should have him in, otherwise he will throw it at the wall."

Petrov shot back a response.

"No, he is not used to the car - he needs more seat time. He will go faster than you, Mr Speed. You must allow him to prove what he can do, and you must accept that he can be faster than you."

Stirling looked at Sam, who responded by pulling one side of her headphones behind her ear to listen to what Stirling had to say.

"You really need to be getting him in. What's he saying over the radio?"

"He's not a happy bunny. Saying that he has no grip anywhere and the car is, well should we say, 'not very good', I think is a rough translation."

Trevor interrupted and pointed.

"I think the rain is here."

A very light drizzle had sneaked up on them and was attempting to make a mockery of the available grip that the track was desperately trying to provide.

The bucking Porsche could be heard searching for grip on the exit of Lodge corner, the available race electronics taking control of the matter and saving the engine as the rev limiter cut in. Sergio grabbed third gear just as the Porsche crested the hill out of Deer's Leap whilst applying left hand lock to keep the car tight on the left-hand side of the circuit. In general, race cars do one thing very well, two things, begrudgingly, three things they may cope with (but at a compromise), and the thoroughbreds start to become divas but give them *four* things to do and they tend to go on strike.

Stirling only had time to say,
"Catch it!"

But the words were lost in the void between Stirling's thoughts and Sergio's now very busy helmeted head.

One. The Porsche was accelerating hard, Sergio was keeping the throttle pinned.

Two. The Porsche was working its suspension hard as it crested the brow and attempted to keep the rear tyres loaded and still in communication with the track.

Three. Sergio applied a slight amount of unnecessary left-hand lock following the marginal direction change of the track.

Four. Sergio pulled for third gear to answer the rev limiters request for another gear.

Instantaneously, the overworked Porsche cried enough and threw its rear end out as a child throws its unwanted toy away. The now slightly dampening track offered no answers to the wayward car, and Sergio's lack of prediction and slightly delayed opposite lock steering input came up wanting. As though to guarantee the expensive accident that was about to happen, Sergio also decided that the best course of action would be to jump off the accelerator, which released any available grip that was still there from the wayward rear tyres.

Porsches are driver's cars and if you don't drive them then they will take over.

The slightly heavier back of the car now took charge of the situation and headed the way it wanted to go. Unfortunately, the pit wall was blocking its route. In a vain attempt to recover the lost cause, Sergio hit his brakes hard. The Porsche, now more determined than ever, made a final lunge for the pit wall arriving there with an expensive and energy absorbing thud. Unfortunately, kinetic energy does not like to change without a fight. The initial impact sent the car spinning to the right until the front of the sorry Porsche made a final assault on the pit wall - the kinetic energy finally accepting defeat and allowing itself to be dissipated into the many other forms of energy that are willing and waiting to take its place in the violence that is a race car accident.

As the red lights around the circuit urgently flashed on, the ever-efficient race control scrambled its safety crews. Trevor held his head-mounted microphone close to his mouth.

"Sergio, are you OK mate? Sergio, how are you? Can you hear me? Sergio?

Stirling inquisitively looked at Trevor, who shook his head and held his arms in a gesture that said, "I don't know".

Stirling swung round to address Sam but was confronted with an empty pair of headphones left on the pit wall. Totally against protocol, Sam had jumped through the opening in the pit wall fence and gone over to the crumpled steaming wrecked Porsche. She was now walking back, her head looking down at the shiny wet track.

Trevor ripped his headphones off and jumped through the rails onto the pit lane to head to race control.

"Stirling, you grab Sam, I'll get over to race control to find out what's going on. This isn't looking good!"

Chapter 15

Sian did not notice the fast-moving Ross Keane through her transparent office wall until her door swung open.

"Richard, where's Richard? He is not answering his phone!"

"He's gone to the glasshouse, Mr Keane. Have we got a problem?"

"Oh yes, and a big one. Sergio has shunted at Oulton and its bad. Can you get hold of the hospital, or anyone, and get as much information as possible regarding Sergio's condition? Can you also arrange for a helicopter to pick Richard and I up from here in 30 minutes, or asap? If you see Richard before me, get him to answer his damn phone!"

The door swung shut then opened again.

"And Sian, absolute lockdown. If the press start ringing reception it's strictly 'No Comment' whilst we get on top of this."

The door closed again and remained closed. Sian decided on the best course of action.

"Stirling, it's Sian"

"Hi Sian"

"What's happened Stirling? Where are you? Ross is looking like he is ready to lay a hen, never mind an egg!"

"Sergio stuck it in the wall and has not come out of it too well. Apparently, he hadn't fastened his safety belts up and he smacked his head big style. They are operating on him at the moment. His dad is in a state of shock."

"He didn't fasten his belts up, really?"

"Apparently when one of the lads went to sort his belts his response was, 'I drive F1, I hardly think a Porsche road car is going to sting me!' Trust me, this is one messed up kid."

"So, what's the plan?"

"Sam is in with his father at the moment so maybe we will have more news soon, but it's not looking good. I have a feeling that Gray Grand Prix will be looking for another driver and, I bet, another cash cow."

"OK, I'll go find Ross and Richard. I am arranging for a helicopter to fly them up. We could do with a meeting Stirling."

"Yeah, I know. Listen, you let Peter Smith know what has happened. I think I have Sam Keane staying over tonight, it's a long story, before you ask. Then, possibly, I am driving her down to her workshop tomorrow, but that may all change, I'll let you know. Either way, I will end up down at Gray Grand Prix tomorrow at some point. We can grab a bite to eat tomorrow night. See if we have got any corner pieces yet for this puzzle."

"OK"

"Sian, can you also chase up the police files that I have asked for from Peter? I am particularly interested in the address where this Rosalie girl lived. Have you dug anything up?"

"Not really. I have had to get my feet under the table, so to speak, but I have managed to have a chat to Richard Gray about her. He is still, after five years, pretty cut up about it."

"OK. Listen, keep me informed of any developments with Sergio and then we will hook up at some point tomorrow, maybe."

Stirling closed the dark green leather case of his phone and looked up to see Sam on her own, walking towards him.

"Wow, Stirling this is not looking too good. Because the little idiot did not have his safety belts on, his head has taken one hell of a walloping. He has what is described as 'worrying' bleeds on his brain. They are saying that the next 48 hours will be critical. The medics are saying that he spoke to you when he briefly came round whilst waiting for the air ambulance. What did he say? Anything that made sense?"

Stirling had become slightly distracted as he scrolled through the contacts on his phone.

"Stirling, what did he say, did he blame the car? This is really not what I need for the team at the moment. I don't know why I agreed to let this test happen."

Stirling gave a reassuring smile to the clearly rattled Sam.

"Sam, please don't worry about the team. Young Sergio has to be the priority at the moment. He just asked me a question. Nothing important and I reassured him. Now if you would excuse me, I have a call to make."

"Well, I am sorry Stirling, but I live in the real world, I'm not a retired multi-millionaire world champion. I have worked hard for my money and I am not going to let some cashed up spoilt Russian kid who can't drive take it away from me!"

Stirling stared at Sam, went to reply, but his international call connected.

A regrouped Mr Petrov approached Stirling just in time to hear the end of his conversation.

"OK that's great."

Stirling looked up only to be met by a pair of fiery eyes.

"Mr Petrov, how is Sergio?"

"How dare you ask how my son is, how dare you? You are the man I hold solely responsible for his accident. You will pay for this Mr Speed. I am not a man to be crossed. You have taken the most precious thing in my life away from me. My whole existence is to be able to give Sergio the best opportunities in life, but now his life hangs in the balance because of you. You will pay for this, and Gray Grand Prix will too, for insisting on this stupid tuition from you. I am withdrawing all my funding from Gray Grand Prix and I will insist that the loan I gave Mr Gray to pay off his debts, which he accumulated building his folly that he calls his 'speed technology centre' be paid off immediately. Your actions have brought great consequences, Mr Speed."

"Mr Petrov, I understand your anger and that you need to kick something or someone, and I am okay for that someone to be me, but you must understand that Sergio's injuries were caused because he chose not to fasten his belts up. He..."

Petrov now leaned forward, his pale and sweating face millimetres away from Stirling's.

"His pain is caused because you insisted on him testing an inferior car not up to his speed, his pain is caused because you chose to drive first, forcing Sergio to drive in perilous conditions. You caused his pain and as result you will receive pain."

Stirling did not like anybody, for any reason, getting into his face. He raised his hand to encourage Mr Petrov to stand back but his arm was instantaneously slapped down by the heavy hand of Mr Petrov's Teletubby bodyguard. Stirling raised both his arms in surrender, turned and walked away from the continuing foul, verbal abuse that chased him down the hospital corridor, verbal abuse that seemed to mock the quietness, orderliness, and cleanliness of the echoing hospital corridor.

Chapter 16

Stirling was surprised to see Sam standing by the passenger door of his awaiting E type.

"Nice to see you're not leaning against the old girl. People do seem to have developed a habit of finding a perch for their posterior against some unsuspecting car's paintwork whilst they text, email or view their ever-so-important social media."

Sam seemed to physically relax with Stirling's comment.

"You are so right; I have noticed that. You'll never get me doing that though, taught by my Dad when a little girl that cars are not to be leaned on, jumped on, or played football against."

Stirling fished for his silver jangly keys from his jeans pocket whilst walking round the long bonnet to unlock the passenger door.

"So, is the central locking not working on your 67 Jaguar?"

Stirling pressed the button on the chrome door handle and swept the door open.

"68 actually. Central locking? If the truth be known the door can be unlocked with a 99p electric screwdriver but I like to keep the pretence up that really you need the keys to unlock it."

"Thanks Stirling. Sorry for the mini meltdown before. The press are going to be all over this and it's going to mean a shedload of extra work for me. I dread to think..."

Stirling looked across the roof of his Jaguar and raised an arm with an upturned hand to back up his next statement.

"Sam, stop! I take it that you are taking me up on my offer for a night trying to outdo each other with stories?"

Sam replied by inclining her head to one side and then mouthing a silent "Please" through a pleading grin.

"OK Sam. You are very welcome, if you are prepared to put today into a box marked 'for attention tomorrow'."

Sam stepped into the old leather scent that filled the inside of Stirling's Jaguar.

"OK, you have a deal Mr Speedy, you have a deal. Now are you sure this is going to start, or should I call a taxi to be on the safe side?"

Stirling stepped into the scented environment; his key already positioned in his left hand to insert into the ignition. He hesitated before turning the key.

"Oh Sam, be careful what you say in earshot of this old girl. Have you ever seen the Spielberg film, Christine?"

Sam laughed at the question.

"I have actually, I believe that is the film where an old Plymouth Fury car takes a dislike to certain people and sneaks out at night to dispose of them."

"Exactly. I suggest that you sleep with one eye open tonight!"

Stirling turned the key and after a moment of carburettor spitting the silky-six fired up and settled into a purr. Sam turned to Stirling whilst locating her seat belt.

"I take it this cat has, perhaps, longer claws than some of the other Jaguars?"

Stirling blipped the throttle to confirm Sam's statement, then eased the cat into first gear and allowed the gearbox to take up the starting torque.

Chapter 17

The helicopter broke free from the ground, hovered for a moment, turned into the wind and with a slight dip of the nose and increase in noise floated into the grey sky. Sian sat opposite the two men who clearly were not happy with their lot in life. In imitation of her two jaded fellow passengers, she reached above her left shoulder, lifting the suspended earphones off their hook, placed them over her head and then positioned the microphone in front of her lips.

Richard Gray was the first to speak.

"Sian, can you cancel the arrangements for tonight?"

"I have already sorted that, Mr Gray, and I have also arranged to have a driver meet us at the heliport. I presume you are both heading to your respective homes?"

Richard replied with a forced grin. Then added,

"Richard. Please drop the 'Mr Gray' thing."

Sian lightly rocked her head from side to side.

"Oops, I know, sorry you have said that before, and I sort of hop between addressing you as Mr Gray and just plain old Richard don't I?"

Richard smiled back.

"You do."

"Oh, not that you are plain Mr Gray, I mean Richard."

Richard continued his smile.

"Oh no, and not that you are old either."

"Sian, whatever you use doesn't really matter. Whatever finds its way out of your mouth will do, OK?"

"OK, Mr erm Rich...ard, don't worry I'll work on it."

Ross Keane spoke up next, in reply to Sian's original statement about heading home.

"We might as well enjoy our homes whilst we still have them, and our shirts on our backs for that matter, because trust me, without Mr Petrov's Rubles we are losing the lot."

Richard broke his stare out of the window and stared at Ross, a stare that said everything without him having to say a word.

Sian, desperate to further open the appearing cracks, subconsciously bit her lip whilst trying to form the next question or statement in her head, the tense atmosphere demanding that just the right words were uttered.

"I think I am going to have a chippy dinner tonight."

As she uttered the words, Sian was really starting to realise that she actually had no idea how her own mind actually worked. What a stupid thing to say.

Richard and Ross both looked at Sian with grins starting to appear on their frowning faces, grins that actually grew into, possibly, slightly hysterical laughs.

Richard drew a long breath.

"Really Sian, what planet are you on? You seem to operate inside your own little world."

"I'm sorry Richard, I am not sure how that came out, but I have to confess that, one, I am hungry and two, I do fancy a chippy meal tonight! Thinking about it, and, maybe given the gravity of the moment, maybe I could have said something a little more constructive. Note to self, try to be more professional."

Richard replied with the remains of a grin.

"No, please don't change Sian, we love it, a breath of fresh air can be nice when you live in the stale toxic air of Formula One."

Richard and Ross looked back out of their respective windows, both no doubt as conscious as Sian was that the noise cancelling headphones that they were all wearing were actually failing to cancel out the clatter of the helicopter as it chopped itself through the disturbed weather outside.

Sian levered some more.

"I might as well enjoy buying my chips whilst I can, seeing as it looks like I am going to be out of a job next month by the sounds of it."

The crack levered open.

Richard continued to smile back at the amusing enigma sitting in front of him.

"Sian, you really don't need to worry about Gray Grand Prix, we always seem to find a way of muddling through to the other side."

Sian kept the momentum going.

"Do you think, Richard, that Mr Petrov will follow through and pull his backing?"

"He is not a man of shallow words Sian, as I am sure you have already gathered. We need to be finding some new backing. I do feel a bit guilty that Stirling is now in his firing line. He is gunning for him as well."

Sian unfolded one of her arms and flicked out her wrist whilst unfurling her fingers at the same time.

"Ah don't worry, Stirling can look after himself. I am sure he can call on a few heavyweight lawyers to fend off Petrov."

Ross spoke next.

"When you are dealing with people like Petrov, legal arguments are the least of your worries. These guys have their own way of getting justice. You tell Stirling to really watch his back with this guy, you do not want to get on the wrong side of him, trust me."

Sian decided to keep the ball rolling now that she had established her 'lack of thinking before opening her mouth' approach.

"Why would you associate with this sort of man, never mind do business with him? Is it not obvious that when you play with vipers, at some point, you're going to get bitten?

"Say it as it is Sian, don't mince your words, my dear, on my account."

"Sorry Richard, I perhaps actually spoke the question instead of just thinking it."

Richard held his right hand up and backed that gesture with yet another smile that clearly indicated that the managing director of one of the largest Formula One teams did not mind one his assistants speaking her mind. Ross decided to jump on the band wagon.

"The thing is Sian, when you are falling down a bottomless black hole you grab at whatever you can. Petrov provided that lifeline. Richard and I grabbed it without considering the cost. I sometimes wonder whether the fall, and then the consequences of that fall, would have been the better option."

Richard interjected on Ross's roll.

"I think Ross is being..."

Ross turned on Richard.

"What Richard, I'm being what, unreasonable, ungrateful? We both used Petrov to climb out of that hole. Afterwards, we should have found firm ground and carefully moved away from the edge, but no, that was not good enough for you. No. You had to hold on tight to Petrov, who proceeded to make the hole bigger so that we were always looking over the edge into the abyss. He played us, Richard, and now he has pushed us back over the edge and let us go. We both knew this would happen one day. I am sorry I ever set eyes on a race car."

Sian sat quietly and blinked her large hazel eyes at Ross as he clenched his fists on his knees and returned to looking out into the darkness that had now swallowed the helicopter.

Richard thought about letting the heavy words hang, but soon came to the realisation that they could not be contained in the cramped, noisy cockpit without further comment.

"I think you will find, Ross, that you had your own reasons for grabbing onto Mr Petrov's coat tails."

Ross rounded on Richard again after a moment's contemplation.

"And you think I don't know that? You think I don't think about that every day when you are forcing me down a route I don't want to go? Sian, I am in this situation because…"

Richard jumped in.

"Ross get a grip; Sian really does not need to see your dirty laundry. I am sorry, Sian, this has all got slightly fraught and slightly unprofessional."

"I am sorry Mr Gray, I feel I have caused unnecessary stress."

"Really, Sian, please. Ross is tired and I think we have all had a difficult day. Ross is making a little more out of this than is the case. Actually, the situation we have with Mr Petrov is quite common in Motorsport. Formula One survives because of two attributes. The first one is its worldwide exposure that is priceless for brands wanting worldwide recognition. Big businesses wanting to get a piece of that action are prepared to pay big money to teams and drivers. The other attractive attribute is its perceived glamorous lifestyle. The Wealthy of this crazy world we live in are prepared to pay millions and millions just to be part of it, and in some cases those millions pay for their sons and daughters to live out their dream of being a Formula One race driver."

Richard hesitated before his next comment and gave a little sarcastic laugh to himself as his mind lingered on the present critical state of Sergio.

"In years gone by, Formula One drivers only had a one in three chance of retiring alive from the sport. Nowadays, the safety in F1 is so good that the rich and famous are more prepared than ever to let their lovable little heirs pursue a funded career in the wonderfully glamorous world of motor racing."

Sian decided to prompt further conversation whilst the going was good.

"I know paid drivers are on the increase in F1, but Mr Petrov has been around Gray Grand Prix for quite some time...surely Sergio would have still been but a boy when Petrov turned up on your doorstep?"

Richard seemed slightly surprised with Sian's knowledge but was happy to continue.

"Well, someone has been doing her homework."

Sian replied with a pretend grin that kept her lips tight and her teeth hidden.

"The moons all sort of lined up and..."

Sian tilted her head on one side, she was not prepared to let anything slip by her.

"The moons lined up? Sorry, what does this mean?"

It was easy to forget that English was not actually Sian's first language.

"A number of situations came together at the same time that made it the right time for us to team up with Mr Petrov."

Ross stirred from his window gazing.

"When Richard says we teamed up with Petrov, what he really means is, he took over our lives."

Richard ignored Ross and continued.

"Ross introduced me to Mr Petrov. Gray Grand Prix had hit some major money issues and was in danger of folding."

Sian interjected.

"But I thought Formula One was effectively a licence to print money?"

"Oh, Sian, there is some truth in what you say, but when you enter Formula One you usually end up with a very large ferocious animal that is as happy as a kitten until it gets hungry - then it turns on its own and devours them. One very successful F1 driver signed for a team that paid him millions per year, but unfortunately, not the same number of millions that his previous team had paid. As a result, his wages did not cover his burn rate even though he still was earning what, in the real world, was an astronomical wage."

Sian sought explanations again.

"Burn rate, what is this?"

Ross replied,

"Burn rate is the money that drivers spend to fund their lifestyle. Their jets, boats, houses, cars, jet setting lifestyle and, in some cases, their gambling habit!"

Richard flashed another look of unexplained disagreement at Ross and then continued.

"Well, you could say Sian, that Gray Grand Prix's income had fallen below its burn rate. I had invested heavily in the technology centre but unfortunately the world's economy decided to have a little hiccup and fall into recession and our main sponsor stumbled into a scandal, so the situations kept lining up. Ross had a little hiccup of his own, and suddenly we were falling down a big black hole. Mr Petrov threw us a lifeline. He had the money and, fortunately for us, his young son had expressed a desire to be a racing driver when he grew up and Mr Petrov now saw a route for his son to fulfil his dreams. It worked for us all at the time. The fly in the ointment was that young Sergio was not, shall we say, blessed, with racing driver genes but, up until today, it was sort of working out."

"No Richard, it was not working out, we needed to pull away from Petrov when we got through our bad patch."

Richard was now clearly becoming agitated with Ross.

"Ross, remember, our issues were separate but we both had an answer, and that answer was Petrov - an answer that both I and you seemed happy with at the time. There are never any free handouts Ross. We had a price to pay for the bail out. We both agreed to the terms, we both…"

"But Richard, the price turned out too high, too high. Now we are left with nothing, so what was the point of it all? Answer me that Mr Gray Grand Prix!"

Sian reappeared from the invisible state that she had apparently taken on whilst the little spat boiled.

"I am really sorry, Sian, you should not have been party to that. Ross is, well Ross..."

"It's OK Richard, Ross, you both are under a lot of stress. I really should have just kept quiet and let you have the flight time to gather your thoughts. I am sorry."

Sian's statement had fallen on deaf ears though, as both her fellow travellers had now removed their earphones and evidently preferred the clattering chatter of the helicopter rotors than the chatter of fellow humans. Sian longed to ask more questions. What was Ross's little hiccup? What happened to the Rosie girl that had occupied her job years before? And what did Mr Petrov do that enabled him to have enough wealth to create a pseudo kingdom of dependant subjects around him? But even Sian realised that her moment of enlightenment had passed. Well, for now at least.

Chapter 18

The hesitant covert drizzle that had dampened the Oulton Park race circuit, obliterated a Porsche race car, and challenged the very existence of a young race driver, had now found its confidence and developed into a long set in downpour. Enough rain was now falling from the dark angry evening sky to cause the subtle undulations in the lanes that Stirling now drove along to fill with water. Stirling tried to navigate around the more expansive puddles but inevitably his slim, by modern standards, Dunlop tyres had to work hard to dispatch the standing water through their tread pattern. Not having the noise-soaking luxurious padding and cosseting of modern cars ensured that the occupants of the E type could hear the tyres doing their work on the soaking roads, the wet noise increasing suddenly as water splashed up on the underside of the Jaguar's long inner arches as another puddle was momentarily dispatched.

Sam cheekily smirked as she spoke.

"You wear driving gloves."

Stirling continued his navigation but afforded Sam a quick glance.

"Leather string back driving gloves at that, really?"

Stirling continued his no comment stance.

"So, you drive a three-hundred-year-old car, listen to something called classical music and wear Stirling Moss driving gloves."

Stirling conceded,

"I do."

Sam responded,

"OK..."

The Jaguar eased up the gravel driveway of Stirling's Drayton House, its aging headlights soon picking up the large old glistening wooden front door through the now relentless rain.

"Do you mind if we go round the back to the garages and put the old girl away? Rain does not do her arthritis any good."

Sam knew that it was more a statement than a question so replied with,

"I do like the sound of 'garages' as opposed to just 'a garage'. Garages belonging to a three-time world champion would suggest hidden treasures inside."

The garages turned out to be a long barn, possibly even an old stable like building, with at least 7 separate garage doors running across its front. Stirling steered the long bonnet towards the nearest door, stopped, pulled on the large chrome handbrake and reached into the back for his waxed Belstaff jacket and accompanying hat.

"So, I presume that Jaguar E type, glove wearing, drivers don't do remote control garage doors?"

Stirling hesitated before opening his door to the raging elements.

"Sam, if we sat here and hit a remote, we would miss the smell."

"The smell?"

"When old cars sit in a garage, they create an aroma that is a blend of oil, fuel, leather and even dampness."

"You mean they all leak."

"Sam, Sam, you should respect your elders."

"Well, you go get your fix Stirling, I'll stay in here out of the rain and try to imagine your joy."

Stirling liked Sam's cheeky honesty and found it refreshing. Very often Stirling found himself surrounded by people that thought they were good at saying what they thought he wanted to hear.

After easing the dripping Jag into dry comfort and closing the garage door against the wet elements, Stirling swung open the back door of the Jag and reached in to retrieve his kit and Sam's overnight bag.

"OK Sam, the elements are sealed outside. You can venture out now."

Sam responded by opening the dripping door, climbing out of the low-slung car and then proceeding to peer into the dark gloom that hid the rest of the lengthy garage space. She then pretended to nose a glass of fine wine.

"Ah yes, I can definitely detect tones of aging oil with perhaps a hint of fuel-stained aluminium!"

"And you think I am weird. This way Miss Keane, I have a housekeeper desperate to fuss over someone else other than me."

"Oh no, hold your horses cowboy, it's not every day that a girl finds herself in Stirling Speed's garage. Looking through your, I have to say, very well set out workshop space, well done, with the obligatory customised snap on tool chest, slightly cliché, but I'll let you have that, I can see a number of covers that seem to hide the treasures of the world! I think it would be very rude not to let me have a little peek."

Stirling put down his bags and walked across the polished red tiled floor to the pure white wall and switched on the first of a row of silver metal light switches. The workshop space lit up with its full car ramp, immaculate work bench which developed into a kitchenette that ended up morphing into a compact, cosy living room. A part wall separated the rest of the garage from this car cave section, on which hung a very large black and white picture of a 1970's Porsche 917 splashing through the rain at a dated looking Brands Hatch. The back wall was being used to hang a large, extremely up to date TV screen, opposite which a cracked brown leather three-seater sofa sat, awaiting occupants.

"Well, I have found my new house. I'll just live in here Stirling and promise not to disturb you. OK Stirling, let's hit the rest of the light switches."

Stirling responded by flicking each switch one at a time, causing the garage to illuminate in sections.

"Oh, my word, what are you on Stirling? We seem to have a kaleidoscope garage. Do you have any pattern to your collection?"

"I have my reasons for each one, I think!"

"OK Stirling, we need to do this in an orderly way. Let's start here!"

Sam walked to the first bay, turned her back to the garage doors and stood facing the two immaculate vehicles, one behind the other, that were now facing her.

"Why?"

"I love Land Rovers. They really showed the world the direction."

"OK, so we have a green Defender."

"Grasmere Green, 90-inch, Heritage."

"Right OK, I get that, I have to say maybe not what I would think a three-times World Champion would choose, but hey, what do I know? OK, but a matching Discovery?"

"Discovery 2 face lift, and the colour does not match exactly, but there you go, a bit of a theme there. A great car. The closest you can get to a Defender but with a bit of comfort thrown into the mix. The launch of the Discovery range saved Land Rover from disappearing down the big black financial hole that so many other English marques had fallen into!"

"Really?"

"To me, the final development of the true Land Rovers before they became 'Chelsea wagons'."

Sam peered under the Discovery.

"Stirling, even the chassis has been sprayed and polished."

"I had some time to kill and chassis have never been Land Rover's strong points."

Sam stood up and ventured to the next bay.

"You really do need to get out more!"

"Take the covers off, they could do with a bit of air!"

Sam, now in a world of discovery, was already exposing the treasures.

"So, what do we have here? Oh...that's a bright and very sexy...gold? Yellow? Aston Martin erm..."

Stirling had decided to sit on his couch and switch on the TV, American NASCAR's were jostling around some far-flung speedway in America. He replied without taking his eyes off the screen.

"It's a 1976 Bahama yellow Aston Martin DBS V8 and under the next cover is..."

"No, no, don't tell me..."

Sam carefully lifted the corner of another car cover.

"Well, it's red and, wow, a Ferrari Dino! Very, very nice. So, why these cars please?"

Stirling was now getting up to speed with the NASCAR race...

"Focus Stirling, please, why these?"

Stirling again replied without looking round.

"The Persuaders."

"I am sorry, The Persuaders?"

"One of my favourite TV programmes. Research it. You will see what I mean."

"OK, note to self; Research The Persuaders! Now to the low line car covers, one a lot smaller than the other and..."

Sam, totally engrossed, now knelt down on the red tiled floor and peered under the cover.

"...and sitting on short chassis stands. Ah, we must be into some poorer stuff now."

Sam pulled the low cover off the smaller car.

"Oh, well, I was not expecting *that*. What is it? I know it is a Formula Ford of some description, I'd go for a Van Diemen?"

"Yes and no. Seeing as the transit into my house is taking longer than anticipated, would you like a beer?"

Stirling pulled open the door of his well-stocked fridge.

"Yes please, I think I could cope with a beer after the day I have had. So, what is it? And why?"

"My first championship winning race car, and it's a Reynard 84."

"Didn't that guy, Adrian Reynard wasn't it, didn't he go on to build Indy Cars in America?"

"Yes. In fact, he was quite a prolific race car builder. FF1600, FF2000, F3, F3000 and, like you say, Indy cars. Don't quote me on this, but he holds some sort of record for his cars always winning their inaugural race, or something."

The last comment fell on deaf ears as Sam had other treasures to discover. Stirling flicked the lid off another beer and walked down with the primed bottle towards the rummaging Sam. It suddenly occurred to him that Sam was the first stranger that he had allowed into his garage, into his space, and he found it nice that he was not unsettled with the idea.

Sam reached her hand out to the arriving Stirling.

"Well, I think you need to be sending this down to my workshop. I'm thinking it is going to be needing some TLC. I'm presuming the tub is ok. Just the left front corner or, should I say, corners, damaged."

"Ah, my slightly bent P34 Tyrell."

"Can you believe that they actually made a six-wheel formula one car? I thought, though, that they were as rare as rocking horse teeth, how did you manage to get hold of one..."

Stirling went to reply but Sam stunted his comment by lifting her bottle up towards Stirling's face in a, 'hang on, here's a thought' sort of way.

"Didn't you crash one of these, one that belonged to Lawrence Troutman, whilst demonstrating it at Monte Carlo?"

"Well deduced my dear Doctor Watson."

"Bend it and you mend it, or at least buy it!"

Stirling laughed.

"Not quite that deal Sam, but let's just say it was a deal easily brokered. I will get it repaired and up and running at some point.

Sam took a considered swig from the bottle.

"Oh, I am quite enjoying myself here. Sorry Stirling, I bet you get fed up of showing people round your car stables."

"Actually, you are the first that I have actually shown round."

"Well, Mr Speed, I will take that as a compliment and an honour. OK, two more covers to go."

Chapter 20

Sergio looked almost relaxed and peaceful as he lay surrounded by machines that monitored his balance between life and death.

The white sterile door of the white sterile private room swished open, slowly. A soft voice accompanied the smiling, caring face that rounded the opening door.

"Mr Petrov."

No reply came.

The nurse approached from the length of the bed so as to prevent startling the crumpled man who was clearly deep in thought. She reached out her hand and rested it on the stooping shoulder. Mr Petrov slowly turned and looked up at the still smiling Nurse, pain eating deep in his eyes.

The soft tones eased through the room again.

"Mr Petrov, the consultant would like to have a little chat to you."

The reply that came out almost as a gasp was smothered with a strong Russian accent.

"I cannot leave my dying son. I cannot abandon him.'

"Mr Petrov, please come and have a chat, I will sit with Sergio."

"If there is any change, you..."

"Yes, yes, Mr Petrov, I will call you straight away. You need to be strong Mr Petrov, be strong for Sergio."

Reluctantly the crumpled figure began to straighten out and finally stood up.

"When you are ready, turn left out of the room..."

"I know where to go."

The crumpled figure seemed to be gaining in size and power.

"People will pay a price for what they have done to my son and Stirling Speed will pay a heavy price for goading my son into this tragic accident. I have made sure people who have crossed me have paid the price in the past and they will again."

The nurse knew not to pass comment at this point and only responded by trying to change her smile into a sympathetic one.

"Keep good care of my son, young lady, and I will reward you. Neglect him, and you will pay."

The intensity of this now fully straightened man ensured that the smile was beaten into submission.

"Mr Petrov, I can assure you that Sergio will receive the medical care he requires."

"'Sergio' is for his friends, his family and his loved ones. To you and all in this hospital that have a duty to care for him, he is MR PETROV!"

The swishing door now swung open and held momentarily on its hydraulic closing mechanism as the now un-crumpled and indignant man swept through the doorway.

Chapter 21

"So, is it a case of best left for last?"

"Really depends on your taste I suppose, but either way I think you should be getting the last two covers off as I am sure I have a housekeeper thumbing through the new jobs page by now!"

Sam chose the cover nearest the garage door and proceeded to carefully unwrap the treasure underneath.

"In my eyes, one of the most beautiful cars to grace our roads. I had to have one."

"Is it not bad form to have a favourite?"

"Oh, I have no favourites, it would cause jealousy amongst ranks."

Sam finished the unravelling.

"Oh, my word, what a beautiful car. I know what this is. Such a vibrant red. Another Italian handsome brute? No, bad description. Gent? No, this beauty is too racy for that."

Stirling smiled at the dazzled Sam.

"I know! Another Italian handsome gigolo!"

"I'm not sure if I quite agree with that description, but I know what you mean, I think. Do you know what it is though?"

"I do. It's an Alfa Romeo 33 Stradale, 1968. Such fantastic proportions, and a sound that can draw unsuspecting drivers, trance-like, to buy one, then have all their money absorbed, keeping the creature in the lifestyle it is accustomed to."

Stirling laughed.

"It's a 67 model and yes, it is, shall we say, high maintenance. Now really Sam, we must go... Really."

"OK, OK. One last cover, please."

Stirling's silence and stance said OK and prompted Sam to make a move to grab the cover.

"This is my dirty little secret that I mentioned at the circuit."

"I think you have a few of those going on, my young man, from what I have seen. So, what do we have here?"

Sam pulled off the final cover. Again, the car was sitting on short stands, its bulbous large wheel arches left empty by the wide wheels that had been removed.

"Ah, this is your guilty little Porsche secret."

"This was my poster car when I was a child."

"The same poster you have in your car cave?"

"The very same."

"Such an iconic car, which, I believe, had a difficult birth according to the early drivers of it. A 1970, Gulf livered, 917 Porsche. Awesome! Does it run?"

"Of course it does! In fact, it is probably ready for a run out at some point. Maybe I can get that Catch Me If You Can race team of yours to run it."

"Now you're talking. We would love to run it."

"Right Sam, can we now go into my house? My housekeeper will get you settled in, then you can tell me why you have a ridiculous name for a race team. I think I've held up my side of the bargain."

Stirling's phone discreetly vibrated with an incoming text as the garage tour finally came to end and a course for the main house was now set.

"Have a good evening Mr Speedy with Sammy ;-) Give me the nod as soon as you know your travels tomorrow. I have seen Peter Smith and he has given me the police files for the Rosie death. This looks like heavy stuff to me. See you tomorrow... if you can tear yourself away from Sammyyyyy ☐

Your loving and ever so affectionate Sian!"

Stirling replied as he walked,

"D'accord mon enfant!"

"Ah he thinks he can speak French all of a sudden. Trust me, I fear growing up, I might end up like you!"

Stirling flashed a glance at the reply, somehow reading it in the French accent that never strayed far away from Sian's English.

Chapter 22

"Mr Petrov, please do come in and sit down. May I first introduce...."

"I will stand, and who is this man? I thought you were the senior consultant. Do not shirk your responsibilities, I deal only with you."

"OK, as you see fit. This man..."

"I do not want him in the room. He looks like a man of little means, a man who could make himself rich by selling stories to your English press about my son's condition. I want..."

"Mr Petrov, please relax, this man is the man that has just saved your son's life."

The proud upright man staggered slightly, just enough for an explorative hand to reach out for the edge of the table in reassurance.

"Please Mr Petrov, sit down, you have been through a lot. You have not eaten or drunk anything. We have a lot to tell you and I really need you to listen and concentrate. We have positive news. Nurse, nurse.... could you please get Mr Petrov a glass of water and maybe a biscuit, please?"

The stern man began to shrink again. The roller coaster over the last few hours proving too much for any flesh and blood to keep up appearances.

"My son is going to live, how? You said to expect the worst and he seems so poorly. I want only what is best for him."

"I know you do. Our initial prognosis was not good, he had a severe swelling on the brain that showed no signs of subsiding but we were contacted by this man who was in Switzerland at the time. He specialises in racing trauma. He talked us through procedures over the phone as he boarded a private jet to fly here. He had been contacted to say that Sergio had been in a heavy accident and had received a severe brain injury. He scrubbed as soon as he arrived and, well, all is starting to look a lot more positive. We will not know exactly what damage has been done, but certainly his vital signs are all looking good and the swelling is regressive. We are hoping to start bringing him out of the induced coma within a few hours."

"Why wake him so soon? Does he not need to rest further?"

The man who had initially sparked fear, now turned hero, spoke up next.

"Mr Petrov, I'd like to get Sergio functioning by himself as soon as possible so that his body can re-calibrate and we can assess where we need to go with his treatment. I am not one who sits on the fence Mr Petrov, but I will qualify what I am about to say by highlighting that this is not an exact science. I am not sure how long it will take for Sergio to wake up and I am not sure of the extent of his recovery, but what I will say is that from my experience in dealing with these conditions, I believe that because we were able to respond to Sergio's condition so quickly, it means that I think the brain damage has been significantly reduced. Fortunately, I was contacted very quickly after the shunt. It..."

Mr Petrov, now round shouldered, reached forward with both hands and clasped one of the hands of the once suspected imposter.

"Thank you, thank you. I will make you a rich man. Thank you."

"Really Mr Petrov, it is a team effort and, as I have said, we are not out of the woods yet."

"I must reward you."

"Really, we are just doing our jobs."

"But your fee, I must pay your fee."

"Please do not concern yourself with that."

"Really, I must at least be able to pay your fee, any fee, I can afford it."

"Mr Petrov, that has been taken care of."

"But by who, how?"

"By the party who contacted me when your son had his accident."

"Party, what does this mean?"

"By the person, the individual who contacted me. The fees have been taken care of. Now, I really suggest that you head off to a hotel. Eat, freshen up and sleep. If there is any change you will be contacted, immediately. I need you to be strong when your son wakes up."

"But this person, this, how you say, 'party' - who is this one? I must know."

"I cannot say. Now go and try to sleep. Please."

The broken man released his clasp and stood up, clearly bewildered. A reassuring hand squeezed his shoulder. Petrov turned round to see his muscled bodyguard who spoke in a heavy Russian accent.

"Listen to them Mr Petrov. I trust them. Let me take you to a nearby hotel, then I will return, and wait should Sergio wake before you arrive back."

Petrov turned without uttering any further words and headed out of the door that was being held open for him.

Chapter 23

"You certainly keep an interesting house Stirling. Designed by you, I read somewhere."

Sam and Stirling sat in a grand, but still homely, living room. Regal, cardinal red walls, sitting above the heavily waxed parquet floors which were somehow softened by a large, exquisite handmade rug that was partially hidden by the soft, almost unstructured, burgundy red leather furnishings that seemed to knock the corners off the room. A roaring log fire ensured that this was a room to relax in post a hearty meal. A meal which had been prepared and served by Stirling's ever efficient but clearly slightly grumpy housekeeper. She did not like her meals being kept waiting. Stirling took a considered sip of his Viognier white wine and savoured the banana and peach characteristics.

"Well, I managed the restoration of the house. I'd quit F1 and suddenly my blinkers were removed, and I really enjoyed, well I suppose, seeing things again. This place had been modernised in the seventies which basically meant many of its original features had been covered up. I set about rediscovering it and making it a place that I enjoyed."

"So, no pad for you in Monte Carlo?"

"Nope. Not for me. I always enjoyed feeling home turf under my feet after I'd been travelling."

Sam eased off her white trainers and swung her feet up to one side, snuggling into her supple leather chair like a cat curling up for a long nap.

"OK Sam, so you have had exclusive access to my private car collection, exclusive access to my, admittedly slightly grumpy, housekeeper's exquisite cooking, a free guest room for the night and a free taxi ride back home tomorrow."

"Stirling you have found me out already... I am just a user."

Stirling pulled up a studded leather pouffe and lifted his legs to use it for its designed purpose.

"Sam Keane, sister of top F1 designer Ross Keane. How did you go from race engineer for a top Italian F1 race team to ending up in prison for stealing sensitive, technical and intellectual property?"

"And then end up a millionaire running my own GT car team?"

Sam interjected.

"Well, I was not going to be quite that brutal, but now that you mention it...!"

"It's really quite boring, but to avoid a room bill for tonight..."

"My housekeeper is making one up as we speak."

"I suppose it all started as a child."

"Wow, this is going to be long story."

Sam responded by raising an index finger as though to make a point.

"Don't be cheeky about my story or there will be no story and it will be straight to bed."

"Really?"

Sam responded with a mock shocked look.

"What would your housekeeper say? Let me clarify, straight to *separate* beds, Mr Speed. I have come across your type before. My story?"

Stirling folded his arms and put on an intense stare aimed right at the curled-up Sam.

"Your story. Please, continue."

It was nice to meet new company. New company that was not uncomfortable with Stirling's previous fame, new company that did not have an agenda. The fact that Sam was a female class of new company, and a pretty one at that, was definitely a bonus.

"Thank you."

Sam smiled then began.

"My Mum died when Ross and I were young. I was the youngest, but Ross always got all the attention, and Dad always had big plans for him. I suppose I just got jealous. I never really had any girly things that I guess I would have had if Mum had still been around. Everything we did or got was always, well, I suppose, for Ross."

"Ross somehow got lucky and got into F1 very young I seem to remember?" Stirling interjected.

"Yes, he did, typical Ross really. He waltzed through university and met Richard Gray at some lecture or something and they hit it off. In what seemed like a blink of an eye, Ross was designing successful F1 cars and being paid millions for the privilege. He met his lovely wife, who deserved so much better in my opinion, had 4 beautiful kids, and bounced through his fairy tale life."

"So, I take it from your tone that things did not run quite as smoothly for you?"

"You could say that. Dad sort of lost interest in me. Even though I was younger, I was there just to look after Ross in my Dad's opinion, but when he left home for Uni, I was sort of surplus to requirements, so I had to make my own plans. I scrabbled my way through an engineering degree and took whatever jobs I could, working around the myriad of UK based race teams. My data engineering knowledge kept me in jobs and, I suppose, was sadly helped by the fact that half the team owners thought they had a chance of jumping into bed with me. They didn't! Boy, I hated that period! Then I met Luca, who was drop dead gorgeous, a well contacted and ambitious Italian man. He was quite a bit older than me, but hey, I liked him, he was going places and I could sit in his wake as his career took off. Oh, and I decided that he could jump into bed with me! All roads lead to Rome as they say, and before we knew it, we were living in Italy. Luca ended up climbing the Italian sports car corporate ladder and I ended up senior race engineer at Stragatti Formula One racing! At this point, Luca decided that he didn't want to sleep just with me, but also his personal assistant! Call me old fashioned, but in my book, three is a crowd. So, I packed my gear and moved out of my rather comfortable Italian farmhouse overlooking Modena, and moved into a one-bedroom stuffy apartment in Modena itself."

Sam fell quiet.

Stirling responded to the pause

"Is that it?"

"Do you have a brandy?" came the reply.

"I am sure I have an extra old somewhere that could worry a glass. Please don't tell me that you want a cigar with that!"

Sam replied with a relaxed smile;

"If you throw a little ice in to knock the corners off, that would be just perfect."

"Extra Old Brandy with ice? I am struggling with that, young Sam."

"Don't be stuffy and get the ice in."

Sam swirled her clinking brandy in the large snifter glass and then offered the aromas up to her nose. Stirling followed suit and took a considered sip, then pressed Sam into continuing her story.

"So how did you get involved with selling industrial secrets to Gray Grand Prix?"

"Well Mr Speedy, I have to correct you there. I never actually got to sell said secrets. Someone blew the whistle and young Sam Keane ended up doing 3 years in one of her majesty's finest prisons. Trust me, I am not a nice person to know."

"I have to say Sam, you do not strike me as a person that would steal secrets from a team and flog them on."

"Well, I did."

Sam took a sip and then looked into the roaring fire. Without looking round at Stirling, she continued the story.

"It started actually as a joke. I needed to fly back to England instead of Italy after a fly away race and Ross and Richard Gray said I could jump on their plane. The Stragatti cars were proving unbeatable. We had developed a material that flexed under set loadings without fatiguing and then perfectly reformed when distressed."

Stirling nodded knowingly.

"Deformable wings, slightly outside the rules."

Sam continued.

"Well, that depended on how you read the rule book. Either way, when at speed down a straight, the wings would flex just enough to stall and not create any drag. As the speed reduced so would the air pressure, the wing reformed and so you had effective downforce again for the corners."

Stirling held out his brandy glass holding hand in a gesture.

"The perfect aerofoil. Downforce through the corners and yet no drag down the straights."

"Exactly. Stragatti had all the other teams scratching their heads. Not only had they found a tweak that no one could spot, even if anyone knew what they were doing, the complexity of the material meant that it would be difficult to quickly copy. It was so secret, only certain members of the team knew about the technology. Most people thought that Stragatti's straight line speed was due to engine and oil developments. I was one of the privileged few that worked on perfecting the wing stall system."

"But you said it started with a joke?"

"Mid-flight, Ross and Richard were pretty stressed that they were so far off the pace and Richard passed the comment, 'I wonder how much, do you think, it would cost us to get your sis to spill the beans on the Stragatti performance? Ross did not see the joke. He could never have entertained the idea that his little sister had more knowledge than him about how to make a race car go fast. But it was the last bit that got to me. He turned to Richard and said, 'do you honestly think Stragatti would let that sort of sensitive knowledge free to roam around in Sam's dizzy head?' Richard laughed and said 'well, if they ever did let her have that knowledge I, for one, would pay handsomely for it'. They talked like I wasn't even there. It was at that point that I thought I would show them what knowledge I had floating around my pretty head."

Stirling sat forward in his seat, still cradling the remains of his extra old nicely warmed Brandy.

"Well, that comment cost you a whole heap of pain!"

Sam forced out a false laugh.

"You could say that again. Three years of pain to be precise."

Stirling sensed the story slowing so decided to help it along.

"But still, there's a big difference between feeling a bit miffed at your brother and actually carrying out industrial espionage."

"Ah, you are now straying into sensitive stuff Mr Speedy."

Sam placed her round and empty glass on a highly polished small side table that had a little green leather coaster strategically placed on it and bit her lip slightly as she looked at Stirling.

Stirling replied with a quizzical,

"What?"

"For some reason, Stirling, I think I will tell you the whole truth and nothing but the truth. I took the full blame for offering the offending information to Gray Grand Prix. Ross and Richard came out of it all as the hurt, innocent party – 'smelling of roses' I think is the expression.

"I do seem to remember Sam that they, at the time, said they had no knowledge of what you were trying to do."

Sam waved an index finger from side to side.

"Not entirely true sir. Ross knew, although it never came out. I told him later that evening that I'd prove him wrong. I told him I, in fact, knew exactly why the Stragatti's were so fast. You might not believe me, but you know, I did not do it for the cash. I did it just to prove to Ross that I knew what I was talking about and that I was better than him. So, I went back to Italy and set about gathering all the secret information from Stragatti that would make me rich and show Ross what a prat he was!"

"But Gray Grand Prix never got that information and suddenly the Italian Armani Police were crawling all over you. It took another season for the other teams to catch onto the trick Stragatti wing. What went wrong?"

"Honestly, Stirling, I do not know. The first I knew that life was about to get a whole lot worse was when I got my apartment door obliterated at 4 a.m. one morning and my phone, laptop, in fact anything I possessed that was remotely digital, was confiscated. In the hearing, a memory stick was produced that I had loaded all the wing spec on, and the rest, no doubt you would have read about in the wonderful press coverage that everyone revelled in. I often wondered if Luca had a hand hammering some of the nails into my coffin, but who knows? Either way, I was definitely off everyone's Christmas card list."

Sam sat back and folded her arms in a that's-me-done sort of gesture.

"So, there you are Stirling, the wonderful life and times of Sam Keane, ex-convict and all-round bad person."

Stirling pressed on.

"As you brought it up, erm, you did seem to do OK out of it all financially. Catch Me Racing doesn't seem too strapped for cash."

Sam released a genuine laugh this time.

"Catch Me Race Team. A play on words that said to people: you might have caught me and thrown me in the clink, but let's see if you can catch me on the track. Although I have to say, every time we win a race or a championship everyone screams that we must be cheating, but you know, you sadly get to the point where you can't give a stuff what people think..."

"And the cash cow?"

"Oh yes, that was my brother. He came to see me at hotel de prison and we had long chats. He suddenly went on this massive guilt trip and started blaming himself for all that had happened to me. On the day of my release, I checked my account to find five million had been squeezed in there. So, my big bad brother that I so wanted to prove wrong turned out to be a very nice little brother with more money than sense."

Stirling pondered, but still had one little irritation that needed scratching.

"And the girl, Sam, where does she figure in it all?"

Sam swung a look at Stirling, clearly rattled by the last question.

"Girl, what girl?"

"The Rosalie girl, that worked for Richard and Ross, she ended up murdered around the same time, she…."

Sam cut in.

"Murdered? Where did you get that from? The silly mare somehow managed to poison herself, I think you will find. Why bring her up, Stirling, why? What is she to you? Well guess what, I might be a stupid girl that tries to sell trade secrets to get one up on her brother but trust me, matey, I am not a murderer!"

"Sam, I am sorry. I did not..."

"Look, I am going to hit the sack. It's been a long day. Hope that my story has paid my room and taxi bill."

Sam stood, staggered slightly and left the room, her back the only part of her body hearing the apology from Stirling.

'Wow, what was all that about? I certainly did not see that crash coming.'

Stirling muttered to himself as he broke his one glass rule and reached for another 25ml of XO!

Chapter 24

Stirling slowed his running pace as he neared the metal gate. The wet floor under foot from the overnight rain made for a slightly uncomfortable run, but the dampness in the early morning air seemed to act as an amplifier for the vast range of countryside aromas that stimulated Stirling's senses. Early morning runs cleared Stirling's carburettors, he liked to tell people. The gate shut with a slightly too loud metallic clang, no doubt rattling the peace for the hidden nocturnal creatures that were scurrying their way back to their hovels. The beaten path ended abruptly and was replaced by a slightly raised wooden track that had been manufactured to protect the sensitive flora from the well-meaning hiking boots that frequented this lush part of the Cheshire countryside. Stirling timed his jogging strides to take in the steps up onto the walkway and then carefully watched his step. He couldn't help thinking that sometimes health and safety goes too far. The wooden slats that went cross ways forming the walkway had been covered with a fine chicken mesh, no doubt to assist in the grip levels on the wet wood. Unfortunately, the chicken mesh was broken in places and had become randomly curled up, ensuring the perfect trip hazard for the unwary!
Stirling had lived through a period in motorsport of great change - financially, technically, and certainly when it came to safety. Thanks to the efforts of drivers like three-time world champion Jackie Stewart, safety in motor sport had improved dramatically. No longer were race drivers to be viewed as gladiators that were eventually meant to pay the ultimate sacrifice for their chosen sport. But just like the wooden track that Stirling found himself jogging on, health and safety can lull you into a false sense of security and motorsport certainly had a nasty habit of biting hard when you took your eye off the ball for a moment. The Oulton Park shunt the day before that had left young Sergio fighting for his life was certainly testament to that.

As usual, whenever guests were staying, the aroma of cooked bacon caught the air as it drifted through the opened top half of the stable door that Mrs B, Stirling's ever efficient housekeeper, always left open when cooking breakfasts, winter or summer. Stirling unlatched the bottom half of the door by reaching in.

"Morning, Mrs B. Morning Miss Keane."

Mrs B got in first with the reply.

"Ridiculously healthy, or substantial breakfast, young Stirling?"

Mrs B was of the firm belief that sausage, bacon, and fried bread never did anyone any harm and was the only way to start a busy day.

"I've pushed hard on my run today Mrs B, and we have a guest so let's go moderately substantial please."

Sam eyed her heavily overloaded plate and realised the error of her earlier reply to Mrs. B that she had omitted the word 'moderately'!

"Well, someone was up early enough to have first pick of the worms, young Stirling."

Mrs B discreetly eyed Sam. There seemed to be a little chemistry beginning to spark between Stirling and Sam and Mrs B was not entirely comfortable with that.

"I've always loved early mornings. Best part of the day for me."

It was now the turn of Sam to eye Mrs B discreetly as she busied herself moderately loading Stirling's plate.

"Erm, Stirling, last night, a little alcohol mixed with a dose of tiredness and stress is never a good combo for me! Sorry if I ended up a little snappy."

Stirling was surprised that this tough stand up for herself girl was bothering to mention it.

"Oh really, no stress, trust me I have had a lot worse and really I obviously touched a raw note, so the blame rests with me."

Sam paused with her reply whilst Mrs B reached between them and placed her rather large moderately substantial breakfast offering in front of Stirling.

"Stirling, I trust you will be travelling today?"

"Yes, I am taking Sam back to her place, then I am off to Gray Grand Prix. I will be staying down there as I am meeting Sian."

Mrs B smiled, hearing the name Sian.

"Oh, do say Hello from me Stirling, and say how come she has not been visiting lately? Will you be requiring a travel hamper?"

"I will, and in her defence, she has been busy working at Gray Grand Prix so it will be nice to catch up with all the gossip and no, I'll be OK without travel supplies. Only off to Milton Keynes."

Stirling refocused on an also smiling Sam.

"I think you are a little spoilt Stirling but…"

Sam's reply was interrupted firmly and by a no doubt slightly overprotective, interjection from Mrs B.

"He deserves to be spoilt."

Sam quickly replied, detecting a little jealousy lurking in the interjection.

"I am sure he does Mrs B, and I am sure you are the perfect person to do the spoiling. May I also thank you for a wonderful breakfast."

"Mrs B does spoil me, and also protects me from anything and everything - so you be careful."

"Stirling, really though, that was rude of me last night. The death of Rosalie, a lovely girl, hit the team very hard but then to have accusations flying around about foul play and it being related to the espionage was just too much for all of us to take in and you can imagine, it left a bad taste. I suppose you bringing it up last night, as you said, just hit a raw wound that I thought had started to heal, but clearly it still needs a sticking plaster over it!"

Stirling gave strength to the acknowledged apology with a pause before replying.

"OK, apology accepted and filed away."

Stirling set to work on his breakfast plate.

"So, what's the plan for today Stirling?"

"I'll get showered and get a few bits thrown in a bag, then I'll give the Jag a fluid check, get her warmed and let's aim for wheels rolling at ten."

Sam smiled again.

"You really do work in your own little insular world don't you, with your routines etc?"

"Years of travelling in the F1 circus. You have to build up your own way of doing things otherwise you end up being everyone's person. I like my set way of doing things, but I am sorry if those ways are not to your liking."

Sam gulped down the mouthful of tea that she had just taken onboard in an effort to speed up her reply.

"No, No, you misunderstand. I love the way you do things, quite cute actually. The world-famous Stirling Speed who really has not been affected by the zillions of pounds thrown at him, as well as the fame."

Stirling felt the slight flush of a blush.

"Oh, you soon learn that the fame thing is a poor veneer manufactured by other people and as for zillions…, I don't think so, may be just a zillion!"

Chapter 25

Ross Keane conducted the exact requirements to fulfil a common expression by using both of his hands one above the other to hold on to the door frame, lean forward and then literally 'pop his head in' to the clearly empty office. A strange action, as just a quick glance whilst walking past the curved glass-walled office would have produced the same information. The action did get the desired effect though, as an employee walking past was able to assess that Ross was looking for someone.

"You OK Ross?"

Ross pressed away from the door frame and swung round.

"Sian and Richard. Looking for both of them actually and they are both proving to be rather elusive at the moment."

"Richard - I am not sure. I know he has not done his usual workshop walk this morning, but his car is definitely in the car park 'cos he's parked next to mine. His space is taken by an old Alfa! Speaking of which, I have just seen Sian - she is in Rosie's challenging some of the lads to some sort of balancing competition or something."

Ross smiled.

"Why doesn't that surprise me? Thanks Tony, one out of two will do for starters."

As Ross walked past the last arch-framed workshop he could already hear the peals of laughter echoing from Rosalie's cafeteria. Entering the room, he could see why. One of the lads was being handed a pot towel from the kitchen area and was attempting to dry himself as water dripped from various protruding parts of his body, an empty, upside-down, suspicious looking large plastic tumbler lay on the floor – deed done. Around him the laughing faces were subsiding. Sian stood smiling at her victim, who was now passing the challenge back to her.

"OK young Missy, let's see *you* try to walk across the room with a plastic tumbler full of water on *your* head."

Sian replied with a cheeky grin.

"Oh, I'd rather not if you don't mind..."

"What do you mean, I would rather not? You said girls were better than men at everything, and you bet that you could walk across the room with a glass on your head without spilling it."

"I know I did. I am so glad that you went first though, otherwise it could have been me looking like a wet drip instead of you."

The room erupted with laughter again.

"You mean you have never tried it?"

"Nope."

"But then why did you suggest it?"

"I thought it was easier than it is. Clearly you have proved that is harder than I imagined."

The laughter now refused to die down.

The agitated victim continued his protests whilst continuing to dry himself.

"But how does that prove that girls are better than men?"

Sian milked the moment and tilted her head to one side, causing her dark shiny hair to lie flat to her face on one side and hang loose on the other. She then raised her right hand to her face and slightly extended her index finger so that it sat vertically across her lips, the rest of her fingers folded away and her thumb resting under her petite chin so as to exaggerate the idea that she was giving some thought to the answer.

"Well, girls definitely make better decisions than boys!"

The victim gave up the attempt to dry his wet shirt with the tea towel.

"What on earth are you talking about?"

The laughter paused for a moment to await Sian's answer.

"Well, it was definitely the right decision to go second in that challenge."

The peals of laughter started again and continued down the corridors as the break came to an end and staff migrated back to their workstations.

Sian also went to leave, but then caught the smiling eyes of Ross.

"Sian! What have you been up to?"

"Oh, just playing with the boys. That one thinks he is God's gift to women and has been a bit 'pervy' with me since I came, so it was time to draw the battle lines. Can I help Ross?"

"Okay first things first. Sergio?"

"Well, much the same as my last report to you but things are definitely looking good and they are well on the way with bringing him out of the coma. I did as you asked, and the press frenzy is now being handled by our press department and so they are sorting the appropriate bulletins etc. I believe they are running them past Richard first."

"Wow, that is good news. Let's hope his recovery is fast and full."

Sian decided to add a little to her report.

"You know that Charles Thomas has been involved? He is some big wig brain surgeon."

"Big wig, yep, you could certainly say that! He is reputed to be the top neurosurgeon in the world! How on earth has he got involved, Sian?"

"Well, that's the strange thing. No one knows. The hospital staff were surprised. He flew in and was there within a couple of hours of Sergio being admitted. Mr Petrov did not know who he was. I know that because Richard was asked if he had arranged it."

"Well, however he got involved it is good that Sergio is getting the top care. Second thing is, I've not really had time to chat to my little sister, Sam, about it all. I know she didn't make it home last night though. Also, I could do with having a chat with Stirling asap. Can you get in touch with them both and set up an informal meeting? Well, not a meeting, that sounds a bit officious, let's go for 'set a time when we can all have a chat'. Can you try your best to get Richard there as well - he seems to have put his head in the sand about it all. Oh and have you any idea where Richard is?"

"OK Ross I will...,"

Sian lifted up both hands and drew some inverted comas in the air with her fingers.

"...arrange a chat. Also, Richard is in the glasshouse. He went in there as soon as he arrived. I think the soil expert guy is in there with him."

"Brilliant. Here I am, beating off sponsors, staff and press, not to mention threats we are getting from Mr Petrov, and Richard is playing with his plants! Nice!"

Sian knew not to stoke the fire so stayed away from commenting about Richards actions.

"I am seeing Stirling tonight, but apparently Mr Petrov is gunning for him. He's already had a letter from Mr Petrov's legal team and a physical threat from his heavies."

Ross rubbed his red brow so hard that faint white traces from the indentations could still be seen for a millisecond after the finger pressure had been released.

"This is getting messy, very messy, and I have a feeling that it is all going to blow up in our faces…Where is Richard?"

Sian pointed in the right direction and then whispered "The glasshouse...?"

Ross relaxed his frown.

"Sorry Sian, you did say. Sorry, stressful times. The joys of running a glamorous Formula One race team, just living the dream."

Chapter 26

Ross entered the glasshouse through an elaborate twin glass door air lock system. The air, temperature and humidity being very carefully monitored and controlled. Ross had never quite come to terms with the amount of money Richard had spent on his glasshouse, but it was his team, his money, and his hobby. 'Extreme gardening' he often joked. A huge selection of plants, weeds, and all things green from all over the world found a habitat in his beloved greenhouse. Richard ensured that phone signals were blocked within his haven of relaxation.

Relaxation seemed to be the furthest thing from his mind at this point though, judging by the exchange of raised voices taking place somewhere in the undergrowth.

"Well, I am sorry Mr Gray but..."

"You're here to check soil quality and pH, not to pass your views on my choice of plants. Just leave and send me your invoice."

"But Mr Gray you don't understand, you can't..."

"Leave, before I have you removed."

Ross hesitated at the air lock doors and was half considering turning back when a red-faced boiler suited man rounded the shrubbery corner clutching a metal case in his gloved hands. He was shocked to see Ross standing there.

"This place needs a health warning on its doors."

Ross replied with....

"Oh"

He decided it was wise not to delay the man's outward plight, even helping him on the way by hitting the button that operated the first sliding door of the air lock. As the first door slid shut sealing in the irate man's back, Ross decided to call out before proceeding.

"Richard?"

There was a slight delay, then Richard's voice floated out on the perfect air.

"Over by the pond Ross."

Ross took the right fork, then a left fork past what looked like a six-foot house plant with shocking red flowers that had a wax-like appearance.

Ross heard the trickle of water into the pond before he saw it. A butterfly seemed to be unknowingly leading the way as it flew erratically in front of Ross.

"You OK Richard? That sounded like fun, not."

"Oh, just some small-minded person sticking his nose into other people's...,"

Richard hesitated briefly,

"Other people's choices."

Richard sat on a bench overlooking his miniature paradise, just staring into the glittering water. Large Koi carp mouths gaped at the surface having detected more movement that could just mean food.

"Richard, we really need to be getting on top of this and you do not seem to be dealing with it. Petrov is attempting to freeze our accounts whilst his people are flat out pulling our funding, I have all the other sponsors jumping like cats on a hot tin roof and to top it all off, Petrov is gunning for Speed legally and apparently, physically. Oh, and there is the small problem that the trucks with the race cars have set off for the test days at Jerez and guess what? We have not got anyone to drive them!"

Richard broke his gaze from his watery view and stared through Ross, then back at the water.

Ross prepared for Richard's response then felt slightly irritated when none was forthcoming.

"Richard!"

Before Ross could continue his planned expression of exasperation, Richard turned back and looked straight into Ross's eyes, decision made.

"Let's get Stirling Speed out to Jerez and let's give the press something to divert attention from Young Sergio. Let's see whether Speed has still got some of his Speed."

Ross mentally took a minute to recalibrate. Maybe this was why Richard was a Formula One team owner and was a survivor. When all the doors were closing, Richard always seemed to find a way of prising one open.

"But Richard, I do see your reasoning, but will Stirling want to put himself back into the circus?"

Richard stood and placed a hand on Ross's shoulder who was now seated.

"Ross, you get on with the test schedule and chase up the development parts. I'll make it happen with Speed."

"But..."

"Ross, can you get hold of Sian?"

Ross remained seated.

Richard turned towards the exit and spoke as he walked away, set on his course of action.

"Let's go, Ross. We have a race team to save and a star driver to sort for our empty race cars that, as you reminded me, are on their way to the test!"

Chapter 27

Stirling held the large, by modern standards, wood steering wheel lightly between his leather clad fingers, the Jaguar almost guiding itself along the sweeping roads to the Hotel that his ever-efficient PA, Lisa, had booked for the night. Stirling had also asked for a room for Sian. It would be good to catch up and compare notes on this latest case that they had been drawn into. Since dropping Sam back at her team's HQ the trip into Gray Grand Prix had taken quite a surprising turn of events. Stirling had been ushered straight into a meeting with an over-caring Richard Gray. Usually, a good indicator that Richard wanted something from you!

"Stirling let me get to the point. I need an F1 driver that's quick and can develop a car. I need a driver at the Jerez tests, and I need *you* to be that driver. How can I make that happen?"

Stirling had replied,

"You mean you need a story for the press to take their minds off the Sergio PR disaster that presently dominates any press story linked to Gray Grand Prix?"

Stirling allowed the cruising speed of the E Type to drop off and then whipped the clutch in whilst blipping the throttle to assist a smooth downward gear change, before squeezing the brake pedal with a more determined effort to manage the Jag's speed for the approaching left hand turn into the long lane up to the sumptuous country hotel.

Rather than one large car park, the hotel had a number of satellite car parks positioned around the grounds that surrounded the hotel. Stirling chose the one nearest the entrance that was reserved for the slightly more exclusive VIP's! The slim Jaguar tyres left the surefootedness of the solid tarmac and ventured on to the noisy, but somehow superior, status of the gravel car park, Stirling only just resisting the temptation to take a slice of throttle and drift the snorting Jag to its night resting place.

"Richard, I really have no desire for a comeback. I am finding that retirement life is ticking all the boxes for me."

"Stirling, I know I don't need to talk big numbers with pound signs in front them. I think that box was certainly ticked a long time ago for you, but Stirling, you are a driver. You have always said it was the driving that came before anything else. I am giving you a chance of four days driving at a circuit where I think you won three Grands Prix, if I remember rightly, *and* in a current F1 car. You know you want to do it."

Stirling really wanted to say that he had no desire to have to study the systems that he would need to understand to drive a modern F1 car out of the pit lane, never mind driving one competently and competitively on the track alongside the best drivers in the world. The test though, would enable Stirling to get closer to Richard Gray and Ross Keane, and therefore closer to the case that Peter Smith had been keen to investigate.

"OK Richard, it was four Grand Prix wins actually. I think you *will* need to get creative with those big numbers though, more for the fact that the press will want their pound of flesh from me, and you will need to get me in your simulator so that I can have a crash course on how to fly one of these modern F1 computer cars. But hey, let's make it happen and remember - I want a window seat on that private jet of yours!"

"Mr Speed, welcome to the Castle. I trust you have parked in our reserved parking? Do you have any more bags that you need assistance with?"

"Just Stirling, please. Yes, I have and no, I do not."

"We have the Caledonian suite reserved for you Mr… sorry, Mr erm, Stirling. I trust you will be eating with us?"

"I will, can you reserve a table for…"

"For two sir, yes, we had a young lady check in earlier. She booked a table for two and wanted reassurance that everything was on your bill, sir. I trust that is in order?"

"A French girl, dark hair and a dodgy English accent?"

"Oui Monsieur, a dodgy English accent… that is considerably better than your French one."

"This is said lady, sir."

Stirling couldn't help but smile as Sian's tones blended into the 'check in' conversation.

"Sian, it looks like you booked in early."

"Dead right, I googled the Hotel when your PA called me, and I thought I ain't missing out on any of this place. The massage and the full spa treatments are just amazing."

Sian paused; a moment of concern clearly etched on her face. She turned to the slightly bemused check in clerk.

You did book that to Stirling's account as well didn't you?

"Yes miss, I did."

"Phew, that's a relief! I forgot to check that before I had everything done."

The clerk turned to the listening Stirling who watched on, smiling at Sian's control of the situation.

"I trust that is OK, Mr…sir."

Stirling went to reply but was beaten to the reply by Sian.

"Ah, don't worry, I am his kept woman. He has a big guilt complex that he spent last night with another woman and now…"

It was Stirling's turn to interrupt.

"That is fine, I am happy to cover the cost for my sort of pseudo cousin, it's a long story, and she does have a habit of talking too much."

Stirling turned to Sian, her head now cocked slightly to one side, a cheeky smile spreading.

"You meet me in the restaurant at 7:30 and in the meantime try not to run up too much of a hotel bill, and let's practice being sensible for a little while."

"Okay Sir Stirling."

Sian saluted Stirling and turned to the clerk,

"He is very demanding and has a terrible temper if anyone calls him Mr Speed."

"Sian!"

Chapter 28

The very attentive and skilful waiter smoothly escorted Stirling and Sian to a quiet table by the window, being careful to take the long route behind cleverly positioned, decorative screens, so as not to excite the already seated diners to the presence of a Formula One Star. They were clearly well experienced at handling the well-recognised who just wanted to sit and enjoy a quiet meal, off duty as it were. Sian looked out through the window, the darkness forcing in on the spotlighted gardens.

"Nice view, if I could see it."
"I believe it is."
Stirling replied.
"So, a little bird tells me Gray Grand Prix has signed a new F1 mega star driver, some old guy!"
"Yes. I am that old guy. They were desperate, and to make it clear, this is not a comeback; it is a one-off test. Sian, please be careful what you say to the press - they will have a frenzy about this!"
"Are you looking forward to it?"
"Honestly, it is a big commitment. To get onto pace again is always going to be a stretch if your mind is not in the right place, but it gets me closer to Richard and Ross. Well, that's what I am hoping..."
Stirling was interrupted as a muted commotion broke out to the left of him. The attentive waiter gently waved his arms up and down, almost like he was interpreting the flight of a graceful bird, his low but clear firm tones could just be overheard.
"I am sorry, but Mr Speed is just having a quiet meal and..."
This time it was Stirling's turn to interrupt.
"Sorry, do we have a problem here?"
The waiter, clearly under pressure, replied.
"I am sorry Mr Speed, I have been instructed by the restaurant manager to ensure you have a peaceful, un-interrupted meal and unfortunately some diners have noticed your presence."
"It's Stirling, and really it does not matter."
The waiter stood back almost apologetically. Stirling hated it when people made a fuss of these things and wished people

would just let him manage whether he minded someone asking for an autograph or whatever. A smart, slim, smiling lady approached, may be mid-forties, dressed in a crisp white blouse and fitted black skirt - a lady clearly comfortable with herself. A man Stirling recognised lurked in the background, awaiting his turn as it were.

"Hi, sorry about that, people make a fuss when really there is no need, can I help?"

"I am sorry, I feel a bit stupid now. My husband is a big, big fan and he will love it when I tell him I spent the night with Stirling Speed."

Sian giggled.

The smiling lady increased her smile whilst Stirling extended a smile back.

"Well, now I feel really stupid because that came out wrong didn't it? Sorry, I meant to say that I met Stirling Speed! I'll get to the point, could I just get you to sign something please, and I will leave you in peace and go be stupid somewhere else."

Stirling laughed.

"Of course, and if you could just make sure that your husband is clear that you *met* me and didn't spend the night with me, it saves me not having to look over my shoulder for an irate knife brandishing husband."

Stirling took the offered pen and pad.

"What's your husband's name?"

"Roger."

Sian looked up from her menu and glanced at Stirling as Stirling looked down to sign and dedicate his autograph.

"Ah, that was my uncle's name."

It was now the lady's turn to take back the offered pen and pad.

"Thank you so much, and I have to say, I am a bit of a fan as well. It's been nice to meet you and your girlfriend, I am sorry I do not know your name."

Sian giggled again.

As Stirling stepped in.

"No, no, we are just sort of half cousins - it's a long story."

The lady clutched her pen and paper and backed away.

"Well, it's been nice. Thank you."

"You *so* need to sort your description of me Stirling. You make it sound as though you are trying to cover a dodgy fling with a young star struck fan."

Stirling rolled his eyes at Sian and then turned in his seat to greet the approaching man that Stirling had noticed blending in.

"Peter Smith, may I introduce my young, slightly outspoken cousin, Sian."

Sian spun round in her seat.

"Peter, I did not know you were here. How did you know that we were meeting here tonight?"

"Sian, you must improve your observation skills. I have been here certainly as long as you have been here today, and witnessed you attacking Stirling's credit cards."

Sian repeated her question.

"But Peter, how did you know we were here?"

Stirling replied.

"Sian, Peter's organisation that you and I are presently in the employ of track some of the most obscure criminals in the world - maybe keeping tabs on us is not beyond their capabilities!"

"That's a very good point Mr Speedy."

Sian replied with few accepting nods of the head.

Waiters bustled and very efficiently produced an extra place and accompanying chair which Peter Smith quickly took advantage of.

With menu consulted, recommendations acknowledged, orders taken and the arrival of the drinks the evening's dining began to take its course.

Peter Smith was the first to abandon the small talk and jump into the deep waters of the case that had brought them all together.

"Sian you have had a chance to look through the police reports for the death of the young girl?"

Sian initially turned to Stirling with her reply.

"I have the report in my room Stirling. I know you were keen to have a look through them."

Sian than turned to Peter Smith.

"I have to say on that front, the Police papers seem clear that it was an accident but, having said that, there is no doubt that

Richard Gray is still, after all these years, uncomfortable with discussing the subject."

Peter Smith quickly chipped in.

"Discussing Rosalie?"

Sian responded.

"Sorry?"

"The subject is Rosalie, never lose sight of the person whose death we are looking into."

Sian repeated her previous response but this time with a different meaning attached to it.

"Sorry."

"Never forget the cases we deal with are real cases of human tragedy."

There was a moment of non-verbal communication but still there was strength in the quietness that said they all had taken on board Peter Smith's lesson of how to ensure that the underworld that they found themselves in did not leave a stench on them.

Stirling broke the moment.

"I will grab that report off you Sian. My dealings with Sam Keane have been much the same. After a pleasant evening with Sam…"

Sian couldn't resist it and jumped into the sentence by turning to Peter Smith and announcing with a sing song voice,

"Stirling has a girlfriend."

To which Stirling replied,

"And Sian has a mental age of ten."

Peter Smith decided to relax and smiled. He liked the banter and relationship that Sian and Stirling had. It was uncomplicated, but there was a strong loyalty and support for each other, and in this sort of job when the going gets tough you take every opportunity to grab at any support offered.

Stirling continued after giving Sian a stare.

"After a pleasant evening…. it all turned a bit sour when the subject of Rosalie came up. I definitely touched a raw nerve and she promptly brought the evening to an end. Her reasons for why she stole and tried to sell intellectual team property all stacked up, and she was quite open that she had made her mistake and paid her dues as a result. To me, the 'baddie' of the scene is our Russian friend Mr Petrov. He has pain written all over him and he is certainly gunning for me as he blames me for his son's shunt. Not good."

Peter Smith seemed to shelve the Petrov subject and pushed deeper into the Sam Keane story.

"And her money?"

Sian looked quizzically at the both of them.

Peter Smith elaborated.

"Sam Keane went into prison on a senior race engineer's wage and came out of prison a multi-millionaire!"

Stirling continued,

"And promptly set up a very plush GT car race team aptly named, Catch Me Racing!"

"Hence one of the reasons why we think she think she got paid to take the drop for the ensuing prison sentence for someone." Sian acknowledged.

Stirling took up his answer to Peter Smith's original money question.

"Sam says that her newfound fortune came from her guilt ridden, and highly successful race car designing brother, Ross. He apparently felt that he caused her to act the way she did, and that in general, as far as being part of the family was concerned, she had always got the rough end of the deal, hence the guilt money!"

"Wow, I wish I had a brother that felt that guilty!"

Sian replied.

Stirling continued.

"I have to say that I found her genuine. She seemed not to want to hide anything. She has clearly worked hard to build up her race team, and an exceptionally good one at that. All her team seem to hold her in high esteem, and as you can imagine she takes no hassle off anyone. She is a proper car nut and seriously knows her stuff. I have to say, she is a bit of an enigma and I suppose there do seem to be some internal battles going on with her. On the outside, a pretty and refined lady, very controlled with her speech, yet when she rolls her sleeves up, literally, she is a tattooed hooligan."

Sian, as expected, jumped in.

"She has tattoos? I have always wanted a tattoo but never actually had the bottle to get one done. I would have an Eiffel Tower with a race car parked in front of it!"

Sian turned back to Stirling and tilted her head to one side, her shining black hair swaying and, with a definite glint in her eye, she prodded Stirling further.

"So, Stirling, did she show you all her tattoos or just the one on her arm?"

Stirling did not get a chance to answer as Peter Smith got in there first.

"Sian, can we please concentrate here, we are on an important journey to bring justice to this case. A girl was murdered in cold blood and someone paid Sam to go to prison for them. So, maybe a little less joking and a little more concentration."

Sian was not rocked by Peter Smith's sudden seriousness and simply replied with a salute and,

"OK Captain!"

Stirling, though, was a little taken aback by Peter Smith's sudden attack on what was Sian just being Sian and thought for a moment about jumping to her defence, but then realised that it was impossible to imagine the pressure that Peter Smith must always be under to get results for his strange undercover organisation. Stirling had, on occasion, since first meeting Peter Smith, wondered who his boss was. How did the organisation have so much influence throughout the world, and where did all the funding come from?

"Peter, I do take your point, but up to now I have to say all looks in order. Sadly, the Rosalie girl died but as of yet there seems to be no foul play and Sam seems to be just a girl who made a mistake and was fortunate enough to have a rich brother."

Sian suddenly engaged. "I am really not happy with Mr Petrov. He has everyone jumping and I really do think he is trouble. Stirling, you watch your back! The other guys, and girls for that matter, seem to be genuine people just surviving the turbulent sea that is life!"

Peter Smith initially said nothing, took a sip of his warmed brandy, slowly rested it on the table again and then made sure that he had their full attention.

"I *know* that Rosalie was murdered, and I *know* that someone is walking around who should be in prison. Trust me when I say that I know for certain this *is* the case, and so we dig and dig until we turn up what has been deeply buried."

Chapter 29

Ross Keane was on edge. That gnawing anxious feeling that all was about to fall apart would not go away. His volcano orange McLaren M4-12C glistened and showed off its different evocative shades as it trundled through the sun-dappled Buckinghamshire lanes on the way to Richard Gray's imposing home. Ross enjoyed his McLaren. He loved its design, he loved the Gordon Murray heritage, a designer he had always secretly admired, he loved driving it. It had always been escapism for his overactive mind that was constantly busying itself with the conundrum of how to make his latest Formula One design the fastest Formula One design! But recently, and particularly today, the McLaren was failing in its task as it purred along, the 3.8 litre turbo charge V8 engine unchallenged and the 7-speed dual clutch transmission happy to be managed automatically. Ross Keane's mind was not on the 12C driving experience but on the meeting that he had been summoned to at Richard's house.

Richard was to be present, Mr Petrov would be present. Ross had been at many meetings where he had made up the trio, but today more people were involved. People that usually Ross never got involved with. People that Richard had always managed throughout all their partnership. People that Ross's creative fertile design mind did not deal with well. Richard Gray and Mr Petrov were there with their considerable and expensive legal teams. Ross got that slight feeling that he was swimming into waters that were deeper than he was comfortable with. Deep waters that he knew, if searched too deeply, could cause a few skeletons to surface.

The V8 engine blipped as the automated systems asked for a lower gear, Ross slowing his charge to make the turn into Richard's gateway. Imposing gates hesitated as a searching camera focused on the McLaren number plate, then searched it's linked databank for a decision on whether or not to allow the large gates to open and allow access to the long winding driveway to Richard's pile. The data banks recognised the familiar number plate and slowly but surely the gates seemed to reluctantly swing open.

The 12C then growled in submission as Ross squeezed the throttle, rolled the McLaren forward and set off up the immaculate driveway surrounded by highly managed and carefully groomed gardens. A manufactured pond that could nearly be classified as a small lake passed on the right. Expensive works of art representing various exotic wildlife, a hippopotamus, crocodiles, and pelicans carefully positioned in and around the water's edge created a false but eye-catching scene. Finally, Ross brought to rest the McLaren on the shale car park outside the steps that led up to the large double doors at the front door of Richard's house. The McLaren was in unfamiliar company as various executive BMW's and Mercedes peppered the exclusive car park. Clearly, the legal beagles had already gathered. Ross reached across to the passenger seat and took hold of the tan-coloured wallet that contained his iPad, then operated his door latch and waited for the gull wing door to smoothly swing upwards. As he clambered out, he took a good look at Petrov's helicopter as it sat cooling on Richard's immaculate lawn. Ross could not help thinking that the innocent helicopter looked almost sinister sitting there. More a reflection of the owner rather than anything the inanimate object had done.

The door was promptly answered by one of Richard's house staff.

"Hi. I bet Richard just loves having that thing leaving indentations on his precious lawn."

The staff member smiled in agreement with Ross's statement and followed with,

"Yes Sir, he has… let's say, made known his displeasure at where Mr Petrov's helicopter chose to land, ignoring the helipad, and he has already issued instructions to have the lawn inspected and any damage rectified immediately."

Ross could not help thinking about that ridiculous statement. Here they were on the verge of losing Gray Grand Prix. On the verge of some nasty buried history being exposed. Their main backer wanting blood and heads in revenge for the crash and injury of his son, and yet Richard still had the capacity to worry about his stupid lawn.

Ross went to walk into the main reception room where the low tones of the gathered beagles could be heard, but before he could swing the door open to enter, the doorman interrupted his path physically and verbally.

Excuse me Mr Keane, Mr Gray has asked if you could visit him in his study first.

Ross partly held out his hands whilst twisting them to expose his palms...

"Okay."

Ross continued down the hallway and swung Richard's study door open only to realise that he was forming the trio again.

"Richard, Mr Petrov."

Mr Petrov made no movement or expression to acknowledge Ross's entrance but Richard got up from his seat.

"Ross, great to see you. Sorry we started a little early. We thought it best that we three have a chat before we get the legal teams agitated. Sit down Ross."

Ross felt uncomfortable, certain in the knowledge that an agreement had been agreed prior to his arrival.

"I'll stand if you don't mind Richard".

Chapter 30

Stirling often struggled with the whole fame thing and was careful not to think too deeply about it. Stirling had loved driving and worked hard to perfect the technique no matter what he was driving. A fire breathing race car, his character-building E type, or driving a truck, for that matter. All had their own individual requirements. The spin off from that simple passion was that he had become a three-time Formula One world champion. The fortune that had come his way he did not have a problem with, as he knew that no matter how much he had earned over the years, there had been others further up the food chain that had been able to jump on Stirling's drive and cash in with far larger sums than had come Stirling's way. So, the money he had no problem with. He accepted that his driving activities had brought interest, debate, enjoyment, and perhaps even a little escapism for many millions of fans around the world. Fans that Stirling had never taken for granted. But what Stirling hated was when people tried to put him on a pedestal above others or tried to give him privileges and allowances that were not fair on others. Privileges and allowances that, if Stirling had been interested in them, he was in a position to pay for.

Stirling had risen early and decided to use the gym instead of going for a run in the unfamiliar surroundings of the hotel. He had warmed up on the rowing machine, slowly waking his body with a steady rhythm that was not over taxing but warmed his muscles nicely. It was not until he stood up, removed his grey sweatshirt, leaving his white tee-shirt underneath, that Stirling noticed that the immaculate well kitted gym still remained empty. A cursory glance over to the gym door entrance revealed a small but gathering number of individuals, dressed for the gym, standing at the entry desk. Some seemed to be emphasising whatever their point was with various gestures. Then suddenly the reason for the empty gym came into focus. Some "management" person had decided to declare the gym out of bounds for everyone whilst a certain Mr Stirling Speed enjoyed his special privilege of having the gym exclusively to himself. Irritation rattled through his bones.

"Do we have a problem here?"

"Ah! Mr Speed! Have you enjoyed your exercise?"

A falsely smiling and clearly under pressure receptionist enquired.

"Just Stirling please, and yes, my 'exercising' is going fine, or more to the point, my warmup is going fine."

A number of eyes peered at Stirling, then back at the now more uncomfortable receptionist.

"So, Mr Spe…Mr Stirl… Erm S..Stirling you have not quite finished yet?"

"Nope. Listen, am I getting the idea that you are keeping these people out of the gym whilst I am in there?"

The receptionist tried to disguise a gulp.

"Well, I have been asked to."

Stirling stopped the answer with a raised hand that then swung down to the door to signal to the small gathering of would-be gym users to pass him by and enter the gym. He accompanied the gesture with a silent but clearly recognised mouth movement to the passing bodies that said, 'sorry.'

The receptionist went to say something, then checked himself.

"There is really, really no problem with anyone using the gym when I am in there. I appreciate you have done an excellent job following your instructions, but if you could get one of the managers to bob up to my room later that would be great. Now I am going to go back in to continue my training. You get yourself a coffee, relax and enjoy the day."

The receptionist smiled a thank you.

Upon re-entering the gym, a number of faces looked up from their exertions and nodded a seal of approval at the way Stirling had handled the situation.

Stirling chose a vacant exercise bike, adjusted it and settled down for a long cardiovascular session that would also give him an opportunity to think over the information and events that had occurred over the last twenty-four hours.

The Sergio accident was unfortunate but racing cars can at times give you a nasty bite, or worse, to keep you on your toes. Sergio was responding well to treatment and Stirling had ensured that he was given up to the minute information of any changes to his condition. Although still unconscious, doctors were making a lot of positive noises. He also took comfort from the fact that he was one of the last to speak to young Sergio before he lapsed into his worrying coma. Mr Petrov was clearly a character not to get on the wrong side of, and at present Stirling found himself in that position. He had had some ugly texts and his solicitor had warmed up his charging calculator as communication of the accusation type had been received from Petrov's legal attack team. Stirling had also been jostled in the hospital car park by someone whom Stirling had presumed must have been part of Mr Petrov's team of 'fixers'.

Sam seemed to be Sam. She wasn't for hiding anything but was clearly uncomfortable with the mistakes she had made. Stirling somehow felt comfortable with her and found himself thinking of another reason why they should meet again. Sam seemed to reciprocate. He'd somehow managed to get her to agree to fly down to the test at Jerez Circuit, Spain, on the pretence that it would be wise for them all to get round a table to talk, all being Stirling, Sam, Ross and Richard.

Stirling agreed with Peter Smith after having read through the police report that something did not sit right about the young girl that had been found dead at her remote property. The cause of death had been poisoning, of that there was no doubt. Young Rosalie had somehow consumed a poisonous concoction, but the idea that she had done it by accident did not sit well with Stirling and he could not shake the shadow being cast over the fact that poison and Russians were in the mix! He had already decided to visit the place where Rosalie Firth had tragically breathed her last breath. The residence was apparently still empty. Rosalie had inherited the quiet cottage location from her grandmother. Being an area of protected nature reserve, it had clearly been difficult for the powers that be to know what to do with it. Stirling planned to start there and see if he could track down any family but preferably her father, who had been obviously vocal at the time of her death, yet somehow was mysteriously absent in the following years.

Where Stirling did diverge from Peter Smith's views was whether there was an issue with the whole spy, payments and resulting prison scandal. As far as he could see, Sam Keane had made an error and paid the price. Ross was on a guilt trip, and Richard Gray, the innocent party of all this, and whose team had suffered the most, to all intents and purposes seemed to have been the perfect gentleman.

Stirling had got into his gym rhythm and his glistening skin and clinging wet tee shirt that highlighted his well-kept body indicated that he was working hard.

Two young ladies and a young man chose to interrupt the rhythm, with an 'excuse me' backed up with a slight tap on Stirling's back by the smiling young man.

Stirling eased his pedalling, sat up, lifted a white towel from the handlebars of the exercise bike and wiped across his perspiring face. A young trio had now gathered in front of the bike, one of whom reached up on her tiptoes and then leaned into the slowing Stirling and put her arm around Stirling's damp back as the inevitable picture was taken. The poor receptionist had done a pitiful job of disguising his run across the gym floor in an effort to ward off the VIP interruption.

Stirling creased his smile on. 'It was you who let them in old boy.' He thought to himself.

Mr Spee…Stirl, erm, Sir, I am sorry, I will..."

"It's fine I have just finished, not a problem."

The second girl now closed in, pen and paper at the ready, the young man again ready with his phone for another picture moment.

Stirling's slight flush of irritation receded as he looked at the excitement deep in the eyes of the beaming face of the girl.

"I've never met a famous person before."

She arched her body and smacked a delayed kiss on Stirling's cheek, the camera clicking away.

Stirling hung his towel round his still muscular and solid neck, the result of many years battling the high 'G' forces of the world's racetracks. He took the pen and paper.

"And to whom do I owe the kiss to?"

"It's Rosalie, I mean Rosie, just put Rosie, put 'to Rosie, love Stirling Speed… please, please, please."

The vibrant excited girl clutched her hands together in a mock begging stance.

Stirling hesitated for a moment as he looked at the beaming young faces in front of him. Beaming young faces that had so much of life in front of them. He autographed the paper and drew his little picture of a ground hog that he always did and followed that with two kisses, much to the delight of the trio. Much to the relief of the gym receptionist the giggling trio gradually withdrew, now absorbed with posting their latest content on Instagram. Stirling found that he had stopped pedalling as he was overcome with a gut feeling of absolute certainty. He was now certain that he was not going to rest until he found the truth behind what had happened to that young, bright smiling light that had been so cruelly extinguished years before!

Chapter 31

"Ross…Ross"

Sian eased over to Ross across the expanse of the room to where he was slumped in a large high backed deep sided chair that faced the window and overlooked yet another of Richard Gray's pristine lawns.

"Réveillez – Vous"

The French request to wake up seemed to register somewhere deep within Ross's subconscious, causing him to stir and force his eyes open.

"Ah Sian! A sight for sore eyes!"

Sian responded by turning her hands outward, smiling, and continuing.

"You English do have some strange expressions. Personally, I get eye drops when I have the sore eyes."

Ross sat up and leant forward, supporting his head in his hands which were supported by his arms, that were supported on his knees. He gave his face a rub and then, after slapping both his hands on his knees, he stood up, wobbled slightly and turned to Sian.

"Well, I'd better get a taxi ordered and find my way home. I don't think a McLaren driven by a slightly tipsy Formula one designer is going to go down too well with the local constabulary."

Sian went to speak but then was cut off by a quizzical Ross who looked around the room and had another little wobble as, in his woken state, he started to recalibrate.

"Where is everyone? Have they all gone? Where is Richard? What are you doing here?"

Sian decided to attack the answers in reverse.

"Richard asked me to come to sort out some arrangements for Stirling's test at Jerez now that the deal has been finalised."

Ross rubbed his face again in an attempt to speed up his recovery.

"Richard asked me to find you and is now on his front lawn inspecting for helicopter damage."

Ross managed to squeeze a smile out with that response.

"Some of the legal beagles are just packing up their tablets, laptops and general electronic devices that have replaced the good old-fashioned file and note pad, which just leaves us two. That could be classified in your first question, 'where is everyone?' Well, we are here!"

"Thank you, Sian, for your comprehensive round up…Now could you by any chance arrange me a taxi?"

"Your taxi is awaiting outside sir, if sir would like to follow, or perhaps it would be better to hold on to me."

"Lead the way, young Sian, I am getting my balance. Slightly squiffy I'll admit to, but legless, I don't think so."

"So, this is my taxi."

Ross stood on the steps of Richard Gray's pile and looked down at the off-white Alfa Romeo junior that looked like a toy when compared to the remnants of the BMWs and Audis that still peppered the large stone shale car park.

Richard could be seen in the middle of his lawn with one of his groundsmen. Upon seeing Ross exit his front door he gave a thumbs up to Sian and held his hand up to his ear, mimicking a phone call, which Ross presumed was directed at him.

Sian skipped down the steps and opened the passenger side door for a now smiling Ross as he steadily descended the almost regal steps.

"Welcome to a proper car, which if all goes to plan will get us to our destination. If not, we can always get a taxi!"

Ross settled on the ox blood aged leather seat, fumbled around finding the seat belt, then prodded around fitting it into the wayward mechanism.

The little eager twin cam engine awaited instruction.

Sian eased first gear into position and looked across to Ross.

"All good? OK let's blast off!"

Ross attempted to warn Sian about how precious Richard was about his driveway and car park but it was too late - Sian had already taken a big slice of throttle and jumped off the clutch whilst holding on to a good degree of right-hand steering lock. Instantly the mischievous Alfa broke traction and threw its short, shapely back end out, daring Sian to catch it. Sian was the match for it piling the opposite lock on whilst catching second gear at the same time and slapping at the throttle again. Carefully manicured stones sprayed up and found new resting places in the expansive car park and some found themselves in unfamiliar places on shiny BMW and Audi bonnets!

"Sian, you are going to be in *so* much trouble."

Richard and his groundsman could only watch with outstretched arms as the Alfa fish tailed and barked its way down Richard Gray's picture perfect driveway.

Chapter 32

"Where did you learn to drive like that, young lady?"

Sian flicked a smile as she negotiated the Buckinghamshire lanes back to Ross's pad in West Byfleet.

"Oh, erm, well, I karted when I was a kid and managed to notch up a couple of championships. You could say it's sort of in the blood."

"I really know little about you Sian, so why is driving in the blood?"

"That really is another story, but a quick round up; The person that fathered me was a waster that wanted to get rid of me on day one and nearly succeeded in the end. I was brought up by two awesome Mums and I have a pretty cool cousin."

"So, the pretty cool cousin is Stirling then, I think I heard?"

"To me, he is my awesome cousin. To him, I am a complicated, slightly outspoken 'half-cousin' I think."

"Two Mums?"

Sian found solace in a dual carriage way after the choking lanes and let the eager Alfa off for a run. The Alfa responded with a bark of delight.

"Yeah, two Mums who were just awesome."

"It's good Sian that you accepted who they were."

Sian decided to show off as she heel-and-toed and whipped the Alfa gearbox into its lower ratios as it approached another roundabout. Timing the gap perfectly Sian slotted into it and accelerated from second up through the specially modified 5 speed box. A present from Stirling, who had insisted that if Sian was going to recycle the car and use it as her everyday car as he did his E type, then it needed to be more user friendly.

Sian suddenly threw Ross a glance.

"Accept who they were? Ah I see where you are going with that one but no, in this case you have travelled up the wrong road there. They weren't together as in together."

"Okay"

Ross blankly acknowledged.

"No, it really is another story, but my fleshly mother was just a close friend of my non-fleshly mother who brought me up because my fleshly mother couldn't bring me up. But when the mother that brought me up died then my fleshly mother was free to be with me as my mother!"

Ross replied with another,

"Okay."

"Like I said it's another story."

Sian began another harsh slug of acceleration from a standing start set of traffic lights. All went well until the thirsty carburettors asked for more of its life blood after a slick change to fourth gear. The bark down the exhaust became blurred and the forward motion slowed dramatically.

Ross looked at Sian who had whipped in the clutch and after a pumping of the accelerator had failed to resurrect an increase in speed. Sian had fallen back to the backup of the starter motor to help with the miracle of resurrection - a task it was up for as the little four-cylinder engine cleared its bout of congestion and fired up again. The traffic that had been left behind initially had now caught up and was determined to show its frustration with an outburst of horns. Sian replied with a wave in the centre mirror, a careful selection of second gear, and another big squeeze of the accelerator to which the Alfa responded to this time.

"You were not joking about 'hopefully' getting to where we are going were you? What was that about?"

Sian patted the dash of the aged Alfa.

"Don't you worry your tired little head, Mr Keane, we'll get you home. Just a bit of newness wearing off. She sometimes starves a little of fuel flow. Probably many years of debris that is floating around in the fuel tank that occasionally gets itself in the wrong place. It's an Alfa, it has character. Embrace it and you'll love it."

Ross answered with yet another but slightly drawn out

"Okayyyy"

"If you do not mind me saying, Ross, I know the last few days have been a little hectic, but you really do seem to have the weight of the world on your shoulders - to coin one of your phrases."

Ross did not respond but looked out of the side window at the flashing hedges.

"You seem to be the nice guy at Gray Grand Prix. I really don't like Mr Angry, I mean Mr Petrov, even though it is very sad what has happened to his son."

Ross responded by flashing a quick look back at Sian, then resumed peering outside.

The silence inside the car was proving louder than the reverberating engine so Sian decided to bring a sharper knife out of the drawer in an attempt to cut through it.

"What was all the spy gate about?"

Ross gave a longer look this time at the busy Sian as she now hustled the little Alfa through a melee of traffic.

Just as Sian thought, her knife had not been sharp enough. Ross responded.

"It was a horrible time for Gray Grand Prix Sian, just horrible."

Ross shook his head as he seemed to replay the events in his head. Making sure the silence did not get a hold again, Sian continued cutting.

"So, your sister Sam decided to help you guys out with a little industrial espionage. I am only just starting to realise, Ross, just how much money is at stake in Formula One. I suppose the temptation is always there. Sam seems to have bounced back from it all."

Ross remained quiet, then suddenly seemed to make a decision and instead of just turning his head towards Sian he actually shifted his whole body round slightly to face her, his left shoulder now leaning slightly on the window in the tight little car.

"Sian, Formula One is a selfish, corrosive animal that devours people's money, time and lives. Try looking under the glamour Sian, under the surface money and what you will see is not nice. You are a nice kid Sian, get as far away from it as possible before it devours you."

"But Ross you have had so much success...You have made a fortune out of it. The press are saying you are in the top three F1 designers of all time. Why do you hate it so?"

"Formula One offers you the world but at what cost Sian, at what cost? I have been paid millions over the years to find a few tenths of a second around a racetrack. Yet what do I have now?

A wife and children that won't talk to me, a sister that ended up in prison because of me, and you know what's even worse, I have no self-respect. I am manoeuvred, manipulated, bought to go in the direction everyone wants. I didn't want all this hanging over me Sian. I paid the price, but it was too high.

Sian went to reply but was cut off by Ross.

"Formula One magnifies everything, money, pain, atmosphere, your talents but also your weaknesses. Formula One took one of my weaknesses and magnified it to the point that it ruled my life!"

Sian realised the tired and still a little drunk Ross was on a downward roll and felt slightly guilty taking advantage of his vulnerable state.

"But Ross, Sam was a big girl who made her own choices."

"It should have been me that went to prison, not my little sister. What sort of big brother allows his little sister to go to prison for him?"

"She paid the price for trying to sell the Stragatti secrets."

"She didn't have secrets to sell Sian. Do you not understand? She was the innocent bystander, yet again looking out for her older brother. I hate myself. I am just the fodder that the Formula One beast produces. Everyone just laughs at me."

Sian couldn't press her victim anymore. He was at his limit and needed time to regroup and so she decided to try and pick the solemn atmosphere up.

"I don't laugh at you Ross. Well, I do a little bit, you know when you are thinking, sometimes you stick your pen in your ear and waggle it around for ages - honestly I don't think you know you are doing it, but I often think of the person that picks up that pen after you, chews it, and gets the distinct tangy taste of Ross Keane ear wax!"

Sian put on her best screwed up face and turned it to Ross who just looked at it blankly.

"Sian you are beautiful."

"Oh no, that was my best screwed up face and you say that I am beautiful, I definitely need to work on that."

"Be careful Sian."

"I know, I drive like a mad woman, but trust me you're better off in a car with a mad woman than a mad man!"

"Rosalie was beautiful. She brought light into every day, just like you Sian. But Formula One devoured her and spat her out Sian. She was just so..."

Sian was shocked to hear Ross bring up Rosalie and looked across when the sentence didn't continue and was confronted by a crumpled man crying into his hands. A timely lay-by proved a saviour for the moment and the Alfa eased to a stop.

Sian undid her seat belt and leaned across whilst pulling her crumpled, heaving passenger towards her. No words could save the moment, only being there for him could help the pain.

Eventually the heaving quelled, the sobs began to soak up and the crumpled figure gradually gained some sort of stature again. Sian said nothing, squeezed in first gear and the shocked Alfa, ready for a launch, actually eased off from rest. Ross resumed his gaze out of the window whilst Sian attempted small talk.

"You'll have that pen waddling in your ear and there will be doodles all over your paperwork by the time we get down to that test, and Stirling has endowed you with his superior three world championship thoughts on how your race car should drive. Trust me, he can be a little superior at times. It's a good thing that he has me around at times to knock him off his perch and exercise his under-worked credit card!"

Sian didn't expect, and didn't receive, a response for the rest of the journey but she hoped her wittering was chipping away at Ross's dark cloud.

Finally, the little Alfa pulled up outside the private gates of Ross's residence, proud that it had completed yet another journey with only a couple of little hiccups.

Ross turned to Sian whilst searching with his left hand for the door handle.

"Sian thank you; I am sorry that...,"

Sian reached out and took hold of Ross's right hand and squeezed it hard.

"Ross, we can get through this together. I am around now, admittedly maybe not your first choice for a team member, but hey, I am loyal - if ever so slightly mad - but Ross, we have Stirling around now too and trust me, that guy gets results and is an amazing guy to have on your team. Things will get better

Ross. Maybe he'll be the one that can lance the boil that has been festering."

Sian wished she'd not said that last bit but in general she was pleased with the rest of her little sentence.

Ross delayed his exit and reached across with his left hand and stroked the skin on the back of Sian's hand that was still gripping his right hand.

Sian bit her lip internally and hoped that this was not going the way she thought it could be and so was relieved when Ross said nothing and pulled at the door handle to open the door. He swung both legs out and used both of his hands to push himself out into the drizzly evening and stood up. Then he turned and bent back down into the tiny, by modern standards, Alfa.

Sian turned with a big smile and looked up at the dishevelled Ross.

"Sian, would you like to come in?"

Sadly, Sian knew exactly what Ross was asking and hesitated with her reply to ensure there was no misunderstanding.

"Ross you are a lovely, lovely man, trust me the last thing you want in your life is a crazy girl like me. I drive myself mad."

"I need company Sian."

"Ross go to bed, have a good sleep, recharge those thinking cells of yours so you can get to work creating the fastest race car in the world, again!"

Ross smiled at Sian.

"You are lovely Sian, don't ever lose that. I am sorry."

"No Ross, no don't say sorry, please don't say…,"

But Ross had already backed out of the door and pressed it shut.

Sian hesitated before pulling off. Ross clicked at his remote and his gates responded by swinging open. He turned to face the headlights of Sian's Alfa, the drizzle now having turned to rain, causing his skin to glisten. He reached inside his pocket, took out a pen, stuck it in his ear and made an exaggerated waggle. He then took it out and offered it to Sian who made another effort at a screwed-up face even though she knew that Ross would not be able to see it through the shiny wiper-polished windscreen and so backed it up with a flash of her high beam headlights. Ross smiled, and much to Sian's relief replied with a cheery wave.

Reverse gear went in with a little graunch, but first gear was ready and waiting. Sian asked for the higher revs and jumped off the clutch, the Alfa leaping forward and sideways with glee!

Chapter 33

"Mr Speed, Mr Gray has asked me to tell you that he will be with you shortly. He has one more business call to complete then will be up to see you. Is there anything else I can do for you?"

Stirling looked up from the notes that Gray's senior race engineer and simulator engineer had compiled for Stirling's crash course on how to drive a modern F1 car. He couldn't help but smile that a lovely, pleasant air hostess had been used to convey the message as, no matter how big an executive private jet was, the message could have been conveyed by Richard Gray simply calling out from his present seated position not ten feet away. Richard had already kept him and his pilot waiting before they took off. The captain apparently having to renegotiate departure times with air traffic control as the time ticked. Stirling supposed that as it was Richard's jet it was his prerogative to keep it waiting if he wanted.

"Thank you, that's no problem and really I am fine, and you can really drop the Mr Speed. Plain old Stirling will get the job done."

Private jets had been one aspect of Stirling's life that he unashamedly always utilised when possible. Some F1 drivers, even though still passionate about driving, still receiving the phone calls where millions of pounds were mentioned in the conversation, still made the decision to retire, citing the constant travel as the caustic cause. One driver who strove for many years to be the best, and finally crowned his efforts with a world Formula One title promptly retired before having a chance to defend or even cash in on his membership of this elite club. One of the reasons behind this unpopular decision was the constant travel. Even when Stirling was racing fulltime he always ensured that he made the journey, the travel, something to enjoy. In Europe he would often be seen driving his E type to the Grand Prix circus where he was the star attraction, stopping off at his designated stop over places. When diary and distance demanded then he always accepted the eye watering cost of using private jets. Not only was the journey enjoyable, his time spent going nowhere at an airport was kept to a minimum, passport and customs only becoming a minor irritation.

"Stirling, sorry I have not had a chance to sit and chat. Joys of running an F1 team for prima donna drivers!"

"Mr Gray, can I get you anything?"

Richard looked at Stirling and awaited his order.

Stirling lifted his glass of fresh orange with one hand and put up his other hand.

"Nope, I am fine."

Richard persisted.

"Something to eat, a snack?"

"No really, I am fine, I need to actually fit into one of your race cars remember."

Richard smiled a response then turned to his employee.

"Can you rustle up one of my favourite sandwiches and one of my favourite drinks."

The air hostess was comfortable with the sandwich responsibility but stalled with the range of favourite drinks.

"I am sorry Mr Gray but drink wise?"

"Something that has a lot of vodka type alcohol in it."

The air hostess smiled.

"I know exactly what you want."

Richard looked back at Stirling who responded by putting down his expansive notes.

"Well, 'The' Stirling Speed driving for Gray Grand Prix. The press are going love that."

"'The' Stirling Speed 'testing' for Gray Grand Prix is a better description. This is no comeback."

"I know that, but seriously, it really is an honour to have you in one of our race cars. I have always been a fan and as you very well know I tried on a few occasions to get you in one of our race seats in the past, but my wallet sadly had boundaries. I still think you had a few more championships in you."

"Trust me, it was not all about the money. If it was then I wouldn't have stopped when I did. I still had a few cash cows out there that were happy to be squeezed. No, it was the right time to stop. Jackie Stewart once said, 'it's knowing when to get into something and more importantly knowing when to get out of it'. Best stop when you are still at the top!"

"Stragatti were making a big play for you when you stopped, I believe?"

"Like I say, it was a good time to stop."

Richard smiled.

"Just like when you drove, you never gave a lot away."

Stirling smiled back.

"There are a lot of predators in F1 that are looking for an easy kill. I was never going to roll over and make it easy."

"Yet here you are, driving for Gray Grand Prix with the first offer I put on the table. Out of character, I think."

"*Testing* for Gray Grand Prix. A big difference. Count yourself lucky that you got me on a good day and that you have a decent driver for a change."

Richard knew the door had been slammed shut and locked. Stirling was not going to give anything away.

Stirling was next to speak up.

"So, the Gray Grand Prix executive jet for the exclusive use of Mr Gray and a certain Stirling Speed."

Richard took the drink off his hostess.

"Yeah, maybe not the best use of company expenses but you did say you wanted a window seat. Actually, Ross has flown ahead of us on a chartered flight. He wanted to get up to speed with the test team. Sian was flying out with him as well, along with some of the support staff, and I even think the delectable Sam Keane is on the flight, thanks to your insistence that we all have a jolly get together."

Richard's phone buzzed to which he responded by cancelling the call and turning it off. He then gestured for the hostess to approach. Can you inform the pilot that I do not want any calls please? I need just a little down time.

"You are uncomfortable with Sam coming out?"

"I suppose I am slightly uncomfortable with paying for the girl that cost me a fortune, got me kicked out of a championship, nearly lost me my main sponsor and, oh, nearly got me locked up!"

"No hard feelings then Richard?"

"It's all water under the bridge. For Ross's sake I dealt with it and moved on. I had nothing to do with it all. Ross had got himself in a mess and Sam thought she saw a gap in the marketplace. I may have pulled off a few dodgy financial deals over the years Stirling, but I have never cheated. I get my kicks out of kicking everyone's backside fairly!"

Stirling delayed his response so that it did not seem as though he had jumped on the subject and glanced out of the tiny window of the multi-million pound money pit as it sliced its way through the warming air.

"Ross got himself in a mess? Meaning he ran out of printer ink? I can't see Ross as a man that gets himself in a mess. He certainly knows how to design a race car."

Richard responded without delay.

"Oh, he can pencil a good car OK but he..."

Richard then hesitated before continuing.

"He has a problem with...."

Richard hesitated again.

"This is not for public consumption Stirling. We have worked hard to keep it under wraps, but Ross has had, or you could say, still has, a problem with gambling."

Stirling opened his eyes wider,

"Really? He does not come across as a risk taker at all. I thought he got his thrills from drag coefficients."

Richard shook his head.

"It is something I have had to help manage and something he has to manage every day."

"Really?"

"I first met Ross at university and trust me, he would bet on anything, he would bet on whether the next person who walked into the room would be a guy or a girl. As his race car designs won more races and I had to find more big numbers to keep him on the pay roll it just fed his addiction into a monster. Sadly Stirling, he is a flawed genius. He is one of the best designers, but he could have been *the* best. In fact, he could still be the best if he could firmly put the habit to bed."

"He's separated from his wife isn't he, Richard?"

"Yes, a lovely lady and lovely kids but when you have heavies breaking into your grounds during the night and threatening your family because of outstanding gambling debts then you know you have a problem. Ross's wife tried everything but, in the end, she had to do what any mother would do and put her children first."

"No way, I never would have got that. He's always been a good guy and talented designer to me."

"He really got in with some bad guys, big international gambling syndicates. When he is working on a new race car or development he is fine, but as soon as he has down time he buckles. I once helped fund a prototype road car called the R1 just to keep him busy between race projects. He still has the car at his home. To me it could have been a long-term project for him to see it all the way through to production and sales, but as soon as it was running, well, he left it alone and fell back to his little kink – or, should I say, big kink."

The jet banked over to the right and the clipped precise voice of the captain permeated the cabin.

"Mr Gray, we have permission from air traffic control to start descending. We appear to have a slot so should be able to go straight into our final approach. We should be down on terra firma in about 30 minutes."

Stirling reached for his lap belts that had slipped to the side of him, clicked the buckle together and adjusted the tension. When he looked up from the exercise, he realised that Richard was looking right at him. Clearly, he had something of importance to say.

Chapter 34

Sian looked around at the elite group of team members that had been chosen to go out on the chartered flight. She had carefully made sure that every one that should be there was, and that all had the passports and laptops etc that were required to do their job. She realised that whilst she worked with some of the best brains in the country, not all of them were endowed with practical life skills. Hence the reason, Sian now realised, why the travel department of the team were quite officious. They had to make sure all details were covered. Testing a Formula One race car was an expensive exercise and critical for the team's performance. It would be a disaster if a key team member missed the test because their passport was out of date or they had left in their office key data required for the test.

Now Sian had completed her job as final checker she sat back and took in her surroundings.

"Well guys and girls, I could get used to this. Only executive suites from now on for young Miss Sian."

Some looked up from the assortment of electronic gadgets that were in their hands and on their knees and nodded in agreement. It was a treat for them to be on a chartered flight as normally they would be on a scheduled flight but things back at the factory had fallen slightly behind schedule. With the Sergio shunt, Richard and, more importantly Ross, had not seemed to be around as much and inevitably things had just somehow slipped.

Sian was just perusing the complimentary cakes and deciding which to obliterate when a young man broke the moment.

"Excuse me miss, could you please step this way."

A smattering of the team looked up again and flung the obligatory comments out.

"Hope your passport is in date Sian!"

"Watch for them putting the rubber gloves on Sian."

The last comment inevitably caused a ripple of laughter.

Sian turned to them all, put on a worried face, then held her wrists together readying them for being bound.

Sian was met by a familiar face in a side room off the corridor.

"Peter Smith! Do you know I am in an executive lounge with complimentary *everything* and you choose this moment to want to meet?"

"Sian, I am just helping you away from some unhealthy eating. I thought a quick catch up would be good. How did your drive home with Ross go?"

"You mean the Ross that has not turned up yet? Apparently, it is quite normal for him to rush into the airport with minutes to go, so I am trying not to stress about it too much. Apparently on more than one occasion they have had to send the company jet back for him."

Although Peter Smith was a busy man and usually insisted on concise answers, he, like everyone around her, had melted into Sian's rambling but somehow effective ways.

"The drive home report, did anything come out?"

"Yes, it did actually, and it was all quite sad really."

"Remember Sian, we are dealing with criminals. And sometimes we need to get close to them to hook them, but always be careful that they do not end up hooking you."

"Peter Smith you are a hard man, but..."

"Not hard, Sian, just experienced, in this unsavoury world we operate in."

"Well by the end of the journey he certainly wanted to get closer to me, but I put that one to bed straight away."

Peter Smith raised his eyebrows.

"Oops maybe that was not the best expression to use. I made sure he understood where I was on the matter, but he does seem a nice man and I didn't want him to feel stupid."

Peter Smith looked at his watch.

"Your complimentary feeding time is reducing fast and you do still have a plane to catch."

Sian raised a finger in an effort to reinforce her next words.

"Good point! Ross admitted that Sam, his sister, should not have gone to prison - he should have."

Peter Smith wanted to keep everything very clear.

"And he actually said that?"

"Oh yes, in fact he was quite upset about it. He said that he should have gone to prison for the spy gate and that no way should he have stood back and let his little sister take the rap. He is definitely pretty cut up by it all and clearly is feeling pressure with the Sergio shunt. He really does not like our ugly Russian man Mr Pretos."

"Mr Petrov,"

Peter Smith corrected.

"Mr Petrov, that's what I said. I do think he felt a lot better for getting it off his chest and I am sure I have got a good rapport with him now, which will help us going forward. I am convinced that he is the man behind the spy-gate. I think he is just a workaholic, obsessed with creating that fastest race car, no matter what the consequences. I think it even cost him his marriage. Yes, I think I can definitely build on the relationship now. It was a good idea of yours to be his taxi. I think he trusts me now. I think his little proposal at the journey's end was just a lonely man, slightly squiffy, stressed and tired, doing what men can sometimes do and make a fool of themselves. I'll make sure he does not feel uncomfortable with it."

Peter Smith waited to see if anything else was going to come out of Sian's babble. When nothing seemed forthcoming he prodded a little more.

"Did he mention Rosalie at all?"

"Yes, he did. He got quite emotional about her as well. He said that I had to be careful with the world of Formula One. He said Rosalie was a lovely girl who brightened up everyone's day. Just like me! Not sure where he got that from. But he said Formula One had eaten her up and spat her out."

Peter sat back in his chair, clearly in thought. Without sitting forward, he continued.

"Nothing else?"

"Nope"

"You have done really well Sian. Now we need to handle this carefully. We need to keep the spy-gate deal on the boil but let's not go deeper on that at the moment. We do not want to spook Ross whilst he's starting to speak up. See if you can draw him on Rosalie."

Peter Smith eyed Sian, who was now sitting back in her chair and twisting a small catchment of shiny black hair with her fingers, who then replied with an

"Okay"

"Sian, trust me, polar bears have a demeanour that invites you to cuddle them, yet they are one of the most ferocious animals on the planet. Your job is not an easy one and sometimes you need to be almost surgical with your actions. I need you to keep focused and safe. Do understand me? If you cannot detach yourself, then sadly this is not the job for you. You need to use Ross whilst he is vulnerable before he has a chance to regroup and close down the hatches."

"I know, I know, but because he has made the odd mistake it does not make him a bad guy, but I know what you are saying. You can trust me, I think."

A knock came on the door and the same young gentleman that had interrupted Sian's earlier cake fest entered.

"Your flight has just been called."

Sian swung round to Peter Smith with a very convincing mock anger face.

"You, Mr Peter Smith, owe me another complimentary executive lounge!"

Peter Smith smiled back with outstretched arms. Inwardly, a little bit of him hoped that whilst trying to train Sian into a hardened field operative, she would not ever lose that quality of not taking anything too seriously.

With a diva flick of her hair and exaggerated arched back, Sian exited the room.

Chapter 35

As can sometimes be the case with private jets, air traffic control had left the Gray Grand Prix private jet high in the stack as they cleared commercial air lines for final approach. The captain had then been chasing clearances by the air traffic team to descend as instructed ready for final approach to the small but efficient Jerez airport in Southern Spain. As the plane lost layers of height clearances Stirling had listened as well as he could to what Richard had to say as his ears and the cabin pressure worked hard to reach an equilibrium.

"Stirling, I have had a meeting with Mr Petrov. He made it quite clear to me that he is gunning for you with both barrels. He feels, as I am sure you have been aware, that you are the cause behind Sergio's shunt. He is a proud man, and he will not rest until he has avenged his son and heir!"

"I know Richard. I have had Mr and Mrs Muscle standing in front of my car door on a couple of occasions. I am not sure what all that is about. I have had some pretty graphic threats and my legal teams are already upgrading their holiday destinations based on the legal threats he has filed. I can handle him."

"Do watch your back Stirling. He has some pretty big sticks to beat people with if they cross him."

"Why, Richard, would you get into bed with someone like that?"

"Basically because of the team. The team has to survive. It was actually Ross who first introduced him to me."

"Thanks, Richard, for the heads up. I like a challenge."

"That's not all I wanted to say though Stirling."

Richard continued.

"He is withdrawing his beating sticks from Gray Grand Prix as long I as do not stand in the way of him coming after you."

Stirling replied with another

"Thanks, Richard"

Which this time had a different meaning to the first 'thanks.'

"Stirling, I have to protect the team. I cannot lose Petrov's backing, not yet at least. But I like to think of myself as an honourable man. I needed you to know that I agreed the deal with

Petrov. You have to know, Stirling. that my allegiance is with Mr Petrov. Ross was no party to the initial meeting, but he has had to agree - although he is not happy about it."

Richard shook his head.

"At last, we get the driver we have always wanted, then we allow our sponsor to screw him over!"

Stirling had then gone on to make all the right noises.

"Okay Richard I appreciate your honesty, I appreciate your position, your predicament."

In actual fact Stirling wanted to say,

'I couldn't give a stuff about your team; I am only driving your car because I have to and shouldn't we all be spending a bit more of our energies worrying about a certain young Sergio battling literally for his life!'

The conversation had naturally come to an end as the captain had announced,

'Prepare for landing please.'

After a visit on board from a pleasant passport control officer Stirling and Richard now found themselves walking up a very plain white VIP corridor to an area that opened up where taxi drivers, friends, family, and work colleagues could be reunited with their travellers.

Stirling knew that Sian would be waiting, with, no doubt, some stupid but funny comment.

Richard was first to recognise a face at the end of the tunnel.

"Oh no, not good! Something's not gone well at the test for Phil our team manager to meet me. He usually sends one of his minions. Well, into the breach we go, my dear man."

Stirling failed to physically acknowledge Richard's comment. He had seen Sian, roaring with laughter.

'Oh no, what has she been up to now?'

As they got near the end of the corridor, Phil stepped forward and took Richard off to one side, his arm around Richard's shoulder.

Stirling was smiling as he turned round to see Sian who had now broken ranks and was running, arms open, towards him.

To his horror he realised that Sian was *not* laughing at all - she was crying uncontrollably. Stirling dropped his bag as Sian slammed into him. He squeezed her hard as she sobbed and looked round at the shocked faces of the Gray Grand Prix staff that had been sent in force to the airport meet and greet. Cameras started angrily flashing, followed by a barrage of indistinguishable questions.

Stirling focused on the first airport official he could see.

"A private room *now* and I want all this press cleared."

Stirling guided the struggling for breath Sian into the makeshift haven of a room.

He sat Sian down, knelt in front of her, carefully cleared the matted hair from her face and helped her ease her emotional eruption.

"Sian, Sian, nice and slow, I am here now, I've got this, now what's gone on?

Sian's creased, wet, traumatised face looked at Stirling. She stuttered in an attempt to make the words that thrashed around her head form some sort of coherent pattern.

"R, Ross, Ross is dead, he is dead, do you hear what I am saying? He is dead and I killed him!"

Chapter 36

Stirling wasn't sure if he should be knocking on the door. The lack of response to the knock was looking like it didn't matter anyway. Peter Smith had been on the ball and had responded quickly to the death of Ross Keane. He had known that Sian would need support and had arrived at Jerez only a couple of hours after Stirling had touched down. Stirling was relieved that Sian was in good hands and it was now down to him to sort out what on earth was going on. Nothing about this case felt right.

Stirling knocked again. Finally, a reply came.
"Can you leave it outside please."
Rather awkwardly Stirling called out through the door.
"It's me, Stirling."
After another smaller delay this time, the door swung open, but not by the person Stirling was expecting to see.
"Richard, I thought you had already returned to the UK?"
"Stirling come in."
Stirling stepped into the hotel room and looked across to the window that overlooked a lush green golf course where Sam Keane sat looking out. She swung her head round when Stirling stepped in, her eyes full of pain and tears, her hair dishevelled.
"Sam, I am so, so sorry. I didn't want to intrude, but just wanted you to know that I can be here for you, for anything."
Sam forced a smile from her red face.
"Life can be a real bummer can't it?"
At which she turned to look back at the empty golf course.
Richard gestured for Stirling to come further into the room and find a seat.
"I am pleased you have called round Stirling; I know you have a lot on your plate with the test. Sam could do with a shoulder to lean on at the moment. Ross's passing has hit us all extremely hard."
Richard hesitated.
"I cannot believe those words are coming out of my mouth."
Richard then took a moment to look out of the window and borrow some of Sam's view.

Now that Stirling was older, retired, maybe even wiser, he wanted to say 'I can't believe that you are going ahead with the test' but he knew that in Formula One the show always goes on. In years gone by, drivers would continue racing past the broken bodies of their fellow competitors, with heavy hearts, but somehow with the false belief that such a thing would not happen to them. As funeral arrangements were being made, other drivers would already be lining up for the vacant seat. Grieving teams would start their selection process knowing that their survival relied on filling the fatal seat to keep the coffers rolling.

Sadly, Stirling knew that even though F1 had now achieved an outstanding safety record, that political correctness resounded through the sport, thanks to the billion-pound sponsor's sensitivities, Stirling new that the same animalistic instinct still ran through the sport. The show would feel the pain at Ross's loss, but the show would definitely go on. Designers within Gray Grand Prix and, in fact, designers throughout the sport would be harbouring dark thoughts of moving into Ross's technical designer shoes. Richard would know that he needed that vacuum filling quickly before his backers, his sponsors, his life support, started switching off.

"Stirling, I really appreciated you going down to the garages like you did to give the lads a pep talk. I know the test is going to be tough, but we have to show that it is business as normal. Phil our team manager is fully briefed and knows exactly what Ro... what we wanted to achieve in the test. I am just pleased that we have you on board."

"I've got this Richard."

"I am going to the airport now to fly back to make... well to make arrangements."

Stirling could see out of the corner of his eye Sam reach for another tissue from the nearly empty box at her side of her.

"Oh, and Stirling, sorry, I forget the relationship between you two, but I have told Sian to take as much time off as she needs. She is a good girl Stirling. I think a family member has flown out to be with her."

"She'll bounce back, she is a strong girl. I'll keep an eye on her."

Richard cautiously continued.

"You know that Sian was the last to see Ross and she is saying that she killed him! I am not sure what she means by that, but she perhaps needs to be keeping that from the press, Stirling."

Stirling felt a slight sting of irritation that Richard was more bothered about his team's PR than Sian.

Stirling tried to hide his irritation in his muted reply.

"Like I said, I'll keep an eye on her."

Richard turned to say something to Sam but as he was only faced with her back, he decided better of it. He bid Stirling goodbye with a nod of his head and left the room.

The silence in the room was deafening so Stirling decided to break the control that the silence had.

"Sam, can I get you a drink?"

Sam eased round on her chair; a smile forced on her face.

"Hope you realised I made an effort with my appearance when I knew you were coming."

She flicked her embattled hair with the backs of her fingers.

Stirling, still feeling slightly awkward, replied,

"Ah I have got you there Sam because you did *not* know that I had decided to come round. So there go, you have your excuse!"

Sam tilted her head to one side and stretched her arms out and down, gripping her hands tightly together in way that helped stretch the tension out of her twisted body.

"I knew you would come, and I am glad you did. You are just the sort of guy to help a damsel in distress."

"Do you want a drink, or talk, or walk?"

"I don't think I am ready to meet the world."

Sam looked across at the mirror opposite the bed.

"And I really don't think the world is ready for me. Sorry Stirling, your eyes must be hurting."

"On the contrary, madam, your appearance is just about acceptable to the eyes."

Stirling joked back.

"Perhaps a talk to start off with. Then maybe a walk and just maybe a drink, although I have not slept at all, so at any point I might just pass out."

Tears flooded up in Sam's eyes again as she suddenly remembered the reason behind Stirling's impromptu visit.

Stirling knew what he had to do, and somehow it felt quite natural. He stood up, walked over to Sam, took hold of her hands and assisted her to her feet. He then wrapped his arms around her. Sam responded by falling into him and sobbed.

Eventually the sobbing reduced to sniffing.

"Come on Sam, get a grip, you've been to prison girl. You can handle anything!"

"Stirling make yourself busy with the complimentary coffee - I'll head to the bathroom and see if I can re-invent myself and stop myself from feeling so bad when you have gone and I take another look in the mirror."

Sam returned, her face looking fresher and her hair combed and pulled back into a ponytail, accentuating her distinctive but soft cheek bones. She walked over to her unopened suitcase and clicked it open.

"Turn away Stirling, if you don't think you can resist my womanly charms."

Sam crossed her arms and went to pull off her well used top. Stirling concentrated on adding milk to the coffees.

Chapter 37

Sam took a sip of her coffee that she held in both hands, then looked up and smiled at Stirling sitting across the little table.

"There is no guarantee on the table Stirling that I am not going to break down into a snivelling wreck again at any moment. I am just warning you."

Stirling picked up his coffee but delayed taking a sip of it.

"It's funny how people view crying as a weakness, especially in men. It's good to cry. It can show extreme joy, extreme sadness, extreme care, but at the very least it's a safety valve that releases your emotions and also, in my experience, women seem better at getting their emotions out, dealing with them and then just getting on with the job at hand."

"It's just so hard. Even though I was little sis, with Mum not being around Dad always relied on me to watch out for Ross, but I haven't been watching out for him, have I? Especially this time!"

Stirling was finding it hard to gauge whether he should talk about Ross or not, and so steered away from him to see if Sam chose to come back to him.

"It was good to see Richard here, making an effort, I presume you two have not always seen eye to eye? Could you not have flown back with him?"

"Flown back to what? The press are going drag everything up again and I am going to get eaten alive. The 'bad girl' sister that...anyway, Richard Gray is the last person I want to be talking about. Trust me, Richard wasn't here to give a consoling hand, oh no, he was here to tell me what to say to the press - and to you, for that matter."

"What do mean, what you are going to say to me?"

Stirling enquired.

"Like I say, if you do not mind, I would rather not be talking about RG or..."

Sam flashed what looked like a genuine grin...

"Or should I call him by what his staff call him behind his back?"

"Go on tell me, as I am sure you are going to anyway."

"They call him King Dick!"

"Really?"

"Yep, King Dick. You ask around when you're testing tomorrow."

"Nice."

Stirling replied.

Quiet tried to enter the room again but was beaten back thanks to Sam's desire to talk.

"Oh, Ross, why would you go and do that, why wouldn't you call me, speak to me, shout at me, anything?"

Stirling decided to jump in with both feet.

"Are they sure he took his own life, it couldn't have been an accident?"

Sam looked up with a slightly surprised look on her face.

"You don't know the details?"

Stirling shook his head.

"Well, no, Richard made sure there was a complete clamp down on information. Until he 'got on top of the situation' I think were his exact words to me, but Sam, I don't need to know the details, really."

Sam took a swig of her coffee.

"No, you do need to know. Sadly, your Sian was the last to see him. After she dropped him off, he went into his garage where he kept his prototype road car that Richard tried to get him to put into production. He rigged a pipe from the exhaust and apparently put on some Phil Collins music and just…. went to sleep."

Sam struggled to get the last words out but was now getting back into control mode and then tried to make light of it all.

"Phil Collins, I ask you?"

Sam dabbed at her eyes again, fighting the pain inside.

"What do you think tipped him over Sam?"

"You know, he had an issue that ate him alive?"

Stirling did not know whether Sam was aware that he had knowledge of Ross's gambling addiction, so played safe.

"Issue?"

"His gambling, Richard told me that he told you."

Stirling could not help thinking that for two people that did not like each other, Sam and Richard had certainly communicated well.

"Addictions are cruel and sometimes it's difficult for others to really appreciate an addict's pain."

"I tried everything with him, but sadly the more successful he became, the bigger the addiction grew, and the nastier the people were that he gambled with. It would not surprise me if some gambling debt surfaces, now he has gone. If it wasn't for Richard and I suppose his own talent for designing fast cars he would have lost his career to it, just like he lost his family to it. OH, ROSS YOU STUPID FOOL! What a waste of a good human being! Why did his addiction have to be so destructive? Why could he not have had an addiction for collecting action figures or building battleships out of matchsticks? Why the gambling?"

Stirling knew not to answer. This was a time for a good listener.

"Oh Stirling, what a mess."

The quietness started to creep into the room again but retreated as Sam stood up.

"Look at the state of me, here I am with exclusive use of a rather dashing three times world champion and all I can get him to do is pass me more tissues. I am sorry, trust me I'll be back to big bad Sam tomorrow."

"Don't be sorry. We all need someone to lean on at times."

The quietness began its assault again.

Stirling really wished that he could take the pain away from Sam, a thought, which he had to admit to himself, he found quite surprising. Stirling had always been very good at building sturdy unbreachable walls, especially with women. Once bitten twice shy!

Sam sat down on the small couch that was positioned to make the best of the view over the rolling golf course that was now shrouded in darkness except for a smattering of white lights that no doubt lit various pathways.

Stirling sat down next to Sam and felt her cuddle deeply into him. The distant sky suddenly erupted with joyous fireworks that somehow made a mockery of the sadness that engulfed the night.

"Please stay with me tonight Stirling."

Sam whispered.

Stirling went to reply, but Sam's breathing had morphed into a deeper, calmer rhythm. At last, Sam had let go of her horrendous day with the knowledge that Stirling would be there for her.

Stirling eased Sam's head onto a soft forgiving cushion, pulled a throw off the bed and gently laid it over the sleeping, tough little sister that had just lost her big brother. The quietness crept back into the room and was now welcomed.

Chapter 38

"Sam?"

Sam looked down from the top of the banking that overlooked turn one at the sun-drenched Jerez race circuit.

"Hi, it's Sian isn't it?"

Sian gestured for Sam to join her.

Even though they had never met before they hugged each other in a way that said a thousand words.

Sam spoke first.

"You OK?"

"Yeah, I think so. I blew apart yesterday, then I picked up the pieces and stuck them back together again so, don't look too closely, or you'll see the cracks! How about you?"

Sam went to reply but was then upstaged by a Formula One car howling out of the pit lane that exited just in front of them.

"I'm okay. I have to be, I have a GT car team that needs running and also, I need to get polishing my armour ready for the press onslaught when I get back to the lovable UK. I've already had to duck the reporters coming out of the Hotel. How's Stirling been doing?"

Sian looked back from the circuit as another car this time crept out of the pits, short shifting up the gear box then back down in preparation for the tight right hand turn two.

"You've not been in to see the team then? I thought you would have been all over the data."

Sam smiled at the innocent Sian.

"Oh, I think the last face the team want to see is one belonging to Sam Keane. Double trouble me, Sian."

"Rubbish Sam, you get in there and face them down. You've paid your dues and from what I have heard from Stirling you ain't no push over."

Sam looked back from the circuit and looked at Sian,

"So, Stirling has talked to you about me?"

Sian knew exactly what Sam was asking.

"Of course he has, you're in there, girl!"

Sian followed up with an exaggerated wink.

"Mess him around though missy, and you'll have me to contend with."

Sam was distracted by the buzz of her phone, another email. Sam glanced at it then reported the message to Sian.

"That's my team manager back in the UK. Apparently, the UK trash press are practically camped outside the workshop desperately trying to find out where I am. Sod them. How has Stirling been doing? I am surprised he accepted the drive. I thought he was done with driving around in circles."

"He has nailed it. They had a few issues first thing during the system checks so he languished at the bottom of the time sheets. You can just imagine some of the 'know it alls' saying, 'I told you he shouldn't have come back'. The press are all over him every time he gets in or out of the car. But then he showed them alright. He has been doing long, full tank runs, and he has not been out of the top five. As it's heading towards lunchtime all the teams are changing tyres and bolting on super softs to go for quick laps to see where they are up to with ultimate one lap pace. Stirling is due out shortly."

Another car chased up the pit lane but then slowed as another car hammered up the straight and braked into turn one.

Sian turned back to Sam who had to lean in to hear as the pit lane started to wake up to more cars ready for their quick super soft runs.

"I am going back to see Stirling after this run. You will come with me. You'll put a smile on his face. I just make him grimace!"

Sam pointed back at the circuit as Stirling squeezed out onto the circuit in front of them.

"I know you are used to all this Sam, but I am just loving seeing Stirling back out in an F1 car again."

"Trust me Sian, watching how he made that Porsche dance at Oulton I can assure you that he has not lost that twinkle in his eye, my word he was quick, straight out of the box."

Sian turned again to Sam.

"What is that sponsor down the side of the Gray Grand Prix Race car?

Sian was referring to the Orange letters that were emblazoned down the side of the grey painted race car.

Sam responded with a roll of her eyes.

"It's a Russian sponsor, all part of our friend Mr Petrov's empire."

"And what do they do?"

Sam shook her head this time.

"Would you believe, they are a huge betting syndicate!"

"Oh"

That was all Sian could reply without being certain that she would not say something totally inappropriate.

Stirling could be seen in the distance entering the start-finish straight but keeping well over to the left of the circuit as Sam and Sian looked on. Clearly, he was awaiting instruction from the team over the radio for a suitable gap in the traffic for him to start his blistering lap. As Stirling weaved up the straight towards them, Sam reached up and put her hand on Sian's shoulder. She appreciated that Sian was trying her best not to say the wrong thing.

"Sian, I am glad you were the last person to see Ross. He was surrounded by sharks that used his addiction to their benefit. You will have made him smile, I am sure, and that's how I want to remember him."

Sian reached across and put her hand top of Sam's.

"Thanks Sam, he sort of opened up to me about some of his issues and I felt bad about that."

"No Sian don't feel bad, it was good that he could talk and get it out of his system. Sadly, he started to get into a big guilt complex about me, but you know I would do everything I have done again if I had to."

Sian smiled and looked into nothing across the circuit as she remembered Ross's parting gesture.

"Sam, do you know the last thing he did before I pulled away when I had dropped him off? He took a pen out and..."

Sam interrupted whilst laughing at the same time.

"He stuck it in his ear and waggled it about....? Why did he always do that? He's done that since he was a kid! The boy needed introducing to ear drops! Also, Sian, if you come across any of his stupid doodles that he used to do when he was thinking, please save them for me."

Sian and Sam were still laughing in memory together as a determined Stirling hustled the urgent and agitated thoroughbred race car out of the last corner and on to the start-finish straight. He was starting a hot lap.

The Gray Grand Prix race car snapped up through the gears, the pulling, screaming, engine not noticing the seamless changes. Stirling tracked gently, diagonally across the circuit under the distinctive flying saucer bridge, in an effort not to induce any time sapping steering input. The sharp front of the car obliterated the timing beacon signal to start another lap, the clock was counting. Stirling pinched a bit of the blue paint that separated the racetrack from the emerging pit lane on the approach to the right hand first turn. The slight positive camber allowed a slightly higher turn in speed, but wind direction changes could have a huge impact on spotting the braking point for a hugely efficient aero dynamic F1 car. Stirling appeared to judge it perfectly. He pressed his brakes hard, the braking system managing huge temperatures as the bullet was hauled to a survivable 'turn in' speed. Stirling pulled for two lower gears with his left hand, the paddle shifts instantly communicating his request to the awaiting gearbox. The instant change of direction of a Formula One car when viewed from the front seems to defy the laws of physics. Sam and Sian could now see why Stirling had been paid the millions as first with a flick of his black and yellow helmet to the right he could be seen looking through the corner, Stirling's eagle like eyes focusing on the exit of the corner, then with huge commitment and total belief in the designer and the dedicated race engineers he hauled at the power assisted steering, bracing himself against the huge G forces and without a moment's hesitation Stirling planted the throttle, the engine screaming out, the super soft tyres desperately clinging on, the simple force of rushing air pressing the car hard into the ground. The car had no choice but to respond to its driver's commitment and pinched a good chunk of the smooth exit kerb. Stirling pulled now for a higher gear, the race car rushing towards the right tight hairpin turn two at a speed that, unless controlled, would result in a huge shattering crash. As the point of no return seemed to have passed, Stirling hauled onto the brakes, grateful for every penny that had been spent developing a braking system that could withstand such abuse, whilst demanding that the gear box kept up to his urgent need to get into the lower gears. Stirling tried to ease his braking pressure as the last possible turning point was reached and he had no option but to input the required right hand steering lock. The right front tyre scrabbled for purchase and came up wanting the result to be a lack of rotation of the wheel. Sian and Sam could see the puff of white smoke from Stirling's front wheel.

Sam, now feeling her competitive juices starting to awaken almost shouted out.

"Stirling no, too fast in! He'll be kicking himself for that."

Sian did not have a chance to reply as she watched Stirling wrestle and hustle the complaining car into the long slow corner. The missed apex was now a given, but Stirling was not prepared to let the throttle off the hook as this time when he squeezed the throttle the car again went scrabbling onto the exit kerb and irritated its out of bounds rough edge.

For a short period, Sian and Sam could hear Stirling's engine as it played to his tune until another car launched at turn one, taking no prisoners.

"It looks like the Stragatti's are on the money today."

Sian excitedly nodded, loving the vibrant, exciting atmosphere that the Formula One cars were agitating, then she pointed up to the large electronic timing screen.

Stirling's name had been tumbling down the order and now sat in 13th place in the list of familiar and famous names as the pre-lunch quick times punched in. Stirling in person blasted into view again at the start of the long straight. Sian almost held her breath as the nose of the race car searched for the timing signal that would indicate another lap completed. Sam found herself grasping her hands tightly together.

"Come on Stirling, come on."

The timing screen had become agitated as names bounced up and down and now some of the names had chequered flags next to them as the morning session panted to the end.

Stirling's name now dropped to second to last as all the chequered flags started to line up at the side of the screen.

Stirling held the car to his right, Sian and Sam's left, as he knew his entry to turn one now had no importance and that it was more important to keep the car in its happiest state, going straight and hard on the power. Finally, the car leapt through its timing signal and Stirling's name launched up the timing screens as the final chequered flag settled next to his name as well.

Sian jumped and unexpectedly grabbed Sam who nearly fell over.

"Third, third. Not bad for an old goat."

Sian babbled out.

Team manager Sam pretended to mock his efforts...

"Third, third what's all that about? If he had not made a rookie error into turn two, he could have been where he should have been, the waster."

Sian had not even heard Sam's response and was busy collecting her bag, bottle of water, and her hat which she had thrown up in the air.

"Let's go grab him before the press get their teeth into him."

Sam relaxed into Sian's excitement.

"Yeah, let's go tell him where he went wrong."

Sam stood for a moment's hesitation, then set off after the almost bouncing Sian, the only blemish in the picture being the two police cars she had just noticed skulking in the paddock behind the rows of colourful race transporters.

Chapter 39

Stirling rolled his hot but cooling and now silent race car into the busy garage. A cordon was quickly put across the front of the garage to hold back the excited press. Sian and Sam stood well to the back of the garage and waited for Stirling to extract himself from the car. From his gesturing in the cockpit, he was still in radio communication with his race engineer whilst the mechanics plugged in the radiator coolers and hydraulic jacks were placed under the front and rear of the car. Another mechanic reached into the car, pulled back the locking collar and removed the steering from the cramped cockpit to allow an easier exit for Stirling, who twisted his central safety belt buckle, unplugged his coms plug at the side of his helmet, and then eased himself straight legged out of the confines of the safety cell he had been 'working out' in.

He stood on his seat, still in the car, whilst he pulled his gloves off and then undid his helmet strap with his now bare fingers. After passing his distinctive black and yellow helmet to a waiting mechanic he, with one hand, grabbed at the top of his under helmet and pulled it up and off revealing his now spiky wet hair and slightly red face. Large fans that were set up in opposite corners of the garage blew a warm but welcome breeze over Stirling's over heated body which was now relaxing back into the world that normal human beings occupy, his hyper-sensitive state being left for the abnormal world that an F1 driver operates in whilst on the track. His eyes rested on his two favourite people of the moment. Sian waved; Sam held up three mocking fingers to which Stirling replied with outstretched arms. He stepped out of the car, had a quick time check with his race engineer and then walked to the back of the garage.

"My two favourite ladies!"
To which Sian replied by looking at Sam and repeating,
"There you go girl, I told you that you were in!"
Sam smiled.
"Thanks, Sian, for me making me feel really uncomfortable."
Sam turned to face Stirling.

"It didn't take long for you to blow the cobwebs off, but I have to say I was slightly disappointed with third."

Stirling turned to Sian.

"Sian, your mental growth seems to have stalled at about 13 years of age!"

To which Sian replied,

"14 actually, that one year makes all the difference!"

Stirling had already turned to Sam as Sian's reply hit his ears;

"Oh, I think the car is better than Stirling Speed to be honest. I tried to take a bit too much into turn two, maybe I didn't have the tyre temperatures quite where they needed to be which stuffed my run out of it, then I had some instability during one of the big high speed direction changes that saw me have to get out of the throttle which will have cost us, but, hey ho, at least we know it's a good car. Just the squidgy bit in the middle letting the side down."

Sam smiled back. She felt good around the down to earth Stirling.

Stirling gestured using his head.

"Come on, let's take advantage of the Gray Grand Prix hospitality unit. I've got about 45 minutes before I need to be in a briefing."

Sam led out of the back of the garage, Sian and Stirling following.

Sian turned back to Stirling.

"Are you enjoying being back? You looked good out there."

"To be honest Sian, with everything that has gone on it was nice to get out there this morning and just drive!"

Sian looked back to be greeted by a view that she had not expected. The route to the large Gray Grand Prix test hospitality unit had become heavily congested with cameras hung around the necks of the world's specialist motorsport press. Stirling recognised one of the old-school drivers, now turned TV pundit, and smiled at him, which was taken as permission to approach.

"Stirling Speed is back with his old speed. With everything that has gone on at Gray Grand Prix, the tragic loss of Ross Keane, the horrendous Sergio Petrov shunt, and the fact that clearly you can still pedal a car, a comeback must be on the cards? Gray Grand Prix needs your speed."

Stirling looked around for Sam who seemed to be holding her own with the barrage of questions she was fielding, then back to his questioner.

"You know, I was pleased Richard Gray approached me and it has been great to get out on track. They definitely have a good car. Ross did a great job on this design. It is just so tragic that he is not here to see how well it went, but trust me, I am on testing duties only, just holding the fort whilst Richard settles everything down. Now if you do not mind this old man needs to get a brew down him before this afternoon's rigorous start."

Stirling took hold of Sian's hand, gestured to Sam to make her way over to the unit, and set off, forcing through the crowding press. Suddenly the crowd thinned and then started to part. Stirling peered through the thinning crowd to discover the reason. Two sunglasses wearing, very official looking policemen were walking directly towards Stirling and Sian. Phil, Gray's team manager was walking behind, his gestures clearly indicating that he had no idea what was going on.

Stirling instinctively pulled Sian closer to him. Finally, the quartet met. The surrounding bodies and Sam fell silent.

Stirling smiled at the two policemen, one of them wearing ridiculous mirror aviator sunglasses.

"Can I help you guys?"

The two policemen in unison looked at Sian, smiled, then looked back at Stirling.

Stirling persisted in trying to move the situation along.

"If you need to speak with me, can you follow me over to the hospitality unit? I need a drink and I am getting a little tight on time."

The one on the right reached into his shirt pocket and took out a folded, official-looking piece of paper.

"Mr Stirling Speed, we have a warrant for your arrest."

Sian took the paper from the policeman.

The cameras hit frenzy mode.

"Arrest me, what on earth for?"

"You must come with us now Mr Speed. We really do not want to use restraint."

"You will tell me first what this farce is all about, or you will need more than restraints."

Phil tried to step in but was pushed back. Sian turned to Stirling.

"It's in Spanish. French, and we'd be okay."

The policeman on the left reached forward to take Stirling's arm.

Stirling stepped away from the approaching arm and repeated his stance.

"You will tell me what I am being arrested for and where you are taking me, or trust me, you are going to have a battle on your hands, boys."

"Mr Speed, please, we are taking you to the local police station and we are arresting you for drug smuggling. A substantial amount of, how you say, Class A drug has been found in your room. You must come with us now!"

Stirling turned to Sian.

"Get hold of Peter Smith, then grab my gear from the transporter and bring it to the police station."

"Sam, I'll need to take a rain check on that drink."

Stirling was then swallowed by the crowd that was now migrating towards the police cars.

Sian snapped into action. Sam looked down towards the floor, took a moment to make her decision, then looked up to see a disappearing Sian.

"Sian wait, I need to come with you!"

Chapter 40

"...and you are?"

Sam had been introduced by Sian to Peter Smith who had hesitated with his reply long enough for Sam to eye the neat grey man in front of her suspiciously. He somehow had a slight air about him that said, 'camouflaged predator'. Sian jumped in.

"This is Peter Smith, he..."

Now it was Peter Smith's turn to jump in,

"I am Stirling's legal advisor - or perhaps some would say legal fixer."

Sian followed up with:

"He's always fixing me."

Sam stepped forward and offered her hand, which Peter Smith shook.

"Well, it is nice to meet you, Mr Peter Smith. I am afraid Stirling has got himself in a bit of a fix."

Peter gestured for them all to sit down, then turned to Sian.

"So, Stirling is languishing in jail on a trumped-up drugs supply charge?"

Sian replied.

"Yes, I visited him with his kit bag after contacting you. They allowed me 10 minutes with him. Apparently, the amount that they found in his room was deemed to be an amount that a dealer would have and certainly not an amount that would be kept for personal use, which is why they are holding him at the moment. The press are all over the police station. They let Sam and I out of the side entrance. I have to say, that Stirling seems quite at ease with everything."

Peter Smith knew that Stirling would indeed be happy with the present situation. He had obviously rattled someone's cage and had provoked a response. Once a corner had been lifted it was always easier to see what lay beneath the surface, but for now Peter Smith chose not to reveal his thoughts.

Sian continued,

"So, what now Peter? I presume we need to find who is behind the set up and prove Stirling's innocence."

Peter Smith moved his gaze towards Sam. Sam replied with silence.

He then continued his progress report.

"I have been making some enquiries. It appears that a small-time local dealer has suddenly been flashing a considerable amount of cash around and has been boasting about his new heights within the criminal fraternity. He is the first link, but this is way outside his normal league. If we tug on his grubby little collar too soon the hatches will be bolted down, and our Mr Big will vaporise."

Sian seemed a little uncomfortable with Peter Smith's progress report.

"But Peter, Stirling is sitting in a prison cell and the world's press are baying for his blood type. Do we not need to nail the under life that has planted the drugs and pressure him into talking?"

Sian looked to Sam for support, but none was forthcoming.

Peter Smith continued.

"Sian, drug dealers do not talk about their pay masters. If they did, it would be one of the last words that they uttered. We need to find out who is behind this Sian, but more importantly, we need to find out *why* they are doing this. Stirling will tough this out. We need to get a name."

"I can give you a name."

Two heads focused on one.

Sam spoke again.

"I can give you the name and the why."

Chapter 41

The Russian accent was heavy, but the English was crisp, clear and to the point.

"You have a persuasive organisation around you Mr Peter Smith. I do not grant many audiences time with me. Usually, my guest are gamblers that yearn for the high stakes so they can become the high rollers, but you, you come to me with a pathetic allegation. Well, Mr Peter Smith, you can accuse as much as your heart desires, but I suggest you come back to me when you have proof. I know this is an area where you have come up wanting, Mr Peter Smith, otherwise you would not be here in person. The police would be here with their proof, not Mr Peter Smith of whatever organisation is supporting your little crusade."

When Sam Keane had released Mr Petrov's name from her lips it had come as no surprise to Peter Smith, his only uncertainty was whether or not Sam would speak out against the criminal world that she had apparently once frequented.

"Mr Petrov, we have a name and can pull in the drug dealer that set up Stirling Speed. He will link you to this."

"Peter Smith, you seem to be a man of the world. You know that any drug man that speaks ill of his paymasters will not long be on this pleasant planet. I can give you his name, address, family connections, even his bank account details, I have no further use of him, but you will never connect him to me. You have nothing on me. Now if you do not mind, I have..."

"OK Mr Petrov, I'll pull the little obnoxious man and squeeze him till I get Stirling sprung, but answer me one question."

Petrov replied by sitting back in his high backed black leather chair and opened his arms.

Peter Smith continued with his question.

"Why?"

"Why is a big question Mr Peter Smith. Why what?"

"Why did you try to hang Stirling out to dry?"

Petrov smiled, then leaned forward in his chair, placing his elbows as support on his desk.

"If I was to get involved with 'hanging' as you say, 'someone out to dry', then it would be for honour!"

Peter Smith was prepared to be patient and play Mr Petrov's game.

"Honour? Please give me an example of how someone could, dishonour you Mr Petrov?"

Patience was not a quality that Mr Petrov had in abundance, and he soon grew tired of his own game, clearly demonstrating this with his change of tone that distinctly moved into deadly seriousness.

"My son is fighting for his life. Do you understand those words? Fighting for his life, and he was put in that situation by Stirling Speed. A man who could not accept that my son was faster than him. My son crashed before he had a chance to prove that he was faster than the so-called 'great' three-time world champion Stirling Speed. Mr Peter Smith, you cannot understand the pain of seeing your child dishonoured and placed in such a situation - it is more than can be described. Maybe this time I have underestimated Speed's powerful friends, but next time, and there will be a next time, my honour and that of my son's will be avenged. Stirling Speed will pay."

Peter Smith was finished for now with this man, so he stood, turned his back on Petrov, who awaited a response but received none, and walked out of the door.

Chapter 42

As the VIP taxi eased to a halt on the sealed, highly polished, decorative cobbled stones outside the luxurious, 5-star, Pine Cliff hotel Stirling knew what to expect. Richard Gray's idea for Stirling to decamp for the gap between the rest of the tests at Jerez to the hotel in Portugal, to avoid the press frenzy, had not worked. The world's press always managed to pick up the scent, possibly much to the hotel management's initial dismay because some member of staff had clearly fallen into temptation and given the game away that a certain Stirling Speed was soon to be resident.

White uniformed staff rushed out of reception to the parked black Mercedes and lifted Stirling's bags out from the gaping boot as Stirling put on his best smile whilst sliding on his aviator sunglasses. Stirling needed to walk the fine tight rope of not getting into discussion or debate with the sensationalist press but not ignoring them and seeming aloof.

"Yes, it was all just a big misunderstanding."

"Yes, the matter is most definitely now closed."

"No, there is certainly nothing else to come out of the woodwork."

"No guys, I have never taken drugs."

"Police think it was just a case of mistaken identity or room mix up or something, but I have been well looked after and they are very apologetic."

"No, I am not meeting Sam Keane here, why should I be?"

Stirling reached the sumptuous double doors of the reception that were swung open by press barring security staff and entered the air conditioned, cool, brilliant white and scarcely populated reception. The smiling duty manager had been pleased to greet and show his publicity machine to his 5-star room. Stirling out of courtesy had mouthed an apology, even though he knew the hotel would now be basking in this unexpected worldwide press exposure.

Now in the shower, Stirling stood, naked, not moving, not washing, just standing with the high-pressure hot water washing away the stain of the stress from the last couple of days. As usual

Stirling had found it irritating that the sensationalist press had the ability of overwhelming the genuine motorsports press. More interested in making a story around,

'The Triple F1 World Champion Drug Dealer'
Or,
'Stirling Speed attempts to distance himself from a relationship with Sam Keane, sister of tragic Ross Keane'.

Stirling's good showing in the Gray Grand Prix race car at Jerez was now history.

Stirling glanced down at his glistening body and eyed the scars from his body-shattering Monza crash. Even now the general press would rather talk about his one big shunt rather than his three world championships. Sensational news over facts.

His short 24-hour prison visit had been hot and sticky but strangely satisfying. He had provoked a response. He was here to crack a case for Peter Smith. Who really should have gone to prison for the industrial espionage? Had the young Rosalie girl been murdered? The fact that Stirling had been set up by Petrov said something - it had proved that he would go to any lengths. Both Peter Smith and Stirling had agreed that this action showed that this was not a good guy for Gray Grand Prix to be involved with. Yet, strangely, they had maintained their relationship with him.

The conversation had become uncomfortable. After being pushed, Stirling had to agree with Peter Smith that he was developing feelings for Sam.

"Be careful Stirling, get too close and it will colour your judgement."

"But Peter, the fact that Sam and I have something together and, to be honest, I really don't know what that something is, but it has meant that I have been able to get under the hard surface that Sam puts up. I do think she just made a mistake with the whole espionage thing and paid the price. People make mistakes you know."

Peter Smith had not held back.

"So, will you be meeting her again on a personal basis? Will she be going to the hotel in Portugal?"

Stirling had unusually felt his hackles rise. Who was Peter Smith to be asking what he was up to in his personal life?

"Stirling, I know you are thinking that I should not be asking these questions, but it is my job to look after my operatives, and whilst you are still on this case then I am afraid that I will look under every stone and leave nothing to chance that could compromise you or the case. When this has all been put to bed then I hope you can take up again the journey you want to go on with Sam. I know that a man in your position must find it hard to find the right and genuine sort of people to be around you."

"I totally get what you are saying Peter, but trust me, I have got this with Sam, okay? Remember, it was Sam that tipped you off about Petrov. She is on our side Peter, and hopefully she will help lead us to the answers we are trying to find."

Stirling had then hesitated but wanted to speak his mind and so continued.

"I have to say at this point we still have nothing, all appears to be just as it was, even though I agree something doesn't feel quite right, but really, we have nothing. The Rosalie death appears to be what it is, just an unfortunate accident, and as regards Sam, like I say, I think she just got caught selling the family silver. The bad guy in all of this, and who has now proved himself capable of, well, anything, appears to be Petrov. I think we should be finding a way of drawing Petrov further out into the open.

Oh, and to answer your question - No, she is not going to Portugal. I have put her on a plane home. Her brother has just committed suicide you know. I am just meeting Richard Gray at the hotel, then as soon as the tests are over, I am heading home. I want to look further into where the Rosalie girl lived."

The room went quiet for a moment as both parties acknowledged each other's stance.

Stirling broke the silence.

"What's happened to Sian? She seems to have gone AWOL."

Peter Smith decided to break down any walls that might be trying to build.

"Okay Stirling, I respect what you are saying. I am just sticking my nose in where at some point it will get chopped off."

The moment of tension passed.

"I know Peter. Maybe after years of absorbing the pressure of F1 I am now having to learn how to absorb a different real-life pressure."

Peter Smith nodded in acknowledgement and then continued, "And to answer your question, I have dispatched Sian back to England to stand watch over young Sergio Petrov. If he takes a turn for the worse and succumbs to his injuries then we need to know instantly, because Petrov will come full bore for you, Stirling. You do realise that. In the meantime you need to keep an eye over your shoulder. It is not a matter of *if* Petrov comes after you again, it is a case of *when* he comes after you."

Stirling reached out, stemmed the water flow, stepped out of the large, granite shower room and reached for one of the weighty white towels that were immaculately stacked on a convenient shelf.

As he towelled himself dry, somehow, he was sure that if he kept pushing and the pressure increased on this case then at some point soon, the lid would blow off.

Chapter 43

Sian smiled at the kind gent and the frowning lady by his side and then put on the best, 'so sorry' face she could muster, her French accent standing out in the so English air.

"I am so sorry; I have just flown in from Spain and have only Euros."

Sian had pulled up at the hospital and realised the expense of parking in a hospital car park.

The aging gentleman had made himself vulnerable by hesitating to look at the pretty white Alfa Romeo and then the pretty young girl that had clambered out from it.

Sian had pounced straight away on the smiling face.

"Pardon monsieur."

The kind gent melted, his wife did not.

"You need to be better prepared young girl. We keep a plastic bag in the car all the time for change specifically for my hospital visits, don't we Arthur? You do know Arthur, that you will never change that Euro or use it for that matter, you know I can't travel with my conditions."

Arthur fished around in his plastic bag and produced exactly the right change for the car park.

Sian offered the equivalent in Euros, at which the kind gent looked at his scowling wife and then looked back into the pretty eyes of the smiling, clearly slightly cheeky young girl in front of him and with a smile in his eyes replied,

"You have the car park on me, young miss."

Sian turned to the lady and tried with her best smile to turn her frown upside down but failed miserably and so replied by stretching up on her tiptoes, reaching in and planting a kiss on the kind gent's cheek.

"Merci Arthur,"

To which Arthur replied,

"You are quite welcome young missy."

"Arthur, please, you are going to have us late for my appointment."

Arthur removed his gaze and smiled at his wife of so many years,

"OK Bec dear, let's get you in."

The lady turned to Sian but now with a slightly more friendly, almost proud, expression and then in hushed tones continued,

"I am having a camera inserted for them to…"

She lowered her tone even more, causing Sian to have to lean in to hear,

"To have a look around,"

The lady made a circular motion with her index finger then pointed downwards.

"The specialists are quite concerned, aren't they Arthur?"

Arthur had by now bailed and was already heading for the entrance.

"Arthur, Arthur, I can't carry my walking stick, handbag, and stool sample all at the same time!"

Sian was now using tremendous effort to maintain her smile whilst trying to banish the terrible visions bouncing around her mind. The lady now had her handbag over her arm, and was clutching onto her walking stick whilst swinging a bag in the air with her other hand to catch Arthur's attention which, by process of elimination, could only have been a bag containing her, 'sample'.

"Merci Madam, I hope all is good with…,"

But the lady had now set off in hot pursuit.

"Arthur, Arthur, wait! Arthur, I am going to drop something, and it will be your fault!"

Upon arriving back from Spain, Sian had got to work on Stirling's request first. He wanted her to arrange for him to visit the house where the Rosalie girl died. By all accounts it had not been lived in since and was in the middle of a protected nature reserve. The drop of Stirling Speed's name and some story about a TV documentary about secluded houses surrounded by nature had, to Sian's amazement, considering she only thought of the idea whilst speaking to the lady on the phone, indeed secured a visit. Now her second task was to get to the hospital and try to secure up to date, accurate information on young Sergio Petrov's condition.

Mr Petrov had made it very difficult to extract information. Even Richard Gray was only receiving information via Mr Petrov himself.

Sian had drawn a blank with the slightly over efficient ward receptionist and had ended up where anyone could go, the waiting room. Sian looked round the dowdy room and hoped that the tatty health advice posters peppered randomly around the white walls would give her some sort of inspiration.

"Is it Sian?"

Sian swung round to see a lanky but distinguished looking man.

"My name is...,"

Sian interrupted.

"I know who you are. You are Charles Thomas the world-famous brain surgeon. How did you know that I would be here? In fact, how do you know my name?"

The lanky frame sat down next to Sian.

"We'll deal with the world-famous bit at a later date, but I had a call saying that you'd be around trying to get through the Petrov information brick wall."

"Well, I *am* here, but I am afraid I am not doing too well. How, really, is Sergio doing?"

"Honestly Sian, I think he is pulling through this. We are being incredibly careful waking him from the induced coma that we have had him in, but every stage is looking very positive. But, as they say, 'the deal is never done until the deal is done'. Sergio has to come back to us in his own time."

Charles took a moment for Sian to absorb the information and then continued.

"I have been told that I can trust you and I have been given your number. Sian, if there is any change for the good or the bad, I will call you straight away."

"Thank you, Mr Thomas."

"It's Charles, please, and trust me, people make more of what I do than is really the case. I suppose I am just doing what I have been trained to do."

"Well thank you Cha...."

"What are you doing here asking about Sergio?"

Sian attempted to make a leap for the high ground.

"Excuse me, and may I ask who *you* are, interrupting a private conversation with Mr Thomas?"

Charles extended his frame and stood.

"This, Sian, is Mr Petrov's personal and not very friendly bodyguard who has been left here to guard our young Sergio. I will leave you two to get acquainted."

Charles turned to leave, then hesitated, turned back to Sian and reached down into the back pocket of his trousers and extracted his aged wallet. After a little rummaging around he produced a tattered business card, put it between his index and middle fingers and flicked them out. Sian reached out and took the card.

"Sian if you need to speak to me please do not hesitate. Sorry about the state of the card. It's probably been in my wallet years."

"Merci, Charles".

Charles looked at the stern bodyguard, went to make a comment, then decided that Sian looked perfectly capable of handling him. He turned, gave Sian a grin and pointed to the door.

"I'll leave this to you then Sian, erm, call if, well, if you need to."

His lanky frame vacated the area and Sian was now left with a Russian bulky frame to deal with.

Sian eyed the bulk in front of her and desperately wanted to ask where his neck was but refrained. Instead, she squeezed on her best ever stern face and waited out the silence, determined not to be the next one to speak.

The Russian accent gave in first.

"Mr Petrov has left instructions that no one is to visit Sergio and no information is to be released. These are very strict instructions that I will implement."

Sian stood up from her seat, walked over, extended an index finger and prodded it into the chest of the now slightly bemused bodyguard.

"Man, you are as solid as you look aren't you? My name is Sian, may I ask yours?"

"My name is no concern of yours."

"OK, Mr no concern of yours"

Sian was sure she detected a slight twitch at the side of her opposer's mouth.

"Are we going have a problem here? I take my orders from Mr Richard Gray and Mr Stirling Speed, not from Mr Petrov. I am here because they are concerned for Sergio. We need to know exactly what is going on."

"I take my orders from Mr Petrov, and if he says no information gets out, then no information gets out, and as for Speed - he is history. Nobody crosses Mr Petrov and gets away with it."

"Mr of no concern..."

"It's Alexei"

"Alexei, let's agree to disagree over the whole Stirling Speed thing. He's sort of my uncle so you are on a loser there, and regarding Richard Gray, surely we do not have a problem here seeing as though they both work together."

"They do not work together. Richard Gray works for Mr Petrov."

"How can that be Alexei when Richard owns a Formula One team that Mr Petrov sponsors? I am afraid, my muscle-bound friend, that Mr Petrov is merely a customer of the Gray Grand Prix marketing department."

"You are wrong young girl, Richard Gray is a mere puppet. Richard Gray is like all Westerners - consumed by greed and selfishness and then when they become vulnerable and fall, like always, it is Russian power, Russian knowhow and Russian money that they grasp at. If Mr Petrov decided to cut the strings, then Richard Gray would collapse into a heap. He holds all the strings."

Sian patted the loyal protector of man and country on his chest.

"Well Alexei, he doesn't control my strings so I will ask and go where ever I want. Boy, you must work out! Just a thought Alexei, try working out those smiling muscles a little. All that frowning will give you wrinkles and a bodyguard with wrinkles is never a good look. You need a stern solid look, not a flabby wrinkly look."

Sian extended a smile in demonstration and then turned to leave.

"Please young lady, listen. You are a nice girl, a funny girl, please take my advice and get clear of this whole situation with Mr Petrov, Gray and Speed. Just stay clear of it all."

Sian turned back and pulled her chin back into her neck.

"What do you mean Alexei?"

Alexei delayed his response, clearly going through a battle with himself.

"There was a once a young girl, just like you. She made me laugh. Well, smile at least."

He paused again, now appearing to be in memory mode.

"She would call me, 'Tubby Trouble'. You remind me of her. She got in between...."

There was another stunted silence and again Sian decided to hold her tongue.

"She wandered into dangerous waters and now she is..."

Alexei looked directly at Sian.

"She is, no longer with us. You stay clear young lady, stay well clear."

Sian decided now was the time to push, hard.

"What do you mean she is no longer with us? She has left the room? She got fired? She changed jobs? She died? She was murdered?"

"I have said too much already. You just stay well clear and please now, please, leave the hospital."

"The Rosalie girl? Is that who you mean? The girl that had the accident?"

Again, a quietness bit into the room.

"It was no accident. What happened to her was wrong. Now, enough. I have said enough. You get clear young, San."

"It's She-arn, you spell it S I A N, Sian."

Alexei nodded.

"You be careful, young Sian"

Sian took hold of one of Alexei's powerful sausage fingered hands and squeezed it. Alexei smiled in response and then added.

"Now go."

Sian slowly made her way to the waiting room entrance, her mind racing with what to do next. Then she thought of the first thing to do. She stopped and swung round and cocked her heard to one side.

"Thank you, Alexei. I think there is a good man hiding inside that bad boy body of yours. Now, let's keep that cheeky smile of yours going."

At that Sian was gone, leaving the big bodyguard to sit down, shake his large head, and wonder what had just left a vacuum in the room.

Chapter 44

Stirling had followed the instructions easily and, except for a quick reverse into someone's convenient driveway, he had managed to guide his battleship grey E Type Jaguar into the nature reserve's public car park. As indicated, there was a gate at the top left of the car park, held shut by a security padlock. Stirling spun the gold numbered barrels with the code he had been supplied with. 1-9-1-4. The padlock remained firmly closed. Stirling had worried that this might happen because Sian had taken three attempts at various numbers before she had convinced herself that she had given Stirling the right pin code that had been given to her. Stirling had said the obvious, 'Sian, why do you not write things like this down?' Sian had replied by pointing to her head and explaining she had it all up there, it's just that at times it all gets a bit mixed up. Stirling looked down at the lock again and noticed an errant number one had not quite fallen into line. He half-heartedly adjusted it and pulled at the lock again and to his amazement the lock fell open. 'Sorry Sian, my mistake.'

Stirling eased his rumbling E type through the gate on to a lane that was obviously not used very often, judging by the overhanging greenery. 'I'm glad my old car has not got the girth of its modern counter parts' Stirling mused. 'Perhaps one of my Land Rovers would have been order of the day'. He shut the gate, locked it behind him as instructed, and stepped back into the old leather interior, squeezed in first gear and gingerly set off up the lane not really knowing what to expect or what to say to the Doctor Campos he was due to meet. After less than five minutes of negotiating the odd pothole and particularly aggressive overhanging branches, the lane opened out into a parking area that was large enough to turn the E type round in one go. The shale car park was overlooked by a quite idyllic thatched cottage, yellow roses growing up the right-hand side of the door that were clearly being looked after. Stirling halted the silky six-cylinder engine and stood up out of the car.

'No Doctor Campos, judging by the fact that my car is the only occupant of this nice, secluded and I suppose you could say, exclusive car park.' Stirling thought. 'I suppose I'd better see if anyone is at home.'

Again, Stirling did not expect to find anyone in as, quite strangely, the cottage had remained empty since the death of young Rosalie years before. Stirling stepped out towards the door but then was halted by a high-pitched voice from the woods.

"Mr Speed, Mr Speed, I'm on my way."

Stirling looked into the direction of the woods in time to see a lady, maybe in her late sixties, dressed well for whatever the weather was to throw at her, a pair of binoculars jangling around her neck as she made large but careful strides through the undergrowth.

"Mr Speed, Eunice Campos at your disposal."

"Doctor Campos, please, just Stirling."

"Stirling, please, just Eunice, I really can't remember what I got my doctorate for these days."

Eunice smiled widely, put one arm behind her back and extended her right arm as a request for a handshake.

"Thank you for allowing me to come, and for giving up some of your, I am sure, valuable time."

"Oh, trust me, not a lot happens around here, this is the highlight of my day, well my week actually. In fact, this is a highlight full stop! Your assistant tells me you are here about a TV documentary."

Sian had neglected to tell Stirling that this was the cover story for him being there, and now having met the smiling, excited Eunice, he felt guilty maintaining the false story.

"Eunice can I be honest with you?"

"You can, young man, but I must tell you I am not the marrying sort."

Eunice laughed at her own little joke.

"Well, I will have to regrettably strike you off my list then."

"Though I could be tempted into a mad passionate affair."

Eunice laughed again, flung her head back, stroked her rather chaotic hair, then continued,

"Well, actually, I am not really a mad passionate affair sort of person either, to be honest."

Stirling gave Eunice a genuine smile back. He had not been sure exactly what to expect but this definitely was not on his 'most likely scenarios' list!

"Would you like a pot of tea, young Stirling?"

Without waiting for an answer, Eunice turned her back towards Stirling and strode off towards the cottage whilst fishing around in her mini khaki coloured ruck sack that she had removed.

"Ah, there we go, tea will be served."

Eunice continued her striding pace whilst jangling a set of keys in the air to demonstrate to Stirling that they now had access to the cottage.

Stirling sat slightly bemused in the bright, clean, well-kept but dated kitchen, having been given an unusually large selection of teas to choose from. Stirling had still not had a chance to mention the real reason for his visit and decided to delay his confession a little longer.

"So, Eunice, you live here?"

Eunice sat down opposite with two gently steaming cups of tea.

"Oh no, no, I am just, sort of, the custodian for the place. Like to keep it as it always was in the past."

Still none the wiser Stirling decided to get into why he was there.

"Eunice, I have to say that there has been a little confusion. I am not here to make a documentary. I am here to investigate the death of Rosalie."

Eunice sat back in her chair, placed her cup of tea gently on the table and eyed Stirling suspiciously.

"Are you from the press?"

"No."

"So, who are you?"

Stirling found it strange saying the next words. He felt almost as though someone else was saying them.

"Eunice, I work for an organisation that investigates injustices that have somehow stepped outside the reach of the law. There is a concern that there is more to the death of Rosalie than meets the eye. Is there anything that you can tell me? I have to say that at the moment, I have nothing."

Eunice took a sip of her tea, replaced it on the table then leaned forward slightly, maybe in an effort to look deeper into Stirling's eyes. Suddenly her scattiness had evaporated, and seriousness had replaced the temporary void.

"Can I trust you Mr Speed? I mean, really trust you? I see sitting in front of me a famous person not part of the world that I occupy. Can you comprehend loyalty? Can you comprehend the pain of losing a beautiful young girl that you have seen grow up into a beautiful young woman?"

Stirling knew that he had to choose his words carefully if he was to get Eunice to open up the wounds that were her painful memories.

"Eunice, I spent a life blinkered to all that was around me. My only focus was to be the best driver in world. But when I retired, I suddenly noticed the world around me, and somehow I wound up involved in this organisation. I got sucked into a case where trust was everything, a case where a broken trust saw the demise of a man's existence. I chose to remain involved with this organisation because I want to do everything I can to make sure that as many injustices as possible can be righted. You ask me if I can be trusted. Eunice, you will never see me responsible for a broken trust."

Eunice sat back, then stood and walked over to the sink and looked out of the window onto the gravel car park towards Stirling's cooling Jaguar. A quietness enveloped the room, a fragile silence that Stirling sensed should not be broken. Eunice was clearly raging a battle in her mind.

"About where your car is, was just about where her father found her body."

Chapter 45

Stirling said nothing and looked at the back of Eunice as she continued.

"This house and the surrounding land belonged to Rosie's grandmother who was a professor at the university."

Eunice hesitated, rounded, and returned to her seat, clearly having decided to trust what she could see in Stirling's eyes and to start the story from the beginning.

"I was a student under her, she really was a wonderful lady. It was amazing, Rosie looked just like her and they both had a wonderful affinity with each other. Rosie loved this place, even as a toddler she trailed her grandmother around and would always throw a naughty tantrum when her mother and father came to her pick her up. She grew up so fast, was very bright, fun, beautiful and..."

Eunice looked through Stirling drifting into her memories, "Happy days."

Stirling gestured towards the substantial tea pot.

"Oh, please do. Let me pour."

Eunice reached over with two hands and picked up the cosy clad teapot.

The now stronger looking tea rushed through the restrictive spout of the teapot and made that unique, gently escalating noise as the hot pouring liquid met the rising level in the echo chamber of a teacup.

"Oh, you would have been popular with Rosie and her grandmother."

Eunice smiled.

Stirling stirred his splash of milk in and tilted his head slightly to one side to exaggerate his quizzical look.

"They both loved their teas in fact..."

Stirling interrupted and pointed to the numerous amount of glass jars that lined one of the kitchen shelves, all carefully labelled up with exotic names of tea.

"Yes, Rosie carried on her grandmother's tea collection and was always experimenting."

Eunice read what Stirling was about to ask next.

"You are wondering why the cottage has been kept just the same as the day Rosie died."

"Well, yes."

Stirling was scrabbling to make sense of anything at the moment but felt that Eunice was going to be the breakthrough that he was looking for.

"I will come to that but let me tell you the story first because at the end of it I need you to believe what I will say."

Stirling sat back and folded his arms in a gesture that said, 'I am all ears.'

"Rosie's grandmother studied vegetation and flora and, in reality, this place became her laboratory and research area. Rosie would spend all her time here and she was always helping me out as I tended to various projects that we were working on. It was always assumed that Rosie would follow in her grandmother's footsteps when she went to university, but from an early age she always had a fascination with motorsport, particularly Formula One. Often on a Sunday afternoon the three of us would sit together to watch you people drive round in circles and Rosie would wax lyrical about strategies and drivers whilst we both tried desperately to keep up with her. So, at Uni she took a business course with a definite ambition to get into Formula One management. Sadly, her grandmother was never to see her fulfil her ambition as she became poorly and passed away. In her will, she left this place to her shattered, beloved Rosie and, much to her mother and father's dismay, Rosie insisted on moving in here when she graduated."

Again, Eunice hesitated whilst she relived a moment in her memory bank.

"I continued my work here and remember one day clearly, with her shouting my name, running through the woods looking for me, to excitedly tell me she had been offered a job at Gray Grand Prix and, by all accounts, she was very good and was soon flying around the world in Richard Gray's private jet as his personal PA. I was very proud of her, as were her mother and father. She was always smiling."

Stirling chose the moment to dig around a little.

"Rosie's parents, what did they do? Are they still alive?"

Eunice sat back in her chair.

"Oh yes, they are still alive, but they suffered greatly at their daughter's death and never really got over it. It was her father who insisted that this place stayed just the way it was. He turned down offers from various trusts and even one from the university to buy it. He asked me to keep it as though it was still lived in and that's what I have always done."

"And do they visit?"

"Rosie's mother never, but her father occasionally comes and just sits where you are sitting now and remembers his beautiful Rosie. By all accounts he travels a lot and once told me the peace of this place calms him, but to be honest, I have no idea what he does. Her mother was teaching, but never continued after Rosie's death. Rosie loved telling me about her job, and I realised that we had also developed a close relationship."

"Was she happy with her job?"

Eunice delayed her reply to express her concern.

"Well initially yes, but I think the team lost a big sponsor or something and some Russian guy got involved. He had a son that he doted on and Rosie really never felt comfortable around them. Then she turned up here just as I was leaving one day. Her dad had just restored an old MG for her. I remember it was sky blue. The strange thing about that evening was that she didn't really want to talk about her new car. She was clearly concerned about something. I delayed my journey home and went back into the cottage to make sure she was OK. Something just did not feel right. Then she told me what had happened."

Stirling felt that he needed to show that he knew how hard this was for Eunice and so halted the flow with a raised hand.

"Eunice, please take your time. I really do appreciate how difficult this must be for you. If we need to break?"

A little twinkle returned to Eunice's saddened eyes.

"OK young Stirling, we can call it quits for now if you like and get back together next week for part two?"

She forced a smile at Stirling who nodded back.

"OK Eunice, whatever is best for you. I don't mind."

"Like hell you don't."

Eunice smiled back.

"I knew you would say that. There are not many gentlemen left in this world. Stirling, us old girls are made out of stern stuff.

If I am right, then I see in you a man of action and the sad 'limbo' that this beautiful and once happy place sits wallowing in needs to be brought to an end and I think you are the man for it. Now, where was I?"

"Rosie had come home clearly rattled over something." Stirling reminded her.

"Oh yes. She had been asked to sort something or other with the designer chappy, Keane, was it? The chap that has just taken his own life. Well, it turns out he gave her the wrong memory stick and on it was technical information from the Italian team, Stragatti. Technical information that was extremely sensitive and it was information that he should not have had. Rosie did not really know what she had seen until an apparently rattled and under stress Mr Keane turned up in her office and offered her a substantial amount of money to forget what she had seen. If he had not acted in such a way Rosie probably would not have realised the gravity of what he had done. Clearly the team was up to no good - they were up to their ears in industrial espionage! Not knowing what to do, she apparently spoke to her father who suggested that she take the matter to Richard Gray first before reporting it to the authorities."

Eunice took a sip of her now cool tea and Stirling filled the pause.

"So, it was Ross Keane who had the information, not his sister, Sam?"

Eunice replied with a quizzical tone in her voice.

"His sister? I know nothing about his sister."

Stirling continued.

"And what was Richard's response?"

"Well,"

Eunice hesitated in thought.

"Well, it was this that troubled Rosie, Richard's initial response. He said that he certainly did not condone it, did not want to know anything about it and that she should make her own decision about how to move forward with it, but if she did report it then she must understand that it would cause a huge fallout. Mr.... erm, Keane, would be finished, but, more importantly, they were in very delicate negotiations with the Russian chap who had already invested in the team. He would not take too kindly to the news that the team's leading designer was cheating. It could have had huge consequences for the very existence of the team. It was a big decision and huge pressure, Stirling, for such a young and caring girl who had her dream job and future. She held the team's destiny in her hands."

"And Ross?" Stirling interjected.

"Ross? Oh yes, the young designer man Mr Keane. Well, Richard said that he would deal with him privately and ask for explanations."

The room went quiet and Stirling knew why. The next stage of the story was going to stab Eunice deeply.

Stirling instinctively slid his hand across the table and squeezed the hand of a lady that one hour before he had never met.

Eunice responded with a fleeting, forced and difficult smile, then braced herself for the pain.

Chapter 46

Peter Smith looked across at the smiling driver as the car he was passenger in urgently danced through the slightly damp lanes, its game and working engine suddenly raising its 'racy' voice as its rear wheels skipped in protest to what they were being asked to do.

"Sian, there really is no urgency, a quick coffee and a catch up was the order of the day, not a race through the lanes."

Sian responded by asking for a lower gear to keep the wildly spinning cams within the little Alfa's engine happy.

After a journey that had somehow only risked one casualty, an irate farmer who had tested the efficiency of his tractor brakes when confronted with a speeding white Alfa Romeo, Peter Smith was pleased to be able to relax his breathing as Sian brought her fun to an end on the car park of her chosen destination, a slightly off the beaten track country pub.

"Sian, I said a coffee after work. Why are we here?"

Sian was in the process of extracting herself from her oxblood leather bucket seat. She delayed the procedure and flashed a smile at her questioner.

"I'm figuring you're paying?"

Peter Smith half nodded.

"Well, why settle for a branded coffee and stale Danish pastry when a brisk drive and a nice meal could be had? I am able to claim my petrol money back?"

Peter Smith looked at the slim, exiting back of Sian as she finished her explanation.

"Don't push your luck, young lady."

Sian ignored Peter Smith's attempt to rein in his 'field agent' as she liked to call herself now. Sian exaggerated her French accent for a little push back.

"A girl on a mission has to eat, you know."

Peter Smith sat back in his chair, his now empty side salad plate looking pitiful across the table from the still partially loaded plate that once proudly just about supported a 12-inch pepperoni pizza.

"How can someone of your diminutive stature devour so much food? In between meetings with me, do you actually eat?"

Sian attempted to regain her pretty little girl demeanour by dabbing the corners of her smiling and satisfied mouth as the last piece of pizza waved goodbye to the world. She pushed the plate away.

"Now, sir, that the important stuff has been dealt with, let's get down to the business of the Gray Grand Prix saga."

Peter Smith chose not to reply with what he wanted to say so as not to risk Sian's present mind flow.

"As I mentioned on the phone, I met with Charles Thomas at the hospital. A very nice gentleman, I have to say. He seemed, I would say, positive about young Sergio's progress but noncommittal. We could very well be in for the long haul or, he could wake tomorrow and wonder what all the fuss has been about!"

Peter Smith interjected.

"I really do hope we have a positive result for all parties involved. Certainly, for young Sergio, but also for Stirling. We are keeping very close tabs on Petrov. He is out for Stirling's blood."

"How dangerous is he? I know he pulled the trumped-up drugs charge trick on Stirling, but physically?"

"We are digging deep Sian. There is no doubt he is a feared man. He basically makes his money lending to gamblers and he has some big-league players on his books. Word is you do not get behind on your payments, otherwise nasty things start happening. He is clever though, because we cannot tie him to any of those 'nasty things' but, mention his name in the circles he operates in and fear ravages the eyes of the interviewee! Your feelings on the case?"

Sian looked at Peter Smith with a rare expression etched on her face, an expression of deadly seriousness.

"Rosalie was murdered!"

Chapter 47

Eunice responded by squeezing Stirling's hand back.

"Stirling, Rosie had made her decision. She was a tough girl. She did not want to be part of someone else's lie."

Eunice let go of Stirling's hand and sat back, somehow strengthened when she recollected Rosie's resolve.

"Stirling, Rosie had spoken to Richard and told him that she was going to report the designer man to the authorities. The FAB?"

"The FIA."

Stirling corrected.

"Yes, yes, the FIA, Federation of... something."

"The Federation of International Autosport. Do you know what Richard's response was?"

"He backed her 100%. He said he admired her strength of character and that she should continue as normal and that she should continue with her plans for the next day when they were all due to fly out on the company jet to a test in Spain, I seem to remember she said. He had apparently said that she was not paid to take on the worries of the team, that was his job. He made it clear that he would set up a conference call with the FIB,"

"FIA."

"Yes, yes, them fellows, he would set up an initial conference call for the following morning before they flew out so that it was not hanging over her. He would pick her up first thing so as they could discuss in the car the exact wording, but he never turned up for her."

Eunice stopped to allow Stirling to absorb the onslaught of information or to possibly comment.

"How do you know, Eunice, that he never turned up?"

Stirling then realised they had reached the climax of the pain for Eunice as he observed her chest heave up and then in an effort to show how 'strong old girls are' she bit her lip.

"Because, young Stirling,"

Tears welled up in Eunice's tired eyes and her voice shuddered,

"My beautiful Rosalie that I had seen dance and smile through life, lay alone, dead, next to the opened door of her little MG for four days before she was found by her father. My girl fought with every sinew and breath and dragged herself out of the cottage, retching in pain as her poisoned body closed down its organs. She died...."

"Eunice, enough. You have said enough."

Stirling stood and went round the table and hugged Eunice's heaving shoulders from behind.

"No Stirling, I want you to know everything. She died on her knees; her beautiful head collapsed on the driver's seat as her body convulsed to its demise. I would give anything for me to have taken her place. She lay there, dead, for four days Stirling, alone, her sweet body contorted in its final struggle. Four days, with nobody to hold her."

Stirling went to speak again but was stopped by Eunice's waving hand.

"The team had flown out, unable to contact her when she did not turn up. In the rush the team in Spain thought that she must have contacted the office and be either working there or off sick. The rest of the team in England naturally thought she was on the flight with Richard and the others and at the test in Spain. It was Richard Gray that eventually twigged that she was missing and so contacted her father, who contacted me. I said that I'd had a long chat with her the night before she was due to fly and that then I had travelled out on a field trip to Cornwall."

Eunice turned round to Stirling who was still standing behind her, holding on to her shoulders.

"Stirling, Rosie's father drove out here and found his daughter dead, can you imagine the horror of that?"

"Eunice I am so, so, sorry but I have to..."

"It's okay Stirling. The Police said that she had accidentally poisoned herself."

"But how did that happen?"

"They said that Rosalie died from consuming a substantial amount of Oenanthe Crocata, or you may know of it as Hemlock Water Dropwort."

"What?"

"It's a very deadly poisonous root."

"But how could that have happened?"

"They surmised that she must have foraged it, mistakenly identified it and made it into tea that she then drank."

"And you agree?"

"No. I most certainly do not."

Eunice had fought through the emotion and now was crystal clear in her speech.

"Rosie had been brought up around here, she had been brought up around flora, her grandma was a professor in the damn stuff, I would teach her all that I was doing. She would not have done that. She was a highly organised girl. She would not have lost her phone. That just was not her, especially living alone in a remote place. I know this place Stirling, I have worked here, played here, I know this place - and I guarantee with certainty there is no Oenanthe Crocata to be found here! They found no evidence of the dropwort anywhere in or out of the cottage, except in a teacup, and incidentally, it wasn't the teacup that she usually used, she always used one her father had bought her. I know these seem like little things, but I knew Rosalie, I watched her grow up, she was like a daughter to me. I would have laid my life down for that beautiful young girl. Stirling, the police fobbed me off as a crazy lady wracked with grief."

Eunice stood up suddenly, flung her chair back and walked back over to the window overlooking Rosalie's final resting place.

"Stirling, please, please believe me. I know with all my heart that my beautiful Rosalie was murdered! Please don't fob me off like the police. There is a killer out there who needs bringing to justice. Trust me Stirling, and I will trust you to tell me if you find anything out."

Stirling could now feel the full weight of this case bearing down on him.

"Eunice, do you have any suspicions of who could have done this to her?"

Eunice lifted both of her hands and ruffled them through her already unruly hair.

"I have thought this through so many times over the years and even tried to make my own enquires. Richard Gray was a nice man and once very kindly allowed me to go in and ask him questions, but I came out feeling a little paranoid about the whole thing. I think maybe the Keane fellow? When I heard that he had committed suicide I wondered, did he do it, because he could not live with what he had done, but I did dismiss him at some point, and I can't remember why. For a long time, I thought the Russian guy may have been behind it all, but Richard Gray assured me that he would not have been involved with him if he suspected for one moment that he had anything to do with Rosie's death. Mr Gray spoke very highly of Rosie and said that he had made his own enquires, but in the end had agreed with the police that it was a crazy, horrible accident."

Stirling delayed a moment with his next question for the information to settle and to make sure he was not overloading this lovely caring woman in front of him.

"And the whole espionage thing, your thoughts?"

"Oh yes, I do remember Mr Keane's sister now. Why had I forgotten about that bit! Mr Gray did tell me but maybe I was too focused on what had happened to Rosie. I remember he said it turned out that it was her that tried to sell some information from another team to her brother. Of course, I remember now. I am sorry, Stirling, I do get a little mixed up in this busy old brain of mine. I think somewhere, somehow, the Russian chap and what must be his grown-up son now, are somehow involved. Oh, I am sorry I have been useless haven't I? Please don't let me put you off Mr Stirling, I really do know that Rosie was murdered."

Chapter 48

Stirling eased the firm clutch in with his left foot whilst his angled right foot busied itself on the brake pedal whilst also giving the throttle a little sharp squeeze causing the straight-six engine underneath the bulging bonnet of his E type to let out a bark at the request. At the same time, Stirling's string-back leather gloved hand felt the short gear stick into third gear. He rolled his firmly sprung Jaguar through the roundabout, then squeezed the throttle again snicking through the gears in the modified five speed gear box as required. As fifth gear settled the engine into a melodic rhythm the hands-free kit that somehow seemed out of place in the 1960's environment of a classic Jaguar sang out. Stirling reached forward and turned the silver knob of his period style radio until it clicked, bringing Vivaldi's four seasons to an untimely demise. A click of the button on the kit connected the incoming call, allowing Stirling to answer.

"Hello."

"Stirling, it's Peter Smith. Sorry for the delay coming back to you. I have been to see Richard Gray to bring him up to speed. He…"

Stirling interrupted.

"Sorry Peter, I am just driving and hands-free devices and old Jaguar E types do not go well together. Let me just pull over. I've just passed a 'lay-by ahead' sign."

Stirling picked up the blue 'P' for parking sign that was rushing up towards him, eased the galloping Jaguar back and proceeded to blend down the gears as his left indicator blinked on and he eased to a smooth stop, pulled on his handbrake and with his left hand reached over to the dangling keys in the middle of the silver dash that hosted an array of beautiful significant dials that, in modern cars, have been done away with and replaced with the watching eye of an all knowing, all seeing and sometimes over reactive computer. He rotated the finger-worn polished silver key to the left and the silky six-engine relaxed and rested.

Stirling reached over and un-clipped his phone to hold it to his ear.

"Sorry Peter, go head."

"You first Stirling. How have you gone on?"

"Well, first of all, I am just on my way back from the Petrov residence."

"Stirling, maybe you should have run that past me first."

"Oh, I had my back up with me, but more of that later. I didn't get past his heavily guarded front gates, but I made it known I was coming for him. I don't like being the hunted. I wanted him to know that he has a fight on his hands if he going to 'peruse his honour' as he calls it."

Peter replied with an air of acceptance.

"Watch those sharp claws when he takes a swipe back."

Stirling continued.

"Before that, I visited the cottage where the Rosalie girl was killed. As you will know, Sian had set it up for me. I met the very pleasant and very helpful custodian of the place, a Doctor Eunice Campos. A little dizzy, but it turns out she doted on Rosalie and watched her grow up. She spoke so highly of her. She sounded like a great girl who must have made her parents proud. They do not appear to be really on the scene and at this point I would rather not contact them and cause them upset. Eunice is adamant that Rosalie was murdered. Everything she says ties into the Police report that the poor young girl died from consuming a poisonous root, which is what the autopsy report stated. The difference is, Eunice is adamant that Rosalie would not have made the mistake of consuming it in a tea and that she would not have found it foraging around the cottage and she also confirmed that it would be totally out of character for her to lose her phone. She was, by all accounts, a highly organised girl and with living out in the sticks she would be aware of the importance of her phone."

Peter Smith interrupted,

"A phone that turned up in the bottom of one her desk drawers!"

Stirling continued.

"It looks like it was a horrid death, and did you know, I can't remember if you told me Peter, but she was found by her father. She had lain there dead for four days after crawling to her car. How awful for her father! Without going through the whole conversation, I am certain that Eunice is right, and that Rosalie was murdered, and it is tied in somehow to the fact that she found out about the industrial espionage and was about to blow the lid. If Ross Keane had indeed been behind it then it would not only have cost the team millions in fines, but they would also have lost their top designer and any hope of the team surviving. Eunice unusually forgot about Sam's involvement but then remembered at the end which seemed a little strange, but she is a bit dizzy. The fact that at this time Petrov was about to bail the team out after they had lost their title sponsor, so that his little boy could have something to play with, does seem to lead one to the conclusion that, given his reputation, he could have got his heavies involved with 'sorting' the problem out. I think that is where we need to focus and find some way of flushing him out."

The delay before Peter Smith replied had Stirling wondering if they had dropped connection and prompted a

"Peter?"

"OK Stirling. First, I agree we should keep Eunice, Dr Campos, in the loop. She seems like a like a good contact and a decent person that deserves answers. Second, I agree that we need to flush Petrov out, but Stirling, I have to reiterate what I have already said to you. These are uncharted waters for you and by all accounts Petrov is not someone you want as an enemy."

Stirling replied quickly in a way that showed his commitment.

"Sometimes Peter, to get the best out of a problem race car you need to push it over the edge of its performance envelope to highlight its weaknesses so that those weaknesses can be addressed. I need to push Petrov over the edge to see where his weakness is. I have promised Eunice that I will get to the bottom of this and I will keep her informed."

Peter Smith delayed again in replying.

"And Sam?"

"Eunice did confirm that Richard Gray had said that in the end, it was Sam who had tried to sell the Stragatti designs to Ross. She just made a daft mistake, Peter, and she paid for it. Ross clearly chewed himself up about it all and thought the only way to help her, compensate her, pacify his guilt, call it what you want, was to give her a chunk of money. Hence the girl that exited the prison was a chastised, wiser and considerably richer lady. I am heading home for a fresh set of clothes and then I have arranged to travel down to see her. I want to clear the air and tell her exactly where I am at with her, and that I am investigating Rosalie's death."

Now it was Stirling's turn to delay. He did not have to wait for Peter to the ask the inevitable question.

"Peter, I cannot lie. I have given it some thought, and I do seem to have feelings for Sam, and I have accepted her past. I appreciate that she has been linked with bad goings on at Gray Grand Prix and she clearly knows what Petrov is capable of, but I really think we can work through this and maybe build something. I have spoken to her over the phone and I believe she feels the same and is keen to meet up. We are trying to keep it from the press for now."

Peter Smith simply replied with an

"OK."

Peter Smith would never usually have allowed one of his operatives to get involved with anyone on a case but, on the other hand, he also realised that when he brought Stirling Speed, three-time Formula One World Champion in on a previous case, he would be taking on someone special who would need to be handled differently. Stirling's fame opened doors, but Peter also realised that Stirling had to negotiate a fragile world of fame. A world that could soon be shattered into flesh cutting pieces. Stirling moved the conversation on.

"So, you met with Richard Gray?"

"Yes. I decided that Sian had dug up all that she could at Gray Grand Prix, and I wanted to tell Richard about the conversation and warning that Petrov's heavy man had given Sian. I wanted to see his reaction.

Stirling jumped in.

"I do not think he will have taken being spied on by Sian very well. Does he know about me?"

"Yes"

"And?"

"Well Stirling there were two things that I found surprising. First, we actually have crossed before in the past, but he did not recognise me. Secondly, I thought he would have a moment of outrage about our surveillance but I saw only a moment of recalibration. He then could not have been more helpful. He commented on how well Sian had done, and that he was sorry to see her go, and that if she ever wanted a change of jobs to come and see him. He then told me that he was starting to have concerns about Petrov, especially when he saw how aggressive he had been towards you. As reported by Sian he is clearly still raw after all these years about Rosalie. He claims to have conducted his own investigation into her death but arrived at the same conclusion as the police."

"And Ross, did he make any comment about his suicide?"

"Clearly he is still in management mode re Ross's suicide. It is quite clear that nothing comes before the team and so at the moment he is controlling the fallout and putting plans in place for moving forward. He is already talking about his new drivers for this year, and a new designer. The speed you demonstrated at the test has certainly got his phone ringing. Regarding Ross, he said that he had never really got over 'spy gate' and the lengths that his sister had gone to in order to get one up on him. He always felt bad about Sam's involvement. I feel the same as you, that Sam did try to sell team Stragatti's design secrets to show how important she was, and that Ross dumped a big dollop of guilt money on her. I do think they all know something about Rosie's death though, hence the reason they are all raw about it. Maybe Petrov let his dogs off the leash and things went too far. We need to keep sparking reactions to see if we can explode this case Stirling."

"One more thing Peter. To come back to the subject of my back up...Why is Sian following me in a Blue BMW?"

Peter Smith smiled to himself and Stirling sensed it over the phone.

"You are hot property at the moment Stirling. I need someone sitting on your shoulder as a backup just in case things start kicking off. It's standard practice in the field to have a wingman, Stirling."

"Why Sian though?"

"I thought it best to pull her out of Gray Grand Prix, now that she has rattled Petrov and after the warning the bodyguard gave her, and also, she has had previous experience following you!"

Peter Smith was referring to a previous case that had brought them all together and Sian had, for a while, followed Stirling around Europe!

"OK"

Stirling smiled,

"You have a point."

"She is a bit of a Rottweiler when it comes to you Stirling and when we told her that she would be following you in a BMW M4 and that she could claim all its fuel back she jumped at the job! Joking apart Stirling, she is a great field agent. She thinks on her feet. I need someone watching your back for you, someone you and I can trust. I presume she is near you now?"

Stirling looked into his chrome rear view mirror and through the slightly distorted view out of the sloping rear window of the Jag.

"She is sitting behind me in the lay-by reading what looks like an upside down Autosport magazine. Oh, and she has just waved at me. I think I might test her a little and see how quickly she can react to a hasty lay-by exit."

Peter Smith continued with a smile in his voice despite the tension that was building with the case.

"Children play nicely! And Stirling, you keep your eyes wide open and if you do get a chance, remind Sian that she is supposed to be covert so that would-be attackers do not know she is there!"

Stirling carefully replaced his phone in its holder, selected first gear, then simultaneously cranked the six-cylinder engine into life whilst dumping the clutch the moment the sparks deep within the engine got into their ignition routine. After applying a little right-hand lock to guide the nose of the Jaguar onto the empty road he instinctively wound on the left-hand lock to catch the widely over steering rear of the Jaguar. A carefully selected second gear soon became order of the day, then Stirling squeezed the throttle pedal hard to the floor, the Jaguar leaping forward with a unique howling roar that only a straight-six on song engine can make.

Covert Sian reacted by first shouting Stirling's name in annoyance, throwing the Autosport magazine to wherever, pressing the start button, pulling the right-hand paddle shift that sent a message to the waiting gear, asked for first gear and hit the throttle hard, allowing the computer to work out the conundrum of keeping the high-powered German speed machine heading in the general direction that Sian intended.

Stirling short shifted into fourth gear, causing the bark to reduce to a growl and allowed himself a little smile.

Chapter 49

"Mr Speed. We were expecting you."

"It's just Stirling, but thanks. I am meeting someone else here."

"Yes, Mr...Sorry, Stirling. Yes, Ms Keane, she has not arrived yet. Would you like to wait for her in the bar area?"

The efficient manager looked behind him as though able to look through walls, then looked backed and leaned in ever so slightly.

"The bar area is a little busy and Ms Keane did say that a little discretion was order of the day."

This was the fame bit that Stirling hated. He fully appreciated that his three world championships made him public property but sometimes it would be nice to just go for a quiet meal without feeling that he was having to skulk around. Stirling smiled in defeat and accepted the manager's good intentions.

"No problem, happy to wait wherever you suggest."

"Thank you...sir,"

Clearly, being on first name terms was a bridge too far at the moment.

"Your car has been parked around the back in a nice quiet area for when you leave later."

Stirling was always a little nervous whenever he pulled up at a restaurant or hotel and a young man or, these days, a young lady stood, hand outstretched, awaiting the keys for your pride and joy so it could be secreted to (hopefully) a suitable parking slot. In an era of parking sensors, reversing cameras and automated gearboxes, 1960 era Jaguars could pose a slight challenge to the modern trained driver. Stirling had also once been shown a YouTube video where a parking valet chanced his arm and took a guest's Lamborghini Aventador for a little street cruise. His moment of enjoyment had come crashing down when he arrived back at the hotel to find the not too happy owner waiting for him. Ouch!

Stirling followed his lead through the highly polished corridor, the parquet floor glistening. Just before reaching the bar area the highly polished manager swung right into a shorter corridor, then opened, stepped through, and stood against the door, allowing Stirling to pass by into the private dining room. Overly sumptuous would be how he would describe it. All of the wood, the floor and the furniture had an unnatural high polish, something that you would expect to find on a luxury yacht or classic Venetian hotel.

"If I may introduce sir to the room."

Stirling was just wanting a quiet meal with a beautiful girl he had decided to get to know better. Simple. Simple could sometimes be difficult in Stirling's life so he smiled and went with the flow.

"You and Ms Keane are of course the sole occupants of the room and you will have a dedicated waiter who is also a sommelier at your service. Should you require attention in between, please ring this bell."

"We will not be needing the bell, thank y..."

The polished manager was evidently partway into his routine and tried, nearly successfully, to hide his annoyance at being interrupted.

"Feel free sir to use the lounge area, the room is yours for the evening. There are suitable magazines and books for you to enjoy."

Stirling stemmed his smile and picked up one of the 'suitable' magazines. Octane magazine...a great magazine, and one that Stirling often read through, but maybe not on a date night!

Stirling replied with a,

"Thank you."

"Now, we have an inside dining table set up for two,"

This for some reason prompted a momentary pause and a little pleased smile from the manager who was clearly proud of this room. He then drifted over to the large window wall that, with little effort, folded together and exposed a veranda that overlooked the rolling hills of Dorset.

"We also have a table for two set up outside, with overhead heaters should you prefer alfresco."

At which point Stirling was slightly caught out by the sudden end of the room introduction.

"Oh, great, thank you."

"I do hope Mr Speed that you are pleased that you have chosen our restaurant for your meal. May we arrange a drink for you whilst you await Ms Keane?"

Appreciating the effort more than the room, Stirling smiled a reply.

"I have to say it was Sam, Ms Keane, that made the arrangements and booked the restaurant but, thank you all the same. Just a tonic water and lemon will be fine."

Stirling settled in the lounge area and picked up the 'suitably selected' Octane magazine. He was looking forward to speaking freely with Sam and was quite enjoying the buzz of anticipation of watching her walk through the door. It had been too long since he had allowed himself to relax around a woman and simply enjoy her company and go with the flow. Maybe this was a sign that he was ready to consider a serious relationship if one came along. He was pretty certain from the texts and phone calls that he had exchanged with Sam that he was reading the right signs and that Sam was keen to take things further. He often wondered whether he over-thought this subject, but a previous short, failed marriage had stoked the gossip columns, stoked the bank accounts of the solicitors involved, and stoked the bank account of his ex! On a previous case, where he had met Sian, the press had very quickly jumped to the wrong conclusion and had him dating a much younger Sian. So yes, he did have to think relationships through.

Stirling looked at his now empty glass and glanced over to the window at the sky that had now darkened within the hour that he had sat waiting for Sam. He checked his phone, no reply to the two messages he had sent to Sam asking if everything was OK. Stirling reached over and actually gave the polished hand bell a ring. Immediately the door swung open.

"Hi. Can you check if you have had any messages from a Miss Sam Keane?"

"No sir, there have not been any."

The waiter had been quietly instructed not to use any of Stirling's names and to stick to, 'Sir.'

"Are you sure? Have you checked?"

"I took the liberty, sir, of checking before you rang as I thought you might ask."

Stirling looked at his phone one more time and then asked, "Could you send the manager in please? Thank you."

"Of course, sir."

Stirling made his apologies and offered to pay for the room that had been exclusively reserved. The manager had politely refused payment but accepted a substantial tip from Stirling that adequately made up for the lack of income from food and wine for the evening. He then refused an escort down to his car, parked at the back of the hotel, and insisted that he would be fine with a few basic directions to the back door. He could not help but feel slightly anxious, rather than annoyed, that he had not heard anything from Sam and was unsure what to do next. Maybe he would try again tomorrow to contact her. He clicked open the door leading onto the rear car park where the Jag patiently waited, reached into his pocket and felt around for the leather fob that held the two aged jangling keys.

The act of removing the keys from his pocket had not been completed before the first crippling blow struck the back of Stirling's legs, causing his pained body to crumple to the ground. Stirling resisted the urge to turn and look at his attacker and tried to draw himself into a tight ball as the next strike of a baseball bat did its worst with a rib cracking blow. As the third blow came swinging in, Stirling's recalibrating body attempted to get control of the onslaught by relaxing the protective ball, forcing himself up onto his knees and coordinating a reach out to grab hold of the sports bat turned vicious weapon, but this plan was instantly thwarted as another bat swung in from behind, the impact creating searing pain across his shoulders, causing his head to snap back. Stirling could now feel himself uncontrollably crumpling to the ground, his mind and vision starting to blur. He fought hard to stave off the unconscious state that was enveloping him, but despite his mind's attempt to send out self-preservation commands, his battered, bruised and broken body, like an exploding race car engine unable to respond to a driver's nailed throttle request, failed to respond to any further mental instruction as his back hit the cobbled floor hard, baseball bat blows now raining in from both sides. Out of the one remaining open eye Stirling caught a glimpse of one of his assailant's black balaclava when, suddenly, the carpark was full of white light and

the sound of a blaring horn. A dark blue car screeched into a rubber-burning donut around the crumpled bleeding body. Then the car noise was gone, replaced with shouts, lots of shouts,
"Get the police!"
"Get an ambulance now!"
"Who were they? Where have they gone?"
"Forget that! Get an ambulance!"
"Stirling, Stirling, stay with me Stirling…open your eyes. It's Sian, Stirling, Sian. You wake up or I will grab your credit card. Come on mate, fight it, I've got you. Try to keep awake Stirling. Oh, Stirling, what have they done to you?"
"The ambulance is on its way and the police, oh my word, is he going to be okay? Can I do anything? Who are you?"
"I work with Stirling. Get me a blanket and take my phone, ring Peter Smith, and tell him what has happened, do it now!"
"Stirling, can you still hear me? It's Sian, squeeze my han……."
The pain, the confusion, the darkness, it all began to close in and squeeze, squeeze, squeeze what? I need to squeeze…,
Stirling suddenly recognised the voice close to his ear and began to relax his grip on consciousness, he could sleep now, no longer any need to fight the inevitable, he was in safe hands, no need to squeeze, no need to….

Chapter 50

Pizza? Why can I smell pizza? Am I hungry? No, thirsty! I am incredibly thirsty, but my eyes are so heavy, where is the pizza coming from?

"Stirling, Stirling! Are you waking up? Man, you have had a 'lie in.' Do you want a piece of my pizza? Oh, erm should I check with the nurse if you are allowed a piece first?"

Stirling managed to win the battle with his eye lids but was now figuring out how to get his eyes to focus.

Pizza, hospital, shunt? Have I shunted a car? Squeeze.

Stirling instructed his hand to move from his side and reach for the small hand on the bed that his eyes had finally focused on.

Sian felt Stirling's hand loosely grab hers and then it began to squeeze.

"Is that a yes you want some Pizza? Come on mate, keep squeezing, good to have you back around, you scared us. What are you saying?"

Sian leaned in and put her partially eaten slice of pizza that she was holding in the other hand back into the cardboard box.

Stirling's vision now started to make sense as he recognised the smiling Sian.

"Man Stirling, you took a..."

Stirling finally got his mouth and tongue to coordinate.

"Sian."

He croaked out. Sian increased her smile and went to reply but Stirling beat her to it.

"Sian, shut up, get me some water and get me the doctor. I want out of here."

Sian swung round to get a glass of water from the white plastic jug sitting on the bed side cabinet.

"Well, that's nice, two days I've sat here waiting for you to put in an appearance and all you can say is 'shut up'."

"Sian."

"What?"

"Shut up, get a doctor, and where is Peter Smith and where are my clothes?"

"Yes sir,"

Sian jumped up and mimicked a mock salute. She turned to the door, happy that grumpy Stirling was getting back into gear and was already waiting for the starting lights on the overhead gantry to blink out! She reached the door, hesitated, then turned back and walked over to the bed as Stirling painfully eased himself up in an attempt to sit up, powering through the pain in his head and the searing pain that emitted from his black and blue bruised flanks.

Stirling grimaced a smile at Sian as various feelings in his mind and body started to re-boot and one was a slight feeling of guilt. Maybe he had been a bit direct with her in his quest to regain control over his conscious state, and now she was coming back for a little reassurance.

"Sorry Sian for being a bit grumpy, I just…"

"Nah don't stress, I'm used to it. I've just come back for my pizza, hospital food sucks."

Chapter 51

Sian had insisted that she be the taxi service home. Back in her little white Alfa junior she had obeyed instruction and kept the pace sedate and smooth, but the fine handling short wheelbase little classic car was not the best for riding the bumps and so Stirling felt every single one. The doctor had insisted on doing some further observations but finally agreed that Stirling could sign himself out. Bruises and cuts would eventually disappear at home just as well as in hospital, and the two broken ribs would repair in their own time. The concussion was well into recovery and scans had revealed that, fortunately, Stirling had a hard head! Sian had taken great delight in her new nickname for Stirling, Quasimodo, a fictional character who among other 'distinctive' features had a distorted face with one eye larger than the other. Stirling had to admit that he was slightly worried that his face would never quite regain the balance and size that it once had.

Stirling's housekeeper had always known how to look after him whenever he had been involved in a shunt. However, she had to admit to herself that she'd never had to deal with injuries received from being beaten up! She had, over the years of his active racing, been on hand to help him beat his injuries on not a few occasions. Even when he'd had his leg and shoulder shattering Monza shunt, Stirling had not liked a fuss being made. He was just determined to get back to normality as soon as possible. She had, however, overstepped the mark slightly when Sian had arrived back with the battered Stirling at Drayton house. He had struggled his way painfully up the stairs. A suggestion that she would take his meal up to his room for him to save him negotiating the stairs again had resulted in a mild snap of a reply.

"I am getting up the stairs, so I am damned sure I can get down them."

She knew it was his way of dealing with injury.

Stirling had conceded that a foot stool could be placed in front of his burgundy leather high back chair and even to another course of pain killers as he held court to his two visitors, Sian, and Peter Smith.

"Well Peter, I think we can say that we have managed to provoke a response. I am afraid I did not really get a chance to avoid that swipe from Petrov that you warned me about."

Sian replied with annoyance in her voice.

"They did a proper job on you Stirling, you did not have a chance. There were three of them, two with baseball bats and a driver in a car."

"Thanks Sian. I think you saved my bacon. That was one big shunt where you just hang on, and wait to find out that what will be, will be.

"I should have been round the back sooner but with you being in that private dining room there was a slight delay before I realised that you had left the building. Then, as I reached my car I heard a muted commotion round the back. I walked round initially, saw what was happening, then thought the only way to take the thugs on was with the car, so I ran back and lit it up."

Peter Smith spoke up.

"That was good thinking Sian, the last thing we needed was you wading in on your own and us ending up with two damaged operatives."

Stirling smiled and looked at Sian.

"Do I remember you doing donuts around me?"

Sian mimicked a cocky attitude and looked down at her nails on her semi clenched right hand, then pretended to polish them on her jumper.

"A pretty good donut I thought, in a BMW that I am not used to, whilst holding onto the horn at the same time."

"So, not only did I survive a good beating, but I also survived one of Sian's donuts around me!"

"I will take that as a compliment Stirling, not bad for a first attempt at a donut!"

"Oh excellent, that was your first attempt. Survived the beating but almost flattened by an out-of-control donut!"

Peter Smith decided it was time to bring order to the room.

"Stirling, your thoughts of who was behind it?"

"It's got Petrov written all over it. It'll take more than that to scare me off from his honour games."

Stirling held up proceedings and allowed a moments quiet to enter the room and then continued.

"I know you are both avoiding the elephant in the room, but I am a big boy. What happened with Sam? I presume she must have been involved in this."

Sian looked at Peter Smith who maintained his eye contact with Stirling.

"Stirling, the night you were admitted to hospital, Sam turned herself in to the police. She said that she had been told to arrange a dinner with you at that venue but not to turn up. She claims that Richard Gray had told her that Petrov wanted a private meeting with you to sort things out. She is adamant that she had no idea that you were going to get jumped. Stirling, I have to tell you that she has blown the lid on "spy-gate." She has admitted to the police that her brother had received the sensitive design information from a disgruntled Stragatti employee. She says she knew nothing of who the whistle blower was, but that her brother had made it clear that if the FIA had found out, his career would be finished, and the team would be finished because Petrov would pull his funding. She claims to have always looked after her brother and so she said yes to taking the drop for him. Between them, they made the watertight case against her. When she found out what had happened to you, she went to the police. She did not want to have any further involvement... She will, I am pretty sure, get a custodial sentence I am afraid Stirling, for perjury!"

Stirling did not allow space for quiet again.

"Stupid girl, she will get what she deserves."

Peter Smith reached into his right hand inside pocket and brought out a white plain, sealed envelope.

"She asked me to give you this."

He reached over and passed it to Stirling.

Stirling attempted to hide his pained grimace and leaned forward, took the envelope and then without looking at it accelerated it into the log burning fire to his side.

"I don't need complications. Now let's focus on how we bring Petrov to his knees."

Sian now took over.

"Stirling, we have something else to tell you. Young Sergio has woken up. His recovery will be slow, but the doctors are confident that he will make a good recovery, all things considered. His father has been to see him."

This time Stirling did allow quiet back in and he also allowed himself a moment to take in the contradicting information. He was feeling anger, even almost a hatred towards Petrov, but felt a huge sense of relief that young Sergio, who had clearly been operating out of his driving depth had pulled through. He let out a small laugh.

"Well done young Sergio, I really am pleased that he has made it. I am sure he is a good kid at heart. I am really pleased."

Stirling looked at Sian and Peter Smith's faces and awaited a response. Behind them the panelled door eased open and exposed a door frame that was now filled by a man wearing a black overcoat. The man's face had a defined jawline and chin that sat below a sharp nose. His cool blue eyes were not sunken as such, but the pale surrounding skin made them look so. Stirling initially struggled to take in who he was looking at, one Mr Petrov, whose heavy Russian accent then filled the room.

"Mr Speed, I believe you when you say that you are pleased my son has pulled through. Mr Speed, if you will allow me, I have an apology to give to you and I think a little explaining. It appears you saved my son's life!"

Chapter 52

Stirling felt out of the loop. Judging by the unsurprised looks on the faces of Peter Smith and Sian, Petrov's entry was clearly expected and even arranged. Stirling swung his legs from their reclined position and went to stand up.

Petrov spoke;

"Please, do not get up on my behalf, whether you are getting up out of respect or, more likely, to do me harm."

Stirling scowled back.

"You'd better come up with a good apology and explanation, and next time you set your dogs on me tell them to have some sort of honour and not jump me from behind."

Peter Smith went to speak but Petrov put his hand firmly in the air to allow him a chance to make a reply.

"Mr Speed, or should I say, Stirling, as you prefer to be called, these were not my dogs. I can assure you that I had no part in this. I will...."

Stirling was in no mood for diplomacy.

"And you expect me, us, to believe you, a man that has had his legal teams costing me a fortune, had me locked up in a Spanish prison on a trumped-up drugs charge and has made it clear that his honour will be had, whatever that means? Get out of my house before I call the police."

Now it was Peter Smith's turn to put his hand up to stop Petrov's reply. Sian moved round to the side of the defensive Stirling, maybe in a move to demonstrate whose side she was on, or maybe as an act of reassurance.

"Mr Petrov is now on our side Stirling. He knows who did this to you. He has the full story. You really need to listen."

Stirling showed a slight acceptance by easing back in his seat, his battered body relieved that no further exertion was required.

Petrov looked at Peter Smith who motioned for him to sit down. Petrov responded by carefully removing his coat which he laid over the back of his chair and then carefully sat down whilst pulling at his crisply creased, immaculate trousers to ensure that he left no knee marks. He then fixed his steely eyes on Stirling's.

"I find myself in an embarrassing situation where I have gravely misjudged you. Mr Peter Smith has told me about his organisation and the involvement in it that you and young Sian have. I now realise that I am in debt to you. Allow me to tell you why I have arrived at this conclusion. Let me assure you that you will be compensated for any expense I have caused you and let me tell you all you need to know about Gray Grand Prix, Richard Gray, Ross Keane, Sam Keane and the tragic Rosalie. As you now know, my Sergio has woken and is on a journey of recovery. I have now found out that you saved his life by responding so quickly to his injuries by contacting Charles Thomas, the world's leading neurologist. He now tells me that *you* paid to have him flown in by private jet and have been funding his fees ever since!"

Petrov paused for a response from Stirling. Sian squeezed Stirling's arm.

"You see, you're not a grumpy old man after all."

Stirling responded to Petrov.

"The kid needed a break."

Petrov continued,

"When Sergio came round, the first words that he was softly able to utter were, 'I beat him dad, three times world champion, I was faster Dad, are you proud of me?'"

Petrov turned to Peter Smith.

"Do you know why my son was able to say these words to me, despite him being slower on that tragic day?"

Petrov allowed no chance for anyone to answer and outstretched his hand in the direction of Stirling.

"When my son's eyes closed before slipping into his terrifying coma the last person to speak to him was Stirling, who reassured him that he would be okay and that he had proved his point by showing he was faster."

Petrov's eyes were watery and risking an overflow as he desperately blinked.

"How could I have been so wrong about a person? How can I ever repay you for the life of my son?"

Stirling didn't like being put on a pedestal and responded again with,

"Like I say, the kid needed a break. I am glad he pulled through. Maybe now's the time to think about where to go with him. I think you have a good guy there, but he drives like he has the weight of the world on his shoulders. He..."

"I am the weight. I thought I was pushing him to be the best. Thank you, Stirling. My son is my life."

"Mr Petrov, instead of pushing him to be the best, why not push for what is best for him?"

"Stirling, let me attempt to repay my debt to you by telling you the story of Gray Grand Prix."

Chapter 53

"Eunice, it's Stirling. Eunice, we have had some developments. Are you OK to talk?"

"I promised I would keep you up to speed. I really think we are making headway as to what happened to Rosalie. The problem we have is that, as of yet, we have no evidence!"

"No, we were all wrong. It turns out that Petrov is not the bad guy, well he is, but not with what we are dealing with. Ross had his own issues. Eunice, this is in strictest confidence, but I said I would keep you up to speed. It looks like the person behind all this is actually Richard Gray."

"I know what you are saying, but all we have is Petrov's version. We have no hard evidence. We are not stopping here; trust me I will keep going until I have this guy."

"Yes, you can help. Think back over that time. Think of anything that could link Richard Gray. Anything out of the norm. Anything Rosalie said."

"We can't do that, we actually have nothing on him, we are not where we started, this is a step forward. I'll get him Eunice, I'll get him."

"The next step is that we are doing some behind the scenes digging around but I am going to confront him and see what his reaction is. Sometimes when you get your target on the ropes they lash out and end up dropping their defence."

"No problem, keep positive. I'll call again soon. Feel free to contact me anytime if you think of anything. You have my number and if I am not available call my housekeeper. Please do try not to worry and be patient. I will flush him out."

Petrov's version of events had left all three in the room almost gasping for air.

Petrov had settled in to reveal all. He had a debt to pay.

"Stirling, you first have to know what my business is. I am a bank to the world of gambling. I supply the loans that give the chance for the low rollers to become the high rollers. You want to gamble big then I will back you. You may be disgusted with that, but my business survives because people want my service, and some have become very wealthy thanks to my loans. Some of the legitimate household names you know today got their original start-up money from gambling with my money. The other, what you might say, more ugly side of my business, are the ones that just keep chasing their dream and losing. One of your very own English football super stars used my money to keep funding his addiction after his retirement. But Stirling, you have to remember that loans need paying back. I cannot go to court for one of your wind-up orders. I get my loans paid by fear. You refuse to pay, and bad things happen. They know what they are getting into Stirling, they are adults.

A big loser was brought to my attention, his name was Ross Keane. The next bet was always the one to set things straight."

Stirling made a gesture with a raised finger to pause the roll of the Russian accent.

"What sort of money are we talking about here?"

Petrov thought for a moment, clearly wanting to show respect for Stirling and not just clutch a random figure out of the air.

"Stirling we are talking a long time ago and I could get you an exact figure, but in Ross's case we are talking in excess of ten million."

At this point, Sian had been unable to keep her mouth under control.

"Bonte divine! We are talking big rollers here, ten million!"

"Young Sian trust me when I say that this figure is only the tip of the iceberg in the world of international gambling. These people have only their lives to offer as collateral! I have to maintain a culture of fear otherwise my business is no more. Ross was fearing for his life when he was brought in to see me. He offered me the only thing he had left, his involvement with Gray Grand Prix! My son was karting, and he said that he wanted to race Formula One. Ross Keane opened up an opportunity for me, and a lifeline for himself. Gray Grand Prix had lost a large sponsor and things were not going well. Richard was fighting for survival; he had invested heavily in his Gray Grand Prix Centre. I had the money to put his team back on the map. The only condition was that one day my son Sergio would race Formula One. Unfortunately, the timing of my approach to Richard through Ross was poor. I soon realised Gray Grand Prix was like a son to Richard, he would do anything to protect it. In an effort to save his team Richard had just paid a lot of money to a Stragatti employee to find out how their successful deflecting wing system worked. Other than that, all seemed good. I had my Grand Prix team for my son, Richard could save his team, and I would write off Ross's gambling debts. But this was all to turn sour with a simple mistake when young Rosalie, who was a, I think you call them, 'PA' to Richard and Ross, was mistakenly given a memory stick by Ross. The memory stick clearly held on it sensitive Stragatti material. Realising what he had done, Ross feared the deal with me would disappear if the industrial espionage was discovered. He panicked and went to see the girl instead of consulting Richard or me first. The girl realised then that Gray Grand Prix had stolen technical information and was put in a difficult position. This is when I became aware of what Richard had done. Richard flew into a rage, screaming at Ross how he could be so stupid. Now all their lives and the future of Gray Grand Prix was held in the hands of a young girl because of stupidity."

Sian had broken the roll Petrov was on.

"Gray Grand Prix was in that position because Richard Gray had stolen intellectual property. He had cheated in a game worth millions!"

"In the end, Rosalie made the decision to go to the Federation of International Autosport and tell them what had happened at Gray Grand Prix. If the news had broken then, the team would have been finished. I would have lost what I required, a future for my Sergio. The deal I was offering to Richard and Ross was then off. I made it clear that to protect my investment we needed to bury the story. I was needing Richard to be completely distanced from the situation. I did not want Ross the chief designer and future of Gray Grand Prix to be involved. I was investing in the team's future and that of my son. So, Ross came up with the idea of involving his sister, Sam. She was having a hard time and, coincidentally, worked for Stragatti. It all fitted. I agreed as part of my investment into the team to pay her ten million pounds to go to prison and take the rap.

Stirling could not hold back. Peter Smith tried to stop Stirling in order to allow the tragic story to continue to unfold, but Stirling wanted answers.

"So, you had the young girl killed for doing what she thought was morally right?"

"Stirling, you must believe me, I had nothing to do with the death of the girl. I create an image that I am a ruthless man, I create an illusion of fear but that is all it is, an illusion. I was in Russia at a time when men in certain positions made a lot of money from the privatisation of some of Russia's resources. I came to the UK and people had already formed an opinion of me. 'This bad guy from Russia'. Stirling, I was a director of a large electricity supplier. I was in the right place at the right time. My money gave me the chance to bolster an image that people already had of me. Stirling, you may see me as a glorified loan shark, a bully, a gangster, but I am not a murderer. You must trust me on that."

Peter Smith remained tight lipped, whilst Sian sat, eyes wide, her mouth slightly ajar.

Stirling continued his uncertain stance.

"OK, so who killed the girl and, why, if you had a plan?"

Petrov did not keep them waiting and replied instantly.

"Richard Gray."

Sian let out an involuntary,

"No!"

Stirling continued,

"And you know this for certain?"

"Yes, Stirling, I do."

"How? How do you know for certain?"

"In my line of business Stirling, you learn to read people, you learn to know what is going on. I know what he did."

Peter Smith now spoke up.

"So how did you know?"

"I was OK with the cover story and Sam Keane was on board with it. She was helping her brother and she would become a wealthy young lady. She had no complaints."

Stirling felt a slight twinge deep inside of him. Petrov continued.

"I did express a concern about just how much the young Rosalie actually knew. Was she aware that it was actually Richard behind the industrial espionage? Was she aware of Ross's involvement with me? I was investing a lot of money. I needed to know that there would still be a team to invest in. Richard replied that he would deal with the matter and make sure that assurances were put in place. Never at that point did I consider what he would do, never.

We were all due to fly out in the company jet to the launch and test of the new car. Richard did not turn up for the flight. I remember that well. Neither did the young girl, so we flew without them. When we arrived, the plane refuelled, turned back around, and flew back to the UK to pick up Richard who joined us later in the day. It was a few days later that the news broke that the poor young girl had been found at her home, poisoned."

The silence in the room at this point was deafening so Petrov continued.

"During the police investigation I refused any comment or to make any statements, but I did become aware that on Ross's statement he claimed that Richard had been on the initial flight, but not the young girl. He was definitely not on the first flight with us. I brought this to Richard's attention. Remember that Richard not only saw me as his lifeline but also, he saw me as a ruthless man to be feared. A man that would go to any lengths to get his money back. Maybe he wanted to play the same game, balance the power maybe, I do not know, but he looked at me and stared at me in the face and I remember he said, 'Whilst you were enjoying the 'in flight' hospitality I was dealing with the matter'. When I enquired 'what matter?' he said, 'you know exactly which matter'. As you may know, Richard has a garden within Gray Grand Prix with exotic plants from all over the world. He is obsessed with the place and we have had many a discussion about the outrageous cost of it. He then referred to this place. He said 'my oasis that you dismiss doesn't just grow pretty flowers, it can protect itself when it wants to, and it just saved our bacon'. I learned later what this expression meant."

Petrov paused for his next point.

"I think the poison that killed young Rosalie was grown there and he somehow tricked her into consuming it."

Stirling went to talk but Peter Smith spoke over him.

"But you still went ahead with your investment, even though you suspected a murder?"

Petrov swivelled on his chair and turned his whole body to face Peter Smith.

"I can only answer, yes, I did. I was desperate to make the deal work. This was Sergio's route into Formula One."

Peter Smith stood up and walked over to the window that overlooked the meadow outside.

Sian spoke.

"All this just to get Sergio into Formula One?"

"Sian, many fathers would do the same. I had the opportunity and the resources to buy into an F1 team. Stirling, you know that these days, fathers have paid millions to see their sons race Formula One, I know families involved in money laundering, drug smuggling, gambling, just to see their loved one race in Formula One. I know families that have mortgaged their homes to see their sons climb to the top of this sport. I am not the only father to have bought a Grand Prix team for their son. I make no excuses. Stirling, you must have seen this."

Stirling replied,

"In my day, the driver made the sacrifices, not the family."

Sian spoke again.

"Forget the 'spy-gate' deceit, a girl was murdered, a young girl!"

"I had nothing to do with the murder."

Petrov then swung his body back towards Stirling.

"Stirling, I am in debt to you. I have told you all I can. I am not here to be judged, I am not here to seek forgiveness, I am here to pay my debt. I will help in any way I can to achieve the justice that you are wanting."

Peter Smith returned from the window.

"Stirling, we need to nail Richard Gray. You confront him full on with the accusation and let's see what response that flushes out. I am going get someone into that Oasis of his and see if we can dig up the poison that killed Rosalie."

Peter Smith then turned to Petrov.

"My organisation has to exist because people like you, Mr Petrov, muddy the waters where bottom dwellers like Gray exist.

Do not think that we are grateful for your speech and exposé. If it wasn't for you, we would not be in this room together dealing with the murder of an innocent young girl who was just trying to do what was right."

Peter Smith then turned to Stirling.

"Do you mind if I stay here tonight? I need a shower!"

He then turned to Petrov and stared deep into his blue eyes.

"Sometimes in my job I feel soiled!"

The room was swallowed in quietness until Petrov stood and left.

Chapter 54

"You should let me drive. Twenty-four hours of rest, I can assure you, has not improved your looks."

Stirling looked across the confines of his E type and smiled at the young and eager Sian. The smile did indeed cause a pain across his bruised and still misshapen face.

"What doesn't kill you, Sian, makes you stronger, or so the saying goes. What the saying does not include is just how painful it is when you are not dead!"

"Go on then, tell me what Peter Smith has come up with."

Sian was referring to a call that Stirling had taken just before they had set off on their journey to see Richard Gray.

"Apparently they have found the baseball bat experts that practiced their profession on me. It didn't take long for them to cave in. They were indeed working for Richard Gray, they knew nothing of Petrov. Peter feels that Richard arranged it to take the heat off him and made it look like a Petrov hit. He has also tracked down the soil expert that Richard had in."

Sian interrupted.

"Excellent. That was my little tip off, thank you very much. I remembered that a soil guy had visited."

"Well done Sian."

Sian tilted her head slightly and smiled approvingly at Stirling's compliment!

Stirling continued after a slight pause to accept Sian's smug smile.

"Apparently Richard has some pretty nasty things growing amongst his pansies, including the root that poisoned Rosalie."

"Wow, so we have him!"

"It does appear that Petrov's story all fits, but there is nothing to tie Richard to the death. At least we have a few things to throw at him. Are you going be okay Sian, being with me, when I confront Richard?"

Sian formed a fist with her right hand.

"To use one of your English sayings, 'hell yes'!"

After a period of contemplation Sian grasped the nettle.

"And Sam?"

Stirling concentrated on the road ahead and replied, "What about her?"

"She liked you, Stirling. People make mistakes. There is nothing wrong with you letting your guard down."

There was a delay before Stirling responded.

"She's a fraud, a fraud that was complicit in the murder of an innocent young girl."

"Will you see her again, now everything is out?"

The Jag suddenly, uncharacteristically, swung out onto the other side of the road, the engine barking as Stirling hung onto each gear change and swiped away a batch of four ambling cars. Sian was aware of the wet road they were on and the right-hand bend that was now approaching at a rapid rate. Stirling swung the howling Jag back on to the right side of the road, dabbed the brake, blipped the throttle and quickly changed down a gear, the exhaust crackling and popping as a result of the overrun engine. Then, as the nose of the Jaguar eased into the direction of the corner, Stirling stroked the throttle. The rear tyres played with the reduced traction that the wet road offered. The balanced but wayward slide helped the car into the direction it needed to go, dictated by the stone wall to Sian's left. The cars that Stirling had just overtaken were nowhere to be seen in the rear-view mirror as Stirling rolled the steering off on the exit of the corner and accelerated up the country lane.

Sian waited for Stirling's response, wondering whether she had overstepped the mark with him.

"I don't deal with frauds. I don't want complications, sometimes all I want to do is drive!"

The security man at Gray Grand Prix recognised the battleship grey E Type the moment it nosed around the corner.

"Mr Speed! Welcome to Gray Grand Prix again. I trust you have an appointment?"

Clasping his clip board more firmly to his chest he stooped down to confront his nemesis.

"Now then, young Miss Sian, could I trouble you for your pass?"

Sian bit her bottom lip, put on her best smile, cranked up her French accent, blinked and replied.

"I am afraid I have not got a pass, sorry."

"And we know why we have not got a pass don't we young Sian?"

"Because I have lost it?"

"No, because you do not work here anymore, do you Miss Sian?"

Sian dropped her smile.

"Really, so you are not going to let me in, yet you're quite happy to let Sir Stirling Speed in without a pass? What's all that about?"

"Because you have not won three world championships and because when you did work here, if you remember, you did not make my life easy did you?"

Sian sat back in her seat and folded her arms.

"Stirling, you need to sort this out. This guy is so grump…"

The security man winked at Stirling.

"On this occasion, Miss Sian, because you are in the company of Mr Speed, I think I will allow you in. Just this once, mind."

Stirling turned to Sian.

"Say something nice to the kind gent Sian."

"'Thank you' is the best you are going to get. Now nail it Stirling and leave some lines on his polished entrance. He hates it."

Stirling thanked the kind man and eased into the car park looking for the visitor's section.

After a little while of sitting in the reception of Gray Grand Prix, Sian got up and started to examine the wall of trophies.

"How come you never drove for Gray?"

Stirling looked up.

"Oh, I was never one for jumping around teams. I needed to feel comfortable with my surroundings and perhaps the right package was never available for me."

"You mean they couldn't afford you?"

"It was always about the driving for me. If I had a competitive car, I knew I would enjoy the driving, and the winning would come easily. With the winning, I suppose came the money, but money was never first on my wish list."

"Mr Speed I am afraid it appears…."

"Can I nip to the loo? I am so bursting."

The overly polite receptionist stopped her apology and turned to Sian, who was emphasising her predicament by crossing her legs and pulling a strange face. The receptionist had never been keen on Sian during the brief period that she had worked there. A little too 'familiar.'

"You know where to go."

Sian did not need any further encouragement and disappeared straight into the offices, instead of using the toilets which were clearly signposted in the reception area.

The receptionist went to stop Sian, then relented and turned her attention back to Stirling.

"Mr Speed, I am afraid there has been a little confusion. I am afraid Mr Gray is not in. He has apparently rushed out on urgent business."

"Please, just call me Stirling. Do you know when he is likely to be back?"

"I am sorry Mr Speed, but I really have no idea. He might head straight home rather than return to the office. I am sure you will have his mobile number. I will also leave a message for him that you have called."

"I do have his number, but he is not answering. OK I'll sit here and wait for Sian. Thank you for your trouble."

The receptionist smiled, somehow falsely and pleasantly at the same time, then returned back to her immaculate glass table and commenced tapping away on her keyboard.

An uncomfortable period of time passed. The receptionist looked several times at the small gold watch on her wrist. Considering that the time was displayed on her computer screen, the sole purpose of this exercise was to show Stirling that she felt that Sian's visit to the toilets was taking much longer than would usually be expected. Stirling smiled back to acknowledge that he agreed, Sian *was* taking too long. Finally, Sian came bustling though the door. She turned to the receptionist without breaking her stride.

"Sorry. Tummy trouble. Not nice!"

Sian then flicked her gaze back to Stirling.

"Stirling, we have to go, now!

Stirling put down the Motorsport magazine he'd been flicking through and turned to say goodbye, but his arm was caught by the returning Sian.

"Stirling, we really have to go now. I think Eunice is in trouble!"

Chapter 55

Stirling backed his Jag out into the car park, grabbed a foot full of revs and jumped off the clutch. The back of the launching Jaguar swung wildly to the left, so Stirling did not waste any time winding on an ample amount of left-hand lock to tame the slide. The security man rushed out of his little glass office leaving his clipboard behind as the din of a hot Jaguar engine earning its living hit his ears. The automatic barrier rose just in time for the sleek body to race underneath it. Stirling found third gear and accelerated hard up the straight tree lined Gray Grand Prix driveway.

"Stirling, I went into my Gray Grand Prix email account which is still live. All of Richard's open business emails were automatically copied onto mine so that I could deal with them, to save Richard having to go through them all."

Stirling busied himself with another gear change and flashed Sian an exasperated look.

"Sian, get to the point and speak up!"

Sian increased her volume to get on top of the Jaguar that was clearly enjoying being let off its leash.

"I noticed an email exchange between Richard and Doctor Campos, Eunice Stirling."

Stirling was now in full concentration mode as his Jaguar ate up the wet tarmac of the dual carriageway they were presently travelling on, at MPH speeds that included 3 figures.

"I know who Doctor Campos is."

"Well, Eunice has sent an email to Richard Gray saying that they need to meet at the cottage. She wanted to discuss the murder of Rosalie. She said that she had found camera footage of the day Rosalie died. She claims it was a nature watch camera that was set up to watch a nest. Stirling, she says in the email that she is open to a deal to keep her quiet. Richard responded straight away and arranged to meet her at 1:30 p.m. That is the urgent business he has rushed out on! He has tried to delete the emails but forgot that they copied onto my email account."

Stirling maintained his silence and thought through the information that he had just been given.

"Stirling what do you think? Would she really be prepared to do a deal with Richard? Do you think she's is in danger?"

The Jaguar panted to a steaming stop for a glowing red light.

"Here, Sian, check the messages on my phone."

Sian flicked through Stirling's phone.

"Nothing on text, nothing on WhatsApp. Should I check your emails?"

"Voice mails! Check them. I am terrible for checking my phone."

"Stirling. you really are ready for an upgrade you know, I can…"

"Sian! The voicemails!"

"Nothing appears to be from Eunice, erm, the only one I recognise is from your housekeeper."

"Put that one on loudspeaker."

The Jaguar reluctantly and frustratedly eased its pace as the road developed a bout of traffic congestion.

The voice of Stirling's housekeeper could be heard loud and clear:

"Stirling, a Doctor Campos has been trying to get hold of you urgently and, guess what? You are not answering your phone! She said she did not want to risk leaving a message in case you didn't get it, and now that is exactly what *I* am having to do. Apparently, she has arranged a meeting with a Richard Gray at 'the cottage'? I assume you know where that is! The appointment is at 3 p.m. She said to tell you it's payback time! Stirling, she did sound a little crazy I have to say, even a little giddy. Anyway, I am sure it will make more sense to…."

The message time had run out.

Stirling angled his wrist up whilst still holding onto the wood rimmed steering wheel so that he could see his watch. The gold IWC Portugieser automatic 7-day power reserve showed 2:35 p.m.!

He pulled out from the congestion, ran a barrage of horns, cleared the junction causing the delay, and hit the loud pedal again.

"3.00 pm? The email said 1:30! What do you think Stirling, do you think she is in danger?"

"I think she has decided to take matters into her own hands and yes, she is in major danger. She has baited Gray. If what we know about Richard Gray is true, he will stop at nothing to save his beloved team! She clearly didn't want us there at 1:30. This is not good Sian."

"She has camera footage?"

"No, I asked her about that. She definitely has not. That's a ploy to hook Gray. I really worry whether or not she has thought this through! Hopefully, she won't go through with anything until we arrive. It's going to be hard to break Gray down. What is she thinking?"

Stirling slid the E Type to a stop at the top of the car park. The gate in the corner blocked further progress.

"Arrgh, the combination, I can't remember it!"

"1-9-1-4. What? Don't look at me like that! I might look a bit dizzy; I might *be* a bit dizzy, but I've got it all going on up here!"

"Leave the gate open Sian, just jump in."

Sian had not shut the car door before Stirling had the Jaguar fish tailing up the country track, spraying mud up the flanks of the classic as if it were a rally car. They were greeted with an empty car park.

"2:56. It looks like we have made it to the party on time and no Richard yet."

Stirling went to shut down the hot and sticky rumbling straight-six engine, then thought better of it.

"Maybe I should park behind the cottage and keep this out of view whilst we talk to Eunice and find out what on earth she is planning."

With the Jaguar secreted away, Sian and Stirling walked around to the front door. Still no Richard. The door opened without resistance.

"Eunice, it's Stirling! Are you around?"

Sian looked at Stirling enquiringly.

"She'll be out in the woods. She is a bit, well, crazy. Actually, she's more than a bit crazy, but in a nice way!"

Stirling allowed himself a slight smile.

"Why are we not all like that? A bit crazy. We'll wait in the kitchen."

Sian looked back at Stirling and pointed to a closed door, questioning whether that was the kitchen, to which Stirling replied with a nod before turning to close the front door.

The door had not completed its click before all sound was obliterated by a high pitched,

"Stirling!"

Stirling knew by the pitch of his screamed name what he was going to see before the horrendous image registered with his eyes. Sian stood, staring, her hand held to her mouth. Stirling followed her stare.

"Eunice no, no, no, no!"

Eunice's hideously contorted figure lay crunched up on the floor, her aging legs showing indecently. Her pained face with bulging eyes and tongue stared back up at the outraged faces of Stirling and Sian. Her unruly hair was matted with her own vomit.

Sian backed out of the room gasping to find a breath. Stirling dropped onto his knees.

"Eunice why, why did you do this? I had this Eunice, I had it."

Eunice's lifeless body held no reply.

Chapter 56

"OK, before we get in to see Mr Gray let's get a few things clear. One. I have no idea why you two are being allowed into this voluntary, may I emphasise, *voluntary*, interview that Mr Gray has agreed to. Two. Remember that we have nothing on Mr Gray, so we have to tread very, very, carefully. And Three. Remember I am the boss here. I don't care what organisation *you* are in charge of, and I really, really don't care how many championships *you* have won driving round in circles."

The balding, possibly fifty-year-old, detective wore his soft collared shirt and tightly knotted but loosely fitting purple tie with distaste. From the moment they had met in the Gray Grand Prix car park he had made it clear that he was only there because his boss had made him be there. He had bypassed Stirling's outstretched hand and spoken directly to Peter Smith.

"It appears, young man, that you have friends in high places. Well, the law is the law no matter what stratosphere your friends inhabit."

He then turned his creased, slightly turned up leather shoes in the direction of the reception and strode off.

Stirling was happy to let the moment go, but Peter Smith who had been showing the stress of the case was not.

"Just remember Sergeant,"

The bait was taken straight away.

"It's Inspector."

Peter Smith was ready with a reply after the expected response.

"Exactly, and if you want to keep that Inspector title, you'd better start respecting your superiors and be sure to do a good job when we get in there, otherwise my 'friends in stratosphere places' will be showing you pity if they allow you to keep even a Constable title never mind a Sergeant one!"

The inspector held back his reply.

Stirling made a note to self:

Must get Peter Smith to take a holiday when this case is finished.

"Mr Gray will see you in the Glasshouse. If you could follow me."

Stirling could not help noticing that this annoyed Peter Smith, but he chose to swallow what he wanted to say. The inspector jumped at the idea.

"Thank you miss, no problem at all."

This unusually also seemed to irritate Peter Smith even more. A man who usually showed no emotion. A man who usually blended into the crowd. A man who usually drifted through the shallows almost invisible until the time was right to strike.

Richard was found cross-legged sitting in front of his pond surrounded by flora exotica from around the world.

"Gentlemen, hello and welcome. I hope you do not mind meeting here instead of my stuffy office. The tragic death of Dr Campos is so difficult to take on board and of course it has brought back the hideous memories of poor Rosie. Please make yourselves comfortable. Stirling, good to see you. How are you? Fancy you being involved in a crime fighting organisation! I never would have foreseen that one."

Richard next turned his head to his waiting receptionist.

"Thank you, Michelle."

Then to Peter Smith and the inspector who had unfortunately ended up on the same bench together.

"The Stirling we all admired during his racing career was scarily focused. If it did not involve making him faster, then he really was not interested."

Richard turned his head and stared into his pond.

"He was a quick boy. If only he could have raced for us. How did you not end up racing for us Stirling?"

Peter Smith got to the point.

"Mr Gray, we have some rather uncomfortable questions for you."

The inspector sat forward in an attempt to start the questions.

"Mr Gray,"

Who replied,

"Tony, good to see you again. The family good?"

"Yes, Mr Gray they are good, thank you. Beth said to say hello."

Stirling glanced at Peter Smith who was looking incredulously at the inspector and appeared almost unable to speak, so Stirling stepped up to the mark.

"You two know each other?"

The inspector proudly turned to Stirling.

"Oh yes. Mr Gray has been a very influential figure as president of my wife's charity. It is a local knitting and crocheting charity that produces garments for people in need and also takes men and women off the streets and teaches them how to make jumpers and things for themselves. Richard, I mean Mr Gray has really…"

Peter Smith had by this point decided he was going to lead the questions.

"Mr Gray, you are aware of how Rosie and now Doctor Campos died?"

Richard Gray put his hand up to his pocket inspector as if to say, 'let it go'.

"Yes, such tragic accidents, I presume the two deaths are somehow linked?"

"So, you know that they were poisoned Richard. Do you know how?"

Richard looked around his glass house at his flora.

"Sadly, I do. My life is my race team. My passion is my flora."

He hesitated, drifting somewhere else.

"When Rosalie came for her interview, we spent more time talking about flora than the job. Her grandmother was a professor at the university and researched lots of flora aspects, you know. Such a lovely girl. She would bring me in herbal teas that her grandmother and Doctor Campos had made up."

"Eunice."

Stirling interjected.

"Sorry?"

"Eunice hated to be called Doctor Campos, she preferred Eunice. So, you knew Eunice."

Richard continued.

"Oh yes, Eunice visited my glasshouse and would unlock the secrets of my garden. She also invited me on a few occasions to Rosie's cottage to show me round the preservation. When Rosie had her tragic accident, she came in to see me and we both had a long chat to make sure we and the police had not missed anything. Rosie was such a special girl and so much more to me and the team than just an efficient PA. We named the canteen and rest area after her. So tragic."

"Maybe you can now have the 'Eunice engine assembly workshop'."

Peter Smith sarcastically added. Richard eyed Peter Smith who reciprocated.

"Mr Smith, you are a private investigator?"

"I head The Special Investigations Bureau, a worldwide organisation. We right injustices, we step up when the police have been left with no more options or, in some cases, do not want to look at more options. We always get our man."

"Or woman?"

Richard added, and then continued,

"I can't help feeling that there is some hostility towards me here. Let's get the cards on the table. I was under the impression that we were here to form a thinktank about these two horrific deaths. I am getting the feeling that there is another agenda here."

Peter Smith went straight for a reaction.

"I think the link between these two murders is *you*, Mr Gray. I think you had these persons murdered to protect your beloved team."

The inspected jumped and nearly fell over his own words.

"Stop, stop! Sorry Richard, this interview is finished. You two, out now!"

Richard again put his hand up to stem the stuttering inspector.

"It's OK."

"No, this interview stops, they have nothing on you, Richard. They are fishing, they are...."

"Tony shut up and sit down or get out!"

The inspector stared at Richard, hovered, then slowly backed up to his seat next to Peter Smith.

Richard looked at Stirling.

"You feel the same?"

"I think there are questions that need to be answered Richard."

"Then let's get these questions answered and then we can get on with our respective and, no doubt, busy days."

Chapter 57

Peter Smith was happy that the politeness games were out of the way.

"You know that both were poisoned by Hemlock Water Dropwort?"

"Oenanthe Crocata, Yes Mr Smith, I do know that."

"A poisonous root that can be found around this very pond that we are sitting around."

Richard seemed slightly wrong footed with that statement and so chose not to cover up his thoughts.

"I am not sure how you know that, but yes, I am sure you would be able to find an example somewhere around here, it is part of my fascination with flora. People think of pleasant-smelling beautiful flowers when they think of flora but actually, flora can bite back if it feels threatened."

Peter Smith continued his onslaught.

"You received an email from Eunice in which she claimed to have identified the killer and made an inference that you were that person and that she might do a deal to keep quiet."

Richard did not seem rocked by this at all.

"OK, let's get all the questions and accusations out on the table and then I will attempt to answer them all, hopefully to your satisfaction."

Peter Smith continued with his statement questions.

"Mr Petrov has gone into great detail regarding the spy-gate, his relationship with you, Ross, Sam Keane and his feeling that you did, in fact, murder Rosalie."

"Anything else?"

"The men that attacked Stirling claim that they were paid by you."

"OK, are you sure that's everything, you don't want to blame any world economy problems on me?"

Stirling spoke up.

"This is not a joking matter Richard. Two people have been murdered."

"I agree Stirling, and I don't agree. I agree this is certainly no joking matter. I do not take kindly to being accused of being a murderer. I do not agree that we are looking at two murders here though. May be an accident and a suicide? But to answer your questions in order,"

The inspector vainly tried to get control of the situation again.

"Richard, I must emphasise, you do not have to answer these questions."

Richard replied with a withering look that clearly said 'shut up'.

"Hemlock Water Dropwort does indeed grow in other places other than around my pond."

Stirling held onto the point.

"None was found near the cottage, Richard."

"None was found at the time of the investigation, Stirling. This particular species likes damp, swampy conditions, that can occur at different times of the year around the cottage. Did you also know that people often get the species mixed up? Firstly, people will get the name mixed up with similar sounding plants, water hemlock and hemlock. Secondly, when foraging, something that Rosie and Eunice did often, it is easy to get the poisonous plant mixed up with similar looking plants such as wild parsnip, sweet flag, or pig nut. I am afraid it was just a tragic, tragic accident."

"Rosie or Eunice would not have made that mistake."

Peter Smith answered.

"Are you sure Peter? You seemed sure that I somehow murdered the two of them. Is that presumption more ludicrous then possibly making a mistake that sadly other people have made? The email? Yes, I received an email from Eunice. I presume Sian saw that when she entered, unauthorised, into my offices to use the toilet. We'll let that go. As soon as I saw the rambling email, I immediately forwarded it to the inspector here."

Stirling and Peter both turned at the same time and looked at the inspector.

"Yes. I can confirm that we received that email."

After a short empty pause Stirling held out his arms.

"And? What did you do with it?"

"We have not had a chance to look into it yet, but obviously it is on our priority list to...."

Peter Smith ignored his pointless response.

"Spy-gate? Mr Petrov?"

"The spy-gate as you call it was thoroughly investigated by the police and taken through the courts. It was clearly shown that I knew nothing of it. The girl behind it all got her just desserts. Ross, who was sadly a flawed genius, racked himself with guilt and paid the price literally, morally and eventually fatally, with his life. As regards Petrov. He wants my team for a plaything for his son. For many years he has tried legally and illegally to wrestle the ownership of my team from me. Clearly his latest tactic is to frame me for murder."

Richard turned to Peter Smith.

"I'm betting the guys who messed up Stirling's world championship looks rolled over easily?"

Peter made no reply.

"I thought so. They were paid to stitch me up by Petrov."

Stirling continued picking.

"Petrov said that you were not on the flight the day the Rosalie girl died? He also said that Ross put in his statement that you were?"

"I admit Stirling, we were firefighting during that period. We'd lost a major sponsor at just the wrong time after I had invested heavily in the Gray Grand Prix Centre. Ross, as you know, had major gambling problems, hence the reason Petrov came on the scene. The Stragatti spy scandal then heaped on yet more pressure. We desperately needed Petrov's Rubles. Ross then dropped a further bombshell on me that he was being chased by another gambling syndicate. I decided that rather than chance losing the Petrov deal I would sort it. Which is what I did when they flew out for the test. I paid off another group of undesirables to get them off Ross's back. I was trying to create a fresh start. We hid that from Petrov and decided that it was something that the police did not need to know about either."

Stirling looked with slight bewilderment at Peter Smith to get insight as to where they should go next.

Peter Smith continued.

"And you can prove what you have just told us?"

Richard Gray sat back in his wicker chair and looked out over his pond, then back at Peter Smith.

"No. I can't."

He left a big enough pause for a reply, but since none was forthcoming he posed a poignant question.

"Can you prove your accusation against me?"

No reply came in the next pause either.

Stirling attempted to balance the discussion.

"OK Richard, we have known each other around the circuits for a long time. Tell me, honestly, what do you really think happened to Rosie and Eunice?"

"You are not going to like what I am going to say, but for what it's worth... honestly, I think you have both been taken on a ride by a crook, Petrov. He has mixed a few truths with a few lies and made a toxic concoction. I think tragically about Rosie that she simply drank a tea made for her, prepared for her, or left for her, who knows the exact scenario? I think that tea was mistakenly made from Hemlock Water Dropwort by Dr Eunice Campos. I am afraid to say that I think Eunice, who could, I think we all agree, be a little dizzy, simply and tragically messed up! She was always experimenting with different teas just like Rosie's grandmother did. Rosie once told me that her father named Rosie after his mother's passion for teas, Rosie-lee..."

Peter Smith interrupted

"Cockney slang for a cup of tea, I believe."

"Yes. Guys, I think Eunice made a tragic mistake. I think she spent years racked with grief that affected her sanity. When you started mooching around it all reared its ugly head again. Then when you told her that it was me who had murdered Rosie, it was not a big step for her to move the blame to me. Peter, Stirling, there is nothing to find here. Petrov wants my company, Sam Keane is now paralysed with guilt after her brother's suicide, and somehow blames me and wants my blood. With poor Rosie it was just a tragic accident and in the end Eunice could not live with it anymore and brought her own pain to an end. I agree it is a horrendous sequence of events but really, I am the innocent one here, just trying to keep my head above water and keep the team that I have devoted my whole life to, from disappearing."

Peter Smith and Stirling both looked out of their respective BMW back seat side windows at nothing, their minds too occupied combing through all the information that needed processing and reprocessing as their driver picked her way through the traffic choked evening.

"Peter."

Peter Smith broke his absent gaze and gave Stirling his weary attention.

"Peter, how did Richard Gray know that I had told Eunice that I thought it was him behind it all?"

Chapter 58

"Your housekeeper said I would find you here."

Stirling broke his gaze from the Super Classic Club Formula Ford race that was raging out on the track and looked down at the smiling Sian.

"You have yourself a good little set up there, Mr Speedy."

Stirling sat high up on the banking at the scenic Cheshire Oulton Park race circuit overlooking the Avenue section of track that ran down to the tricky, critical left-hand corner, Cascades. He sat on one of two low-slung orange deckchairs set up, actually, in the back of his car - the large back door of his Series 2 Green Land Rover Discovery swung open giving a clear view of the track but not allowing passing race fans a clear view of the three-time world champion of their sport.

"Jump up young lady and enjoy my exclusive seats."

Sian climbed onto the sprung hydraulic assisted step, onto the rubber bumper and then swivelled round and down onto the low-slung chair.

"What a grandstand."

Sian's voice was drowned out as the buzz of angry jostling Formula Ford single seater race cars appeared over the brow and chased down towards the entry of the third gear left-hand corner in what can only be called a tangled side-by-side mess. As the multi-coloured cars and bobbing helmets negotiated the undulating entry, amongst pops from the exhausts and downward gear changes amazingly, the what seemed like inevitable crash was avoided as all the cars found some sort of order as they understeered and oversteered their way towards the late apex and then screamed off, jostling for position again up the climbing straight.

"Wow, that's close racing! Awesome."

"We'll see who's leading when they come over the brow and into view, about now, as they go down the back straight."

Stirling became aware that Sian was not looking at the circuit and was looking directly at him.

"You OK Stirling? You've been hard to get hold of lately."

Stirling broke his gaze of escapism and looked directly back at Sian.

"I hate losing Sian. I hate it. Have you spoken to Peter? Any news?"

"He's taking that break that we both told him to take, now that we can't go any further with the case and, no, there has been no further news. Like Peter said, we don't always get our man, if there is one to get that is. Maybe when we back off cracks will appear and eventually the whole truth will seep out. Sam has been in touch with me again. They reckon she will get a custodial sentence but the fact that she came forward herself will go in her favour. Petrov has stepped back into the shadows, kept his funding in Gray Grand Prix and Sergio is under private rehabilitation care now. He will be OK, thanks to you. Stirling...."

The jostling snake of race cars passed again, registering in Stirling's eyes but not in his brain which had now travelled somewhere else.

"Stirling, Sam is desperate to speak with you. She practically begged last time I saw her. She is a strong lady. She wants to apologise face to face. She is not looking to make excuses for herself, she wants..."

Stirling came back into the here and now.

"I know Richard Gray is living a murderous lie, I just know it. I know Eunice was genuine. She would not have harmed a hair on Rosie's head. She said to me that she would have died for that young girl, and I believed her. I just cannot get it out of my head, Sian."

"But if we can't prove it.., like Peter said, we take on difficult cases. If we can't pull a clean open and shut case, then we have to leave it to another time. The organisation cannot be compromised, it cannot be dragged through the courts. The Police have warned you not to pursue Richard or any other related matter anymore. You have just got to let this one go and move on Stirling."

The buzz of the Formula Fords had now changed to a low rumble as the marshals clapped the winner as he drove by, hand aloft. Stirling didn't even recognise the colour of the winning car;

his mind was scrabbling for ways to manage this latest frustrating sense of failure.

Sian grabbed Stirling's arm and shook it.

"Come on, you brooding oaf. How about I race you back to your place? First back gets to choose the film tonight!"

"So, you have invited yourself round have you?"

"Yep, all arranged with your over-caring, Stirling-spoiling, housekeeper of yours."

Sian was first to spring through the large heavy wooden front door of Stirling's Drayton house.

"Accept it, you lost, you lost, you lost. Little girls in sporty Alfas eat world champion driven Landys, fact. So, I think that means I get to...."

"You found him then, young Miss Sian? I have aired a guest room for the night for you as I presumed you would be staying."

Stirling put on a mock surprised look.

"All arranged is it? Yes, Sian will be staying thank you and eating with us if that is alright."

Stirling's housekeeper did have a soft spot for Sian but was not going to show too much of it.

"So, you found him where I said he would be?"

"I certainly did. Stirling you 'saddo' you are so predictable."

Stirling sarcastically replied,

"I sometimes find it peaceful there!"

He then turned to his waiting housekeeper

"I'll go have a shower and be down for...?"

Stirling turned his back on Sian, awaiting an answer.

"Should we say 45 minutes? Oh, and Stirling, this came for you whilst you were out. It was a special delivery from a courier. I had to sign for it."

Stirling reached out and took the white envelope and looked at the address. It simply read in handwritten letters 'To Mr Stirling Speed. For his attention only. Private and confidential'. Stirling looked at his housekeeper, and then at Sian.

"Why are you both looking at me like that? It'll be some sort of loft insulation sales gimmick or some long lost fan professing their un-failing love for me."

Stirling went to put it on the rustic hip height table that had been formed from two used wooden railway sleepers, one of which had been cut in half to make the legs.

Sian went to grab it off Stirling but he snatched it back before her fingers had time to grip it.

"Okay, I'll open it."

Stirling's face was hard to read as he looked down at the short but to the point handwritten letter. The first two sentences stopped any further reading in its tracks until a supportive seat could be found.

Dear Stirling

Oh dear, If I have not been able to tear this up and it has been delivered to your house from my solicitors then I must be dead! Oh by the way please keep reading it because this is or I should put was Eunice no, no 'is' because I am still here whilst I am writing it, anyway this is Eunice.

Chapter 59

Peter Smith waited for Stirling to answer his phone.

"Sorry Stirling for the delay getting back to you. The age-old excuse would you believe, I was in the shower. My team has briefed me and said to expect a call from you. Richard Gray is now in custody. Apparently, he was picked up at the airport, he had a ticket for South America. He claimed he was heading out there for a meeting with a potential sponsor. The police will handle everything now. His phone apparently showed that he received a tip off about the latest developments. So, things moved fast."

"The police must have moved fast to pick him up at the airport!"

"Apparently Mr Petrov had privately put 24-hour surveillance on him. As soon as he found out that the police wanted Gray he was able to say exactly where he was."

"Well done Mr Petrov! Hope he doesn't do much more otherwise I will end up being in his debt again, not good! It is all so surreal to finally be in possession of the hard evidence that will convict Gray of the two murders. It is so hard to accept that he lived the lie for so long!"

Peter Smith, although at home, was still very much on the case, making sure his latest catch did not wriggle out of the net.

"Forgive me asking, but did you tamper with anything before the police got there?"

"No, I did not even drive up to the cottage. I waited in the main car park. I didn't want to confuse any tyre tracks up there or anything."

"I was allowed to enter the cottage with the new investigating officer who was very efficient. Apparently, Richard Gray's friendly inspector has been suspended, pending further investigations. Sian went to Gray Grand Prix with another inspector and his team whilst they sealed that place as part of the investigation. The police seem to have been very keen to make sure nothing was going to be left slack this time."

"Good. And everything was as Eunice said in her letter to you?"

"Yes, exactly as she said. Our dizzy Eunice must have got off the phone from me knowing exactly what she was going to do. She researched and planned how she was going to trap Richard. She even planned who was to find her, she arranged to see Richard, but gave me a later time. There were covert surveillance cameras set up in the car park outside the cottage, in the entrance hall, and in the kitchen, exactly where the diagram showed in the letter. There were two microphones set up. She had used the latest gadgets available, to the public at least, and they had all been set meticulously. She then deposited a letter with her solicitor that was to be forwarded to me in the event of her death. Hence the delay before I received it. Eunice was not as dizzy as she would have us all believe."

"She was a professor, Stirling. A smiling, slightly bumbling, but extremely clever professor! Richard Gray had no chance of outsmarting that one once she had her claws into him!"

Stirling said the inevitable reply.

"He still managed to murder her."

"She *allowed* him to murder her, she knew what she had to do the moment she emailed him. She wanted Rosie's death brought to undeniable justice. So tragic."

"She needn't have made the sacrifice though Peter. We could have been there for her. Such a waste!"

"Sometimes, when desperation kicks in you have to take matters into your own hands to make absolutely sure that the job gets done."

"Wow, how do you cope with these cases Peter?"

"Stirling, when you sat in your race cars you knew you had a job to do. You knew you had to be all in, or you might as well hit the quick release button on your belts and get out. In this job when you are into a case, no matter what, you have to be all in! When that job is finished then you get out and have a long, hot shower and recover. Just as there were always more races there are always more injustices that need people like us to sort them out."

"You have seen the footage?"

Stirling asked.

"No, I have no need. Have you seen and listened to everything?"

Stirling had decided that he did not need to see everything. The end of Eunice's life would have been horrific, and he pitied the police officers that had to painstakingly go through everything.

"I saw enough for Richard Gray to hang himself. The footage shows Eunice excuse herself from the room. She purposefully gave him the opportunity, Peter. During her absence you clearly see Richard empty a small bag of what we now know for certain was a large quantity of ground Hemlock Water Dropwort into Eunice's tea and stir it in. When she returns, she picks up the cup and drinks it all down in one go. She then stares at Richard and simply says, 'you have just poisoned me, haven't you?' and Richard simply replies, 'yes.' She sits down and grimaces slightly. She then says..."

Stirling hesitated as a lump formed in his throat.

"My word, what a brave lady. She then says, 'you killed our beautiful Rosie didn't you?' Richard has tears cascading down his cheeks at this point and says nothing. Peter, Eunice reaches out across the table for Richard's hand and takes hold of it and says..."

Stirling took a deep breath to get control of his emotions.

"...And says, please tell me what happened before the pain becomes too great for me, please. Then it was like Richard was at a confession. He then says that he offered everything to her. Everything to keep quiet, or at least to keep quiet until all had settled with Petrov. She would take no money, no promotion. He offered to buy the cottage. He then almost pleads with Eunice. 'She gave me no choice; she gave me no choice. Just like you have given me no choice.' He is crying at this point and continues, 'This is not my fault, I have my team and I have my plants, I have to do this for them. I gave Rosie time to sleep on it. She called me and said that after speaking to her father, who I know she adored, she had decided that she had to go the authorities. I had no choice'. At this point Eunice starts to choke and struggles out 'thank you, young man'. I could watch no more."

Peter Smith replied instantly, which shocked Stirling, given the hideous story he had just unfurled.

"Well done Stirling. You and Sian, we, got a result. Richard Gray is finished, and Rosalie can rest now."

Stirling felt slightly irritated with his 'job done' attitude.

"Peter, you once said to me never to forget that we are dealing with real lives that have been cruelly taken away, real lives that have left families and friends destroyed with grief, and all you can say now is that we 'got a result'!"

"Stirling, learn to protect yourself, learn how to keep yourself sane within this disgusting world that we have to pick ourselves through. When you had your Monza crash, or any of your crashes where your life could have been extinguished, your mind will have had a way of coping with that trauma, otherwise you would never have pushed a race car throttle again. I have to say to myself 'we got a result' and move on, or I would never pick up a case file again."

"No Peter, I am sorry, but this is not a silly race. A beautiful young girl was murdered for the sake of a stupid race team and some stupid plants and a wonderful person sacrificed her life to bring a selfish murderer to court. As I went through this case, I often found myself wondering who paid the price here? Young Sergio, nearly killing himself to make his father proud. Petrov himself, for the millions and millions he has squandered chasing a ridiculous dream for his son. Sam, for being so desperate that she would live a lie and go to prison to protect her brother. Ross, for putting everyone in this position because of his selfish gambling. No, Peter, this is not a case of 'we got a result.' These selfish beings did not pay the price, Rosie paid the price and Eunice paid the price."

Peter knew that there was nothing he could say to make the hurt that Stirling was experiencing go away, and so allowed the silence to start the healing process.

"Peter, I'm off to see Rosie's parents tomorrow. They need to know that Rosie can rest in peace now."

"OK Stirling, you do that and, Stirling, take the long route down to see them. Go for a drive, recalibrate. Don't make visiting Rosie's parents about something you have to do for *you*, make it something you want to do for Rosie and Eunice."

Chapter 60

Stirling had enjoyed the drive down to Dorset and had enjoyed driving along the coastal route to his destination. The Jaguar was happy to purr and breathe in the fresh sea breeze.

Rosie's parent's house was at the end of a tarmacked single track road with high hedges on each side. The wide country gate was open and so Stirling was able drive into the spacious parking area and to pull quite close to the front door that sat in the middle of the painted, white, symmetrical, neat and tidy house. As he waited for the door to be answered he thought about what he had decided to say and then realised that it would be totally unsuitable. Before he had a chance to think of something else the door opened.

"Hello, I'm Stirling Speed. Can ..."

The lady in front of Stirling interrupted in a pleasant manner.

"Thank you, Stirling, thank you so much for all you have done and taking the trouble to come to see us. We have been expecting you. Maybe you should speak with my husband first. He is in the garage. The side door is open."

Stirling smiled a reply back and followed the direction that had been gently gestured.

Stirling found the side door and stepped through the shiny black painted wooden door and into the immaculate garage. The middle of the garage was taken up with a small, by modern standards, immaculate baby blue MGBGT sports car. Stirling could see someone sitting in the driver's seat.

"Mr Firth, your wife said I would find you in here. It's Stirling Speed."

The door opened and the man slowly clambered out and turned to face Stirling.

"Peter, what are you...?"

Suddenly everything clicked into place.

"Peter, Rosie was your daughter wasn't she...?"

Peter forced a pained smile.

"Yes."

Peter Smith nodded.

"Stirling meet Peter.... Firth, Rosalie Firth's father who you know as, Peter Smith. Stirling, thank you for getting a result, I just knew you would. I decided that I owe it to you for you to know everything. I trusted that you..."

Peter wavered slightly and leaned against the MG, his shoulders starting to shake, his mouth desperately wanting to say something but struggling to form the right shape.

Stirling remained rooted to the spot; his body initially unable to take in the scene before him.

Peter Smith had finally dropped his guard, his protection, his escapism, his detachment, and his body slowly crumbled into unrestrained grief.

"Stirling she is all I had, she was my life, she came to me for advice and I should have protected her, I should have protected her, I allowed this disgusting world to murder my own beautiful Rosie! I didn't protect her Stirling, I never...."

Stirling stepped over to the heaving broken body in front of him and pulled it tight into him in an effort to control the heaving sobs.

Stirling now knew who had paid the price.

About the author

Stuart Jones is a championship-winning race driver and a qualified international race driver coach. Whilst still at school he was singled out for his writing.

A number of his young scribblings found writing competition success. All assumed that his writing would continue after he left school. At 52 years of age, he picked up the pen again. A life of traveling the world, driving race car exotica and mixing with the fascinating people that populate the glamorous motorsport industry has provided him with fertile material that demanded that he should recommence his long-dormant writing.

Stuart has worked extensively in the broadcasting industry, including the BBC as motoring correspondent and as driving expert for various car shows.

In forming the main character, Stirling Speed, Stuart has brought the male hero character up to date and smashed the James Bond womanising, heavy drinking stereo type. His female characters are empowered, strong and take the lead in his story lines.

Printed in Great Britain
by Amazon